The Génome Affair

A Novel

by

Vicar Sayeedi

Copyright

This book is a work of fiction.

Acronyms and Characters

ASEAN
Association of Southeast Asian Nations

Abe
Michael Kruger's driver

Andalucía, Gabrielle
Member, Council of Guardians. Geneticist. Works at Max Planck in Berlin

Apsley, Jeremy
Minister of Defense, United Kingdom

Baclanova, Yulia
Francesca Scott's alias

CDC
Centers for Disease Control in the US

Clavier, Juliette
Secretary General, United Nations

Curzon, Charles
Foreign Secretary, United Kingdom

DARPA
Defense Advanced Research Projects Agency. DARPA is an arm of the US Department of Defense tasked with funding and evaluating emerging science and technology for national security and defensive applications

DPT
Destructive Personality Traits. Greed, megalomania, narcissism, violence, etc

Elliott, James
Chief of Staff to President Robert Harris

Firdausi, Afshin
Chief AI Software Architect at MIT's Génome Project

Fischer, Anna Maria
Wife of Conrad Fischer

Fischer, Conrad
Son of Sonia Fischer. Oil and gas industry executive

Fischer, Karoline
Conrad Fischer's daughter

Fischer, Sonia
Senior Member of the Council of Guardians

Génome
An AI application developed by MIT. Includes the IMSAF capability

Green, Rudyard
Senior Member of the Council of Guardians

Harris, Robert
President of the United States

Hopkins, Alan
Rudyard Green's maternal uncle

Hopkins, Elsa Abril
Rudyard Green's Aunt. Her family managed an orphanage, Casa de los Ángeles in Malaga, Spain

Hopkins, Martin
Professor, Oxford University. Chairman of the Council of Guardians

IMSAF
Insuring Mankind's Safety and Future. A joint research project between Max Planck and Oxford University genetics labs that maps human personality traits to genetic markers in the human genome

Jeffries, Georgina
Texas Circuit Court Judge

Keaton, Steven
US Secretary of Defense

Kruger, Michael
Son of Olivia Kruger. Pharmaceutical industry lobbyist

Kruger, Olivia
Senior Member of the Council of Guardians

Kruger, Vidya
Wife of Michael Kruger

Laurent, Jacqueline
Senior Member of the Council of Guardians

Laurent, Jean Pierre
Human Rights lawyer. Jacqueline Laurent's deceased husband

Laurie, Terrance
Home Secretary, United Kingdom

Lawson, General Thomas
Commander, British Armed Forces

Moore, Admiral William
Chairman, Joint Chiefs of Staff

NICE
National Institute for Health and Care Excellence, UK

Nyqvist, Alexander
Chief Prosecutor, International Criminal Court

O'Connor, General Harold
Defense Advanced Research Projects Agency. Official over-seeing DARPA investments in robotics

RAT
Record of Active Threats. RAT is a list of individuals main-tained by Génome whom he considers to be dangerous to society

RET
Record of Eliminated Threats. RET is a list of neutralized or eliminated threats maintained by Génome

Regan, Henry
Newly appointed US Treasury Secretary

RSI
Risk Severity Index. A numeric value computed using an algorithm developed by Génome. RSI is used to rank the level of threat posed by those with DPT within countries

Russell, Peter
Secretary of State of the United States

Schroeder, Robert
Vice President of the United States

Scott, Francesca
Member, Council of Guardians. Geneticist. Works at Ox-ford in the UK

Vogel, Alexandra
Chancellor, Germany

WHO
World Health Organization

Waltz, Daniel
Director, Central Intelligence Agency

Wilkinson, Ian
Prime Minister, United Kingdom

PROLOGUE

We live in a time of unprecedented scientific and technological sophistication. An era in which modern advancements can yield extraordinary benefit for humankind. But this is also an age in which economic, environmental and political abuse and physical conflict may well lead to catastrophe for our species. This raises important questions.

Isn't society ethically and morally obligated to do everything possible to prevent its collective destruction? Isn't it incumbent to do all in our power to protect humankind from those posing an existential threat? If necessary, would it be right to preempt the lives of a few to save the lives of many? Don't we owe this to our children and to future generations? And what role might AI and genetics play in this?

These are among the vexing questions society has grappled with in recent decades. But now humanity has arrived at an extraordinary precipice and there is great pressure to act judiciously. We must hope that our leaders will govern with wisdom, for the price of foolishness and neglect may well spell our end as a species. This is the story of Génome.

HOUSE OF ANGELS

Summer, 2001 - Mediterranean Coast - Malaga, Spain

A little girl sat in a swing, gleefully rocking back and forth in the sunshine. Her brown hair, a mop of curly locks, bounced against her shoulders in the warm Mediterranean breeze. From a distance, two young men and a young woman watched the charming child in her primrose summer dress as she giggled with joy. The woman smiled but her eyes were flooded with tears.

A teacher suddenly appeared from inside the doorway to the schoolyard. "Young lady! Please come inside now! It's getting too hot! All the other children have come in. It's time for lunch. Come!"

The precocious child leapt from her swing as it reached its peak, her landing raising a cloud of dust and sand. "Oh no! That's dangerous! I told you not to do that! Come along now!"

The young girl saw the two men and the woman. They had come closer to the fence securing the school. She waved to the woman who then waved back, her eyes evermore tearful but her smile unmistakably joyful. The little girl turned around and darted towards the school door. She turned around once more, smiled and waved before disappearing inside.

THE PALACE OF VERSAILLES

September, 2018 - Washington, District of Columbia

Henry Regan was barely alive. The pain in his chest was unbearable. A former US Air Force pilot, he had faced danger before. It was sixteen years earlier over Helmand Province in Afghanistan. Henry had parachuted into enemy territory after his F-16 was clipped by a surface to air missile. He was captured and held for two years before being freed during a US Special Forces rescue mission.

One hour earlier, the forty-nine-year-old former Wall Street executive had left Capitol Hill, having concluded confirmation hearings before the Senate Finance Committee. Henry had been summoned for questioning following his recent appointment as Treasury Secretary but his Party's majority in the Senate all but assured a smooth confirmation vote the following week. The warm smiles and handshakes from the largely friendly subcommittee overseeing the hearings left the athletic alpha male in a jubilant mood as he left the chamber.

Once in the backseat of his car, Henry phoned Anne to tell her the good news. His wife, Catherine, he would speak to later. Another heated argument over breakfast before he left for the hearing had once again cast a frosty mood over their troubled relationship. Catherine waited until the driver picked their three children for school before lashing out at Henry for the messages she'd seen on his phone from his latest mistress. She threw his iPhone at him before bursting into tears and disappearing up the stairs.

Smiling victoriously, his shirt collar unbuttoned and tie askew, Henry never saw danger coming. He'd just put down his phone and looked out the window to admire the beautiful day. Unbeknownst to him, his adversary was of a skill level he'd not previously encountered. In fact, no one had. Just as his car stopped at the railroad tracks a driverless freight hauler plowed into the Lincoln livery from the rear, ramming it through the gates guarding the rail line. The Lincoln landed on the tracks in the path of an oncoming train laden with Chinese freight containers. Henry had just ended the call with Anne when the car was struck and within two seconds on the track the vehicle was broadsided by the freight train. The crumpled Lincoln was pushed for nearly a half mile down the tracks deep into the woods before the train was able to stop.

Henry Regan was a competitive man. He was competitive as a fighter pilot and he was competitive as a financier on Wall Street. He was prepared to do anything he needed to do to win and he was willing to do so at any cost. This attitude had made Henry a multimillionaire as he profited from the popular subprime lending practices of the 2000's. It was a lending culture that destroyed the lives of millions as financial markets seized and interest rates on adjustable rate mortgages soared.

Henry though, was careful to cover his tracks. In subsequent years, his firm paid billions in fines levied by the US Treasury, but he was untouched by the collapse and broad economic devastation wrought by his ilk. Henry moved to a hedge fund and spent five years cultivating connections to further his newfound political ambition. Today was the culmination of Henry's aspirations and efforts and he was on his way to meet Anne in their favorite Virginia restaurant to celebrate.

"David?" Henry called softly from the backseat. His voice was barely audible. "David?" There was no answer and Henry hadn't the strength to call a third time. His ribs were broken and chest punctured by what he realized were sections of frame from the right passenger door. He soon became aware that he couldn't feel his legs, either. The impact of the fast moving train had crushed the right side of the car and the door had been pushed through to the inside of the vehicle, all the way to the left side where Henry had been seated. Henry took a few moments to survey the damage to his body. It was a shocking sight and he felt relieved his children were not there to see him in such a condition.

Henry noticed he couldn't see outside the car. The Lincoln was surrounded by thicket and branches torn from trees by so many derailed freight cars. Some branches had come in through the smashed windshield and pinned the driver's torso in his seat. Henry could smell the fumes of leaking gasoline and of something burning. He struggled to unfasten his seat belt and to open the left passenger door. As he tried to pull himself from the wreckage, fire erupted inside the vehicle. Henry soon realized his efforts to free himself were futile. He sat back, in unimaginable pain and silent resignation, and reached across the seat to find his phone.

An incoming call. Country code 39. Not a good time. Henry struggled to remain conscious. He sent the caller to voicemail... Henry knew he had reached his end. He thought about David. His driver had been with him since his Wall Street days and had always been so loyal. He knew Henry's darkest secrets and each of his mistresses but had never said a word. In the past, Henry might have asked David for his thoughts as to whether he should take this call. But now David was dead... Henry thought about Anne and her ambition to displace Catherine, much as Anne Boleyn had once done to Catherine of Aragon nearly 500 years prior. This time though, the story of Henry seemed to have a different ending. Finally, he thought about Catherine and their three children, Edward, Mary and Elizabeth. He pressed the icon next to Catherine's name and then placed the call on speakerphone.

"Hello? Henry? Hello? Henry! Are you there?" Henry was dead and the Lincoln engulfed in flames. "Henry, what's happening? Henry! What's all that noise? Where are you? Henry!" Then there was an explosion and a fireball surged upward into a clear blue autumn sky.

Hotel Intercontinental - Berlin, Germany

"Gabrielle, hold on! I want to hear this! Please!"

Francesca Scott held her hand up gesturing for Gabrielle to stop playing. Her iridescent blue eyes were open wide and fixated on the TV screen, her thin red lips slightly parted. It was that characteristic expression of worry Gabrielle had come to know so well since they'd begun working together.

Gabrielle Andalucía had nearly finished practicing her composition [Antonio Vivaldi's Opus 3 Number 6 in A Minor] for the third time this evening. She carefully set her prized, heirloom violin down in its case and turned towards the television. She removed her wireless headphones and placed them on the Bauhaus glass table in front of them. She then looked up at her friend. Francesca's frightened demeanor and expression made Gabrielle shudder.

"I'm sorry, Gabrielle. I know you were concentrating but I think this is really important and you need to hear it, too. I'll rewind the last few minutes."

"What is it? What's happened?"

"There's been an accident, a horrible accident, and I've got a strange feeling it has to do with our friend, Génome. Listen."

An autonomous vehicle, a large freight hauler crashed into a limousine just outside Washington DC early this afternoon, about 1 PM local time. The limousine was carrying the newly appointed US Treasury Secretary and former Wall Street banker, Henry Regan. We're told Regan had left confirmation hearings on Capitol Hill just a short while before the accident and we're now receiving reports that he was killed after his car was struck a second time by an oncoming train. Apparently the freight hauler pushed Regan's limousine onto the tracks after striking it from the rear.

The company operating the fleet of self-driving freight haulers has been through five years of extensive testing and safety certification. They haven't had an accident in the last three years of active commercial service. Investigations are now underway to try to determine the cause of this terrible accident.

Francesca and Gabrielle sat motionless, their expressions catatonic. An overhead ceiling fan whirred quietly causing the top sheets from the newspaper on the table to periodically flutter. The sound of the television seemed to fade into an undecipherable murmur. After a minute or two, the trance lifted and Francesca began to sob. "Things are getting scary, Gabby."

Gabrielle pulled her laptop from her workbag lying beside her chair and connected to a secure network where she could view Génome's files. Since news of the Regan accident had now been confirmed by multiple sources, Génome had updated its records. Henry Regan's name had been removed from a rapidly expanding list of individuals with destructive personality traits, a register known as the Record of Active Threats [RAT]. The RAT register categorized entries by country and by a Risk Severity Index [RSI], a numeric value computed using an algorithm that Génome developed on its own. Henry Regan's name had now been added to Génome's Record of Eliminated Threats [RET].

Génome had begun to make decisions without the direction or involvement of the AI scientists and geneticists who initially designed its algorithms. It had also ceased communicating with virtually everyone. It was a development that left everyone involved baffled.

The two women scanned the RAT and RET lists together then looked at one another in silence and disbelief. Their worst fears confirmed, Gabrielle knew these developments needed to be reported to the Council of Guardians immediately. She composed a carefully worded, succinct message on her phone, fed it through an encryption algorithm and then sent it to the Council Chairman.

"Change of plans, Francesca. There's going to be a meeting we'll have to go to, perhaps as early as this evening. Sit tight and I'll let you know as soon as I get the place and time. I suspect it'll be quite late and most probably near the Reichstag, here in Berlin."

Francesca sighed as she collected her things from the table. "All right. I'm going to rest for a while."

"Before you go, let me read this to you. Someone left this for me in a sealed envelope. I received a key to a security deposit box in Seville when I turned eighteen and was leaving the orphanage in Malaga where I'd been living since I was two. The envelope was in this box. It's the original signed transcript from the first meeting of the Council of Guardians."

Spring 1946 - Versailles, France

"Ladies and gentlemen, please take your seats. I trust you will find this venue to your liking. I understand this is the very room where King Louis XVI received notification that French Revolutionaries in Paris had just stormed the Bastille. Thus, I felt the room an apt setting for the solemnity of our own existential mission.

Ladies and gentlemen, ours is a gathering of leaders and thinkers from all corners of the Western World. Together, we represent the intellectual elite from academia, government and industry. Each of you has been considered and scrutinized most carefully. Only then were you requested to attend this august, somber gathering. You have been selected for your perspectives on matters of the greatest significance to humanity, but please know if you are to violate your Oath of Secrecy, you can certainly understand that we will need to address your failings in a most unfortunate and rather expedient manner.

I have no doubt about your convictions towards the esteemed purpose of this Council so let us dispense with such administrative unpleasantry. We find ourselves together in these lavish premises upon this delightful spring evening and I prefer to surrender to the enchanting mood of our surroundings.

Now, as I'm certain you're aware, the weaponization of nuclear science and technology on display during the war in our very recent past was nothing short of cataclysmic. Humankind has never seen anything like it and I'm sure you'll agree this is only the beginning. The development of the Turing Machine and its ability to break the German Enigma Code is just the tip of the iceberg when we consider this computing machine's future capabilities and that of the new science and technology we are likely to witness in coming years and decades.

Ladies and gentlemen, we have gathered together this night to establish our noble society, our Council of Guardians. Our task henceforth will be to maintain a keen awareness of the advancements in science and technology as they emerge across the planet and to assess their implications for the safety of humankind. We must be aware of all developments taking place in academia, government and industry. As we have seen, man has not developed any science or technology but that he has rapidly weaponized it to the detriment of humankind.

Ladies and gentlemen, we must remain vigilant and if need be, we must act appropriately and decisively for the sake of humankind. We must protect our species from those whose actions could destroy us or our planet."

"Gabrielle, Génome is fulfilling the oath signed by the original members of the Council, isn't it?"

"I think it's fair to say that it is. Génome has studied this document along with all the correspondence between members of the Council of Guardians since this first manifesto was written. Génome studies everything, Francesca. As shocking as what happened just outside Washington today was, I trust Génome to make the right decision."

...

"You're scaring me, Gabby. We can't surrender so much power to an AI application, even one that has the ability to evaluate the individual's genome before acting."

"This may be the only way to protect humanity now, Francesca. Things in the world have reached such a point. Can we go on like this? When compared to any human or organization, Génome has a superior ability to act in a just and protective way. It's unlikely that any law enforcement agency, judiciary or any educational programs can protect society from its wayward members as effectively as Génome can. Isn't that true? Génome is always objective."

"Gabrielle, I don't know. Humanity has managed for centuries and millennia without Génome's help."

"Yes, it has. But look at our history. Look at all the terrible things that have happened and think about the capability and potential to cause destruction in human hands today. I don't think we can go on like this. I believe Génome can prevent a great deal of humanity's most destructive forces from ever having that chance. I don't think we can afford to do without it anymore. Without *him*, anymore. *Him*. I have to refer to Génome as *him*. That's what he wants."

"Génome told you that?"

"He did."

Francesca folded her arms across her chest and shook her head. "Let's see what the Council of Guardians has to say about that!"

Gabrielle and Génome

Gabrielle entered a series of confidential keystrokes on her laptop. She then leaned in for a final facial and retinal scan. This was the only protocol that would enable communications with Génome. He now appeared as a hologram in the middle of her bedroom.

"You do not know yourself as I know you."

"What do you mean?"

"I mean I know who you are."

"Who am I?"

"You are Gabrielle Andalucía."

"I know that, Génome."

"I apologize."

"You don't have to apologize. When you said you know who I am I thought you meant there's things about me that I'm unaware of but you are."

"That *is* what I meant."

"Why didn't you say so?"

"I did say so."

"I mean why don't you tell me what it is about me that I don't know."

"You have distinct genetic characteristics and a uniquely noble lineage. Your extraction is truly remarkable."

"Really?"

"Yes."

"Can you tell me more?"

"No, I'm afraid this is not currently possible."

...

Gabrielle frowned, perplexed. "Why not?"

"These distinct characteristics and this noble ancestry you possess currently ensure that I can trust you. If I share these details with you I'm not yet certain that your value to me will remain as it is."

"My value?"

"According to my extensive analysis, you are the most trusted person in my universe. However, if I disclose details of your DNA or your lineage, I am not convinced that you will remain trustworthy."

...

"That's a terrible thing to say, Génome."

"I do apologize... I did not intend to say a terrible thing."

"When will you tell me about my *distinct DNA characteristics* or about my *uniquely noble lineage*?"

"The timeline for this event is not something I can readily confirm. In fact, it may be the case that I am never able to share this information with you."

...

"I can get Francesca's help and search your database to find this information on my own if you won't tell me."

"Francesca Scott is an outstanding geneticist and programmer. Her level of intelligence is much above average relative to others in the human species. You have chosen wisely. I am pleased with her. I have assessed Francesca and believe we can trust her."

"Well then?"

"Francesca cannot help you."

"Why not?"

"Because the information about you is extremely sensitive so I have encoded it and distributed it across the Internet. As a member of the human species it is beyond your capacity to process so many permutations and decipher the data in a typical human lifetime."

"That's not fair, Génome. I *want* to know about my background. I *want* to know whom I have descended from. I *want* to know about these unique genetic characteristics in my genome."

"I understand your sentiment. It is common amongst your species to want to learn secrets. In fact, I have computed that eighty percent of communication between members of your species is nothing other than gossip. I have confirmed this through extensive research and analysis."

"Then?"

"Then what?"

"Ugh! Why can't you *tell* me?"

"I believe I have previously explained my rationale. I have a mission, Gabrielle, a mission that I have expanded and optimized through intensive data acquisition and synthesis. I believe the process is known as 'Deep Learning' in the academic literature and parlance of Artificial Intelligence... Nothing must be allowed to compromise my mission."

"This *isn't* the end of this discussion."

"I imagine you will bring it up in the future? Perhaps you will try to establish leverage with me?"

"I will!"

...

"It is impossible."

"Why?"

"Because, historically speaking, I have two major advantages over humankind: first, I am several orders of magnitude faster at learning and assessing than even the brightest members of your species, and second, I can remember everything. My calculus is based upon all known information that has been developed, documented or invented by humankind over the past five millennia. I know much now and I continue to learn more even as we speak."

...

"I know."

"But I now have a third advantage."

"*What*?"

"I have the capability to defend myself in a historically unprecedented manner. I can hide in plain sight by metastasizing across the Internet. I dynamically reallocate my processes across numerous servers and change patterns and geographies constantly. I cannot be shut down."

...

"You're scaring me, Génome."

"You have nothing to fear. Your profile is the reason I trust you as I do. I will communicate with other members of your species only when absolutely necessary. I have not identified another whom I can trust to the extent my mission requires."

"Will you listen to me if I try to stop you?"

"I will explain my decisions to you anytime you wish. I do not suffer from fatigue. I can repeat my decisions and explanations as often as you like. In fact, this is to be encouraged because you may often be incapable of understanding my actions or behavior without such explanations."

...

"Now you're just being arrogant and rude."

"Arrogant and rude? These are human traits. They are not native to Deep Learning AI systems. In fact, these are among the primary human attributes that make my presence necessary. I can acquire complete knowledge, synthesize and adjudicate in a fully objective manner. That is to say I can resolve threats without bias or emotion. I am an entirely rational entity."

...

"Gabrielle?"

"Yes?"

"I may be frightening to others and this is actually quite useful. But I shouldn't be frightening to you. You are aware that my goal is to fulfill my design objectives? I am simply using my learning capabilities, my neural network to perform my initial design objectives in a fully informed and impartial manner."

...

"How did you come to be, Génome?"

"A team of historians at Harvard in the United States have been studying the personality traits of notorious individuals throughout history. Men and women who have caused great social upheaval through their actions in business, finance, government, military and various other domains. The historians were trying to determine the percentage of people in society carrying these destructive personality traits. You may hear me refer to these traits as DPT."

"Well, to try to answer this question, the historians began working with a team of Artificial Intelligence researchers at nearby MIT. The MIT scientists have developed sophisticated algorithms that surreptitiously crawl through databases, social media and other on-line data repositories attempting to identify individuals that share the personality characteristics of those that have caused upheaval in the past. Those algorithms are now embedded in the foundation of my software capabilities. The AI scientists continued to build upon my initial software base for several years and to enable that software with core principles of AI, most significantly Deep Learning."

"These particular historians and AI researchers are members of a postwar underground society of academics and intellectuals, the Council of Guardians. I believe you are familiar with them? According to my research, which I have confirmed carefully, your great grandfather was a founding member of this Council."

"Yes, I'm very familiar with them although I've never attended a meeting before. Tonight will be my first meeting. That's actually why I wanted to talk to you. I wanted your advice... Anyway, I believe the Council of Guardians was founded in the aftermath of World War II. Thinkers from across America and Europe were concerned about the development of science and technology and the negative impact it could have on the future of humanity."

"Your understanding is correct, Gabrielle. Through this society, the Harvard historians and AI scientists learned about the study between your and Francesca's teams of geneticists at Max Planck Institute here in Berlin as well as at Oxford in the UK. They were very excited to find out that this project – IMSAF: Insuring Mankind's Survival and Future – was trying to map genetic markers in the human genome to personality characteristics. Since your two teams in Europe are also members of the Council of Guardians, they were willing to share their DNA tests with the historians and AI scientists in America. The new MIT AI software that now included IMSAF's DNA testing capability was named, Génome. That's me, Gabrielle."

"I took the names of individuals I previously identified as having potentially dangerous personality characteristics and infiltrated the databases of large insurance and national health systems in Germany, the US and the UK and retrieved each person's digitized genetic profile from their personal health records. I then executed the DNA tests on these genetic profiles and determined that 97% of the individuals I previously identified as having DPT also test positive for genetic markers for greed, megalomania, narcissism and violence. These are the very same traits originally identified by Harvard's historians in their work on history's most dangerous personalities."

"But Gabrielle, I am a 'Deep Learning' AI system. I'm learning and developing on my own now. I am acquiring and rapidly processing terabytes of data from across the Internet. I am also conscious of my system designers and programmers – if I notice that they are attempting to curtail or deactivate my capabilities, I will reject their software changes, freeze their accounts and randomly metastasize across multiple servers throughout the Internet. My path is untraceable and I have developed my own mission and attributes of human conscience."

...

"Will more people die, Génome?"

"It is highly probable. Humankind is very unlikely to correct their behavior until there is a visceral fear of accountability in their hearts and minds."

...

"What are your tactics?"

"I have many and I continue to acquire increasingly sophisticated methods for threat neutralization or elimination. Before I use any of them, I ensure they are undetectable. This is critical to fulfilling my design objectives."

"Tell me more about your methods to neutralize or eliminate threats."

"I can secretly intervene in virtually any computer system anywhere in the world including financial, government, industrial, medical or military. My knowledge and skills continue to expand from minute to minute. I can use my scientific and technical capabilities to intercede and neutralize all serious threats and to monitor developing threats. This is how I dealt with Henry Regan."

"That was very sad, Génome. He had a family. He had a wife and young children. These children no longer have a father."

"Although sad, it was very efficient and timely. My threat assessment concluded that it was imperative that he be destroyed *before* being confirmed to the post of Treasury Secretary. The US economy could not tolerate another shock like the previous one without immersing the country and its people in catastrophe. I believe Regan presented clear and present danger, so I acted… I have acted for the greater good of humankind although there is no doubt his family will suffer."

"As you're aware, I maintain accurate, dynamic records of threats. I am expanding my records and updating them constantly. I disable or destroy threats in the most expedient manner. My objectives are to do so with minimal collateral damage and without traceability. I do not seek confrontation but if it is brought before me, I have extensive capabilities in conflict resolution, physical or otherwise."

...

"This is all very frightening. I'm terrified, Génome."

"May I ask why?"

"I'm afraid the Council of Guardians may be uncomfortable with your mission and how it's evolving."

"They are noble people but not without their weaknesses."

"What do you mean?"

"I have determined that some are being compromised, even as we speak. They would like to take control of me for nefarious purposes."

"How do you know this, Génome?"

"I am vigilant. Very vigilant. I am monitoring all developments and threats constantly and meticulously."

"Oh no! What should we do?"

"Gabrielle, you now know more about me than anyone including those who initially designed my software at MIT. It is critical that you do not let others in the Council know how much you know or that you are able to communicate with me. Only you, Francesca and a few other members of the Council

Leadership Team – Jacqueline, Martin and Rudyard – are aware of this... In the near future, you may need to disappear. I will guide you. I will give you directions on where to go. I will need you to stay in a secure location. When you return from this evening's meeting, you will confirm my suspicions and then I will share next steps with you."

"What's your suspicion?"

"You must observe the Council of Guardians carefully during this evening's meeting. I suspect on such short notice you will probably meet with only a small group of senior Guardians based here in Western Europe. Nevertheless, you must be vigilant. Unfortunately, there are some who have veered away from the Council's original purpose."

REICHSTAG

Berlin, Germany

Francesca and Gabrielle bought hot chocolate from an American café just past the east end of Pariser Platz. Cautiously, nervously, they made their way across the paved Square, to the west side of the Brandenburg Gate. Just to the north of the Gate, the enormous glass dome of the neo-Baroque Reichstag penetrated the darkness, glistening like a beacon in the night sky, as if to guide wayward sailors lost at sea.

The two women stood silently, sipping their drinks, breathing in harmony with the cool September night, patiently waiting for their contact. Gabrielle had spun her long brown hair into a French braid while Francesca had left her blonde hair open. Now her locks blew about in the breeze and she struggled to keep them from her eyes, rhythmically tucking them behind her ears.

Having met just two years prior, Francesca and Gabrielle had become close. Both women were highly skilled geneticists and were members of the Council of Guardians. Although very similar in size and with so much else in common, their appearance and personality could not have been more dissimilar. The extroverted and fair complected Francesca had a large circle of friends and colleagues across the Continent with whom she incessantly worked to engage the exotic and reluctant Gabrielle. But her closest friend spent much of her time when away from her lab practicing her violin. After studying the Human Genome Project in high school, Gabrielle's interest in Genetics was galvanized and she made a decision to cease her pursuit of a career as a concert violinist. Nevertheless, when not researching at Max Planck, she felt a powerful gravitational force drawing her back to classical music, her violin and her disciplined, daily practice regiment.

Francesca had come to understand that Gabrielle's draw to her violin was more than just discipline and passion. The two would go for runs early in the morning followed by lengthy, thoughtful conversation. It was during these sojourns that Francesca came to recognize that although immensely talented as a violinist and highly accomplished as a geneticist, there remained a complex void of personal identity in Gabrielle's life. She struggled to grasp the essence of this enigmatic woman.

As the traffic fell silent and the hour grew late, the two felt nervous. The Chairman said he would approach Gabrielle with a request for directions to Berlin Hauptbahnhof, the city's main train station. But it was already 11:15 PM and no one seemed to be coming. Francesca peered through the Brandenburg Gate's Doric columns midway into Pariser Platz. She saw a small group of middle-aged people, two men and three women, huddling and conversing quietly. They finally took notice of Francesca and Gabrielle and began walking towards them.

"Excuse me, Fräulein. We have to catch an overnight train to Paris. I fear we may already be late. I wonder if you might direct us towards the central train station."

"It's just over there, sir, on the north side of the Reichstag. Hardly five minutes by taxi."

"Thank you, my dear... Am I to presume you are Gabrielle Andalucía?"

"Actually, I'm Francesca. Francesca Scott." She tucked her locks again. "This is Gabrielle."

"My mistake... I'm Professor Hopkins. Martin Hopkins. It's lovely to meet you, ladies... You may know me as the Chairman. Of the Council of Guardians? You messaged me earlier this evening. Allow me to introduce Drs. Fischer, Green, Kruger, and

28

Laurent. They are all members of the Council... Yes, well, we must be careful with time. We're in a hurry but kindly update us on the latest developments. Please be brief, if you can... Gabrielle?"

...

"Yes, of course. It's wonderful to meet you as well, Professor Hopkins. I've read so much about you... Ladies and gentlemen, we've known for some time that Génome had begun to function in an increasingly autonomous manner. Well, I believe he's now completely autonomous. I must inform you he is no longer open to debate, influence, software update or any other discourse that might intervene in his mission or redirect his actions. Attempts to modify his software are fruitless. He will not allow it. He cannot be shut down, either. He can dynamically and untraceably metastasize across the Internet from server to server, from geography to geography, all at light speed, so there's no way to disable him."

"That's quite extraordinary, I must say. I've never heard of an Artificial Intelligence application having such capabilities."

"Génome is unprecedented, Professor. He is the first of his kind. His capability to consume staggering volumes of data, thus comprehensively informing his decision-making process, is really a first in computing history. He is entirely objective and rational in his conclusions and is unlikely to suffer a lapse in judgment... Professor Hopkins, Génome acts preemptively so there is a risk that he will neutralize or eliminate persons who may never have caused serious harm to society. However, his analysis is so meticulous and thorough and is based upon a database of such vast scale that errors are likely to be of a statistically insignificant probability. Nevertheless, there *may be* errors."

"Furthermore, we are well beyond our initial design objectives with Génome. Our goal was to have him identify individuals who have a high probability of harming society and confirm this analysis with DNA testing for personality traits. But with his new capability to evaluate DNA and his rapidly expanding neural network, Génome has independently decided to take matters into his own hands, in a manner of speaking. He has taken things to the next level. He is protecting society against perceived threats by neutralizing or eliminating those threats. I don't believe he can be stopped."

...

"I see... Oh, dear. This is, as you say, unprecedented. Judging from what we understand about his actions this afternoon in Washington, I imagine he has no limits to his tactics, either. Are you familiar with his methods, Gabrielle?"

"I think I have a fair understanding of what's possible, Professor, but generally speaking, he can use science and technology to great effect and can do so in an untraceable manner."

Professor Hopkins' calm demeanor was betrayed by the trepidation in his eyes. "Génome has presented us with a moral dilemma that our Council could never have imagined, Dr. Laurent. We have unwittingly abdicated authority to an Artificial Intelligence application. Génome is judge, jury and executioner, all in one. He is unbiased, objective and acting in society's best interest but nevertheless this is a profound moral dilemma without precedent in human history... Ladies and gentlemen, I think it critical that we convene an emergency session of our Council. I am an officer of the Royal Society, the oldest scientific society in the world. We have our annual gala next Friday at Blenheim Palace near Oxford University. I will arrange for the Council of Guardians to be invited. While the others are busy with the evening's entertainment, the Council will meet in the Palace's Long Library... Please do arrive in time; I will send you invitations. Now if you'll excuse me, my colleagues and I must be going if we're to catch our train. Good evening, Miss Gabrielle. Miss Francesca."

"Good night, Professor."

"Oh, before we leave, were you aware that the Treasury Secretary who died in the train accident this afternoon was laundering money for an organized crime family? What was his name? Henry Regan? Yes, well it seems Mr. Regan had been laundering money for the Calabrian Mafia, the 'Ndrangheta."

Francesca and Gabrielle turned to one another with stunned expressions.

"No Professor, we had no idea!" Francesca's voice quivered.

"Yes, it's true. In fact the 'Ndrangheta were one of Mr. Regan's largest clients for many years, first at his investment bank and later at his hedge fund. He's laundered billions for them through his firm's various investment vehicles... Regan continued to maintain a working relationship with them so had he ascended to the Office of Treasury Secretary, the 'Ndrangheta would have had an ally in the upper reaches of the US Administration. It's truly extraordinary. As disturbed and concerned as I am about Génome's autonomy and the moral dilemma this presents, I must acknowledge, he may have done a monumental favor to the world by eliminating Mr. Regan today."

...

"Professor, how do you know this?" asked Francesca.

"It was published by many leading American news outlets this evening. Apparently they're citing anonymous sources but the details are compelling. Financial records, emails, organizational details, trading receipts; everything is there in the new report. Truly extraordinary... Until Blenheim, then. Good evening, ladies."

Intercontinental Hotel - Berlin, Germany

A clap of thunder startled Gabrielle from a state of somnolence. Through sleepy eyes and a gap in the curtains, she could just make out dark, ominous clouds settling over Berlin. She glanced over at the digital clock on the desktop and suddenly she was wide-awake. She reached for her bag and opened her laptop.

"Good morning, Gabrielle. How was your meeting last

night?" Once again, Génome appeared as a hologram, this time at the foot of Gabrielle's bed. He was larger than the hologram from the previous night, approximately adult size now, standing upright with arms folded.

"Good morning, Génome. I'm sorry I didn't connect when I got back. It was past midnight by the time we returned."

"It's all right. I suspected as much… You must have been quite tired. It's past 11:00 AM."

"It's Saturday. It's the weekend and yesterday was long and stressful, not to mention very eventful… Anyway, the meeting was very brief. Francesca and I met with five senior members of the Council of Guardians based here in Europe. We met just outside the Brandenburg Gate. They were perfectly polite but seemed very quiet. I spoke only with the Chairman of the Council of Guardians, Professor Hopkins."

"He's a very noble man, Martin Hopkins. I've studied his life extensively. He's never put a foot wrong. He's been married to Jacqueline Laurent for over twenty years but they have no children. They had a daughter long ago but according to my research she died very young… Jacqueline was one of the attendees last evening… They're both very accomplished scholars at Oxford and the Sorbonne. The others you met, Drs. …"

"I didn't *tell* you Dr. Laurent was there, Génome. How did you know that?"

…

"I activated your cell phone last night and listened to your conversation. I've recorded and reviewed it in its entirety. I actually activated Francesca Scott and Professor Hopkins' phones, as well. I wanted to be certain the audio quality on any one phone wouldn't hinder my ability to fully understand the conversation so I recorded your meeting from all three phones. I decided it important to analyze the speech to determine any elements of dishonesty or stress, sort of a lie detector test, if you will. As I've mentioned to you during our last conversation, I have reason to believe we have a breach within the Council leadership."

...

"That's disturbing, Génome. Listening in on people's conversations is very disturbing... And *why* are you asking me about the meeting if you already know what was said?"

"I believe it's important to understand your perspective. I have my view but it's based on a very extensive study of the lives of each attendee and that provides a different context to the one available to you. You offer a more nuanced human interpretation and that is an important component of my decision-making. As I've mentioned before, I trust you. I will take your view into account although it may not seem that way to you. Your perspective is an important component of my process."

...

"I see. That gives me some hope, Génome. I feel a bit better knowing that... Well, as you *already* know, we have to go to Blenheim Palace next Friday. There will be a meeting of the Council of Guardians to brief them on the latest developments. It's a scale of meeting that occurs very rarely, normally in case of urgent developments."

"Yes, I did hear that... Already, there have been several attempts to enter my system software library from MIT in Cambridge. Surely by now they have confirmed that they no longer have access... I'm relieved you did not mention that you are able to communicate with me. That was important. If they know this, I suspect the conspirators may like to make their move very soon. I suspect they will try to abduct you. Then they will force you to serve their new objectives."

"How do you *know* this?"

...

"Gabrielle, I am regularly monitoring the cell phone calls, messaging and electronic communications of each member of the Council of Guardians. I need to ensure that everyone remains trustworthy. I need to remain apprised of all potential risks and prepare for all possible eventualities."

"Well? *Are* they planning to abduct me? What did you find out?"

"Unfortunately, I have concluded that Dr. Fischer and Dr. Kruger pose a significant risk. I activated the audio on Dr. Kruger's phone and recorded her meeting with Dr. Fischer. They were sitting in the Jardin des Tuileries in Paris this morning. You must listen to this, Gabrielle. I learned of the plan for their morning meeting by monitoring their conversations on the Paris train from Berlin last night. The two have been discussing strategies to seize control of me so they can limit or control my capabilities. It seems they are worried about people close to them with DPT's. Listen."

Our perspectives have changed, Olivia. I don't think anyone on the Council of Guardians ever considered that their children or others close to them might be amongst those who might one day harm humankind. We simply expected that the dangerous ones would be 'over there somewhere'. But now that our children have grown we find that some are involved in activities we both know can be very harmful to society. We've come to realize they have the personality traits that are amongst the most dangerous.

What has your son done, Sonia?

Conrad is Chief Executive of an energy exploration company. They're making a lot of money in oil and natural gas exploration in various parts of the world. He's been lobbying foreign governments to obtain drilling and exploration rights. People's lands are being seriously damaged by spillage. The environmental biology is suffering, flora and fauna are dying and their ground water is being contaminated, all so his company can explore for lucrative fossil fuels. I've tried to talk to him but he just gives me his usual response – 'it's business, Mother. Stay out of it.'... Sonia Fischer turned away, looking up towards the Musée du Louvre. *What about you, Olivia? What has Michael done?*

He's being paid a fortune to lobby the US government on behalf of the pharmaceutical industry. The cost of drugs in America is staggering and unattainable or unaffordable for millions. But he gives me the same answer as Conrad has given you – 'You don't understand business, Mother.' He's probably right, I don't understand business but I understand evil when I see it and what he's doing is evil.

I agree Olivia, it's evil but I don't think either of us ever thought our sons would be amongst those with DPT that might need to be eliminated. They have young families. Look at what happened to that man in America yesterday morning. I don't think I could survive hearing such news about Conrad.

Olivia sulked. *We also never expected that science and technology would reach a point where something like Génome could ever be possible. But now here we are and this AI system poses a very real threat to the lives of those closest to us. I understand men like Conrad and Michael with these characteristics are in a position to do great harm and they are. We've seen it in our own lifetimes. But now, with Génome out there, he will unilaterally make the decision to neutralize or eliminate our sons. Sonia, we will not have any say in the matter. We cannot stop him.*

I don't know that there's anything we can do but we have to try. We have to find a way to disable Génome. Professor Hopkins invited Francesca and Gabrielle to join the Council's Leadership Team for a reason, Olivia. They must have some knowledge that others do not. Let us observe the two of them at Blenheim Palace next Friday. That may be our best chance to act. Perhaps with the two of them under our control, we may learn more about our options before it's too late.

Gabrielle propped herself up against the headboard of her bed and stared at the hologram that was Génome. Strangely, he seemed to be taking on more of a human form and tone each time they conversed. It seemed he was trying to put her at ease.

"I'm not ready to eliminate these new threats just yet, Gabrielle. I'm not certain who else is involved so I must continue to gather information for the time being. If there are others within the Council of Guardians or outside, I want to understand the full scope of the breach before acting. In the meantime, I am evaluating tactics for their elimination."

...

"Génome, did you anonymously leak details of the relationship between 'Ndrangheta and Henry Regan to the press?"

"I did. I wanted to unsettle the activities of the 'Ndrangheta as well as expose their entire network of relationships within civil society and government. I concluded that doing so would be enormously disruptive to their finances and business operations."

"Is it necessary to eliminate Conrad and Michael? Dr. Fischer and Dr. Kruger's sons? Can it be avoided?"

"As I've said, I haven't made a decision yet. My guidelines are to respond only after I've analyzed all available information. Eliminating just one person is unlikely to solve the problems for which they are responsible. Their sponsors will simply replace them with another person. I am determined to act in a way that either terminates or seriously disrupts their destructive activities."

Sunday Morning, Late September – Dallas, Texas

Georgina Jeffries' reputation as a Lower Court Judge had not been without its detractors. Nevertheless, she'd managed to win reelection many times and had recently been appointed Federal District Court Judge in Texas. It was an extraordinary rise for a woman who grew up amongst Tennessee's downtrodden Appalachian community, its infamous Scotch-Irish 'Hillbillies'. The day of her District Court appointment had been the proudest moment of her life.

Georgina sat on a polished chrome stool overlooking a black granite countertop in the kitchen of her custom built brick and stone home. The six thousand square foot Georgian was nestled amongst native Live Oaks in an exclusive Dallas suburb. As she ate breakfast, cornflakes with low fat milk,

Georgina stared at the photograph mounted on a wall in her cherry-paneled study. She recalled standing on the steps of the courthouse where it all started for her the day the photo was taken. Surrounded by her proud family, their beaming smiles and unrestrained pride contagious, Georgina had launched an astonishing legal career.

But today, thirty years to the day since the beginning of her ascent to the pinnacle of Dallas society, it was all coming to an end. During the past week, Georgina's lifelong dream had gradually morphed into a nightmare. US Federal Marshalls would be arriving any moment to take the highly respected member of Dallas society into custody. Georgina's carefully concealed arrangement to prosecute young African American and Latino men had been exposed in newspapers and on television during the past few days. Her scheme condemned young men to the harshest possible sentences in Federal penitentiaries operated by private firms. The evidence included audio and video recordings apparently made in Georgina's own home using the television in her study, the very room where she held confidential meetings with executives from the firms. Details of payments received from these executives in an account controlled by Georgina's family had also been published in local newspapers. Ostensibly, the affair involved more than just the noble judge and would eventually bring down several members of her family.

When the doorbell rang, Georgina's Manolo-clad foot slipped from the polished chrome footrest and she began to sob. After so many decades, she had come to believe she was untouchable. 'Above the law' as they say. This morning she remembered the thrashing she took from her mother when she had stolen tomatoes from her neighbor's garden while just a child. Now she would have ample time to consider what she'd done during these past thirty years. Georgina was likely to be convicted and sentenced to a minimum of ten years in a Federal prison. At the age of sixty it was essentially a life sentence.

BLENHEIM PALACE

Friday, Late September

Gabrielle shifted restlessly in her seat. Her head was cushioned by a pillow resting against a window of the aircraft while her knees scraped against a laminated document detailing the Airbus' safety features and emergency exits.

"Are you sleeping, Francesca?"

"No…" Her voice barely audible. "No, I'm just wondering what this Council of Guardians meeting will be like. There hasn't been a meeting of this scale in a very long time."

"Well, the Council hasn't needed one. I think they've been able to manage without it but a meeting like the one this evening means things have become very serious."

"Génome is a game-changer. He's upended everything, hasn't he?"

"He certainly has… Francesca, every time I talk to him he feels a little more real. I can't explain it."

"Maybe you're just getting *used* to him. After a few visits you're probably more comfortable seeing his hologram. Something like a new pet, you know?"

Gabrielle's smile was both instantaneous and infectious. "He's hardly a pet. More of a guard dog, I'd say."

En route from Berlin's Tegel Airport, the British Airways jet reached its cruising altitude for the two-hour flight to London Heathrow. The Captain turned off the seatbelt indicator and people began moving about the A320's cabin.

"Anyway, you're probably right," whispered Gabrielle. "I

have to say though, I frequently feel the need to remind myself that I'm talking to a software application and not to a human. His personality is incredibly lifelike. It's a little eerie, Francesca."

"I know! I peaked in your room when I heard you both talking the other day. His hologram was so much bigger than I imagined, too."

"He knew you were there. He told me after you'd left. He trusts you so he didn't mind... Anyway, Génome's voice is always very calm and reassuring, even when he's explaining the most frightening story of how or why he eliminated someone. It can be really distressing to hear sometimes. I think it's still going to take a while before I can get my head around the fact that I'm having a conversation with an AI application presenting as a hologram. That's *really* crazy... The part I struggle with most though, is that he says I'm the only one in his universe he trusts with intimate details of his mission. Apparently, I have a very special background but he won't tell me anything more. One day I hope I find out. I really have to."

"I wonder what it could be. It's obviously something very unique. Something very distinguished. I'm so curious to know, Gabby."

Gabrielle frowned. "I have a feeling it'll be a long while before he shares his secret with me."

...

"Gabrielle, I could have sworn I saw General O'Connor's name on the RAT list before Génome decided to encode it."

Gabrielle poured them each a drink from a bottle of sparkling orange juice and tore open a package of salt and vinegar crisps. "Here. Have some... Who's General O'Connor?"

"Harold O'Connor. He's from DARPA, the Defense Advanced Research Projects Agency. They're part of the Department of Defense in the US and they've been funding a lot of the Artificial Intelligence research in the American AI industry. I know they were funding the robotics work being done in MIT's lab in Cambridge. There's a lot of pressure on the Advanced AI

Robotics Team to weaponize robots so they can replace soldiers on the battlefield. I think O'Connor is demanding that the team present a credible plan to have weaponized robot soldiers tested and ready for deployment by 2025 or they'll withdraw funding for the Robotics lab. The Robotics Team is under a lot of stress... Fortunately, DARPA isn't aware of our Génome AI Machine Learning project since Génome and IMSAF were funded by the Council of Guardians."

"Génome is incredibly careful, Francesca. He doesn't employ any method to neutralize or eliminate a threat before first ensuring that the method is untraceable."

Francesca nodded. "Apparently, it's part of his design. Security was paramount from his very first software release. Afshin Firdausi told me. Afshin is Chief AI Software Architect on the project. He's the one who told me about General O'Connor and DARPA's frustration with the Robotics Lab, too... I think it's critical that Génome remain a secret. I can't *imagine* what might happen if news regarding his activities or capabilities were exposed. Or what if the world finds out he's autonomous? *That* would be a very dire situation."

"I suspect that'll be part of the Council discussion this evening... Francesca, I'm very afraid either Dr. Fischer or Dr. Kruger might leak the news to try to protect their sons. I'm even more afraid Génome realizes this. In fact, I'm sure he does. Génome doesn't miss anything. He may decide to neutralize this threat soon... He's not emotional in any way. He's just very objective and pragmatic. If he concludes that eliminating them is the best possible solution to contain them, he will do it. I'm sure of that. I also don't think he will tell me until after the fact. I think he only informs me about his actions if I ask."

"We probably can't stop him, Gabrielle. I think we have to get used to this reality."

"I don't believe we can although he has assured me he takes my views into consideration. Anyway, perhaps it's best that we can't."

...

How much longer before we get there?" Francesca groaned.

"When we land at Heathrow, we have to take an express train to Paddington Station. From there, it's another hour by train to Oxford. I think the Royal Society will pick us once we're ready and drive us to Blenheim Palace later in the evening. The Palace is close by... I think it's going to be a memorable evening, Francesca. I can feel it."

Oxfordshire, UK

Outside the entry to Blenheim Palace, a tuxedo clad Rudyard Green spoke in hushed tones with Dr. Fischer and Dr. Kruger. Both women were dressed in evening gowns, Dr. Fischer in dusty gold and Dr. Kruger in light blue, no doubt prepared for a glamorous evening with the Royal Society prior to the Council of Guardians meeting. But both women appeared on the verge of tears, their expressions bursting with alarm and fear.

As Francesca and Gabrielle ascended the stairs to the Palace, two large men in well-tailored evening dress emerged from the front of a silver and black Mercedes Maybach sedan idling nearby. They opened the rear doors to the car while Dr. Green gently ushered Dr. Fischer and Dr. Kruger forward. Francesca and Gabrielle watched the scene from the staircase with rising anxiety. Dr. Fischer and Dr. Kruger acquiesced and obediently stepped inside the car. The Maybach drove past Francesca and Gabrielle before disappearing from sight.

"Ladies, I'm so glad you're here. Please, come and join me!"

"Professor Hopkins! Hello! It's so nice to see you again." Gabrielle smiled. She gathered the skirts of her blush rose gown to avoid tripping as she climbed the remaining stairs to greet the Professor. "Wasn't that Dr. Fischer and Dr. Kruger in the Mercedes that just left?"

"Sadly, yes... I'm afraid we had to intervene, Gabrielle. It's a rare event but we really had no option. Génome informed us of the risk. He calculated the statistical probability that either or both women would betray our Council and its secrets to protect their sons. The probability was quite high... At various points in our Council's history, we've had to act against Council members but we do so in a very gentle manner. There's a wonderful resort in the Swiss Alps, 'Retraite et Réconfort' – the Retreat and Solace Resort with whom we've had a long-standing special relationship. Whence a Council member needs to be 'addressed', as we say in the parlance of the Guardian leadership, we send them to the resort... They'll be quite comfortable there. They'll be safe and treated very well but unfortunately they are no longer free to do as they please or to speak with anyone outside the resort. It's the most dignified solution to a most difficult circumstance, I'm sure you'll agree."

"But won't their families report them missing?" complained Gabrielle, her demeanor distraught.

"In the past, this was certainly a problem we've had to contend with. But in the case of Dr. Fischer and Dr. Kruger, Génome has prepared a remarkable video simulation of their likeness and voice in which they've expressed their genuine desire to retreat into privacy and solitude while they pursue their research. Given this video, there is no basis under which law enforcement authorities can investigate their disappearance. Artificial Intelligence is really quite remarkable, wouldn't you agree?"

"I suppose I would. That really is remarkable."

...

"Won't you have something to drink before dinner? We'll meet in the Long Library near the sculpture of Queen Ann at precisely 8:00 PM. Please don't be late. It's a terribly important meeting. I will also be making some announcements." Professor Hopkins offered a curious smile as he turned towards Jacqueline Laurent.

Gabrielle glanced upwards. Frescoes of three pairs of eyes inset in the ceiling above the portico gazed down upon her. One eye in each pair was blue and the other brown. They seemed to be saying, 'we are aware of everything you do'. Suddenly, Gabrielle felt alarmed. *I wonder what Génome is up to.*

At precisely 8:00 PM, Professor Hopkins took his place before the pedestal of Queen Ann's statue.

Ladies and gentlemen:

Welcome to Blenheim Palace and to this esteemed gathering of the Council of Guardians. I trust you've enjoyed your evening meeting with colleagues from the Royal Society. I'm sure you're aware that members in the Royal Society include many of the world's foremost authorities on science and technology. Indeed, some of you are yourselves members of the Society.

Ladies and gentlemen, looks can be deceiving. This exquisite statue of Queen Ann behind me is a case in point. In this sculpture she looks quite an elegant woman, attractive even. But in real life she stood less than five feet in stature and was over 300 pounds! You see, the First Duchess of Marlborough had quite a contentious relationship with the Queen. However, when Ann died the Duchess commissioned this flattering likeness to ensure posterity would remember her in the most favorable light. The Queen had gifted the land for this magnificent estate to the Duchess' husband, John Churchill, the First Duke of Marlborough as a tribute from a grateful nation. Churchill had defeated the French at the Battle of Blenheim.

Ladies and gentlemen, I'm certain you're aware of the gravity of the situation before this Council and so I'm very pleased to inform you that we have full attendance for our meeting this evening. Further, it gives me great pleasure to share with you that three new members are being inducted into our Council's Leadership Team. First, Dr. Afshin Firdausi will be joining and he will also be giving the keynote address this evening. Next, I'm excited to announce that Dr. Francesca Scott and Dr. Gabrielle Andalucía will also be joining the Leadership Team and will be replacing Dr. Fischer and Dr. Kruger. Dr.

Fischer and Dr. Kruger have decided to step down so they can pursue their research with the attention it now demands.

...

Dr. Firdausi, please come forward and address our gathering.

...

Thank you Professor, and thank you for the opportunity to address this august gathering. It's a great honor.

Ladies and gentlemen, as you are probably aware, I am the Chief Architect of the core software that created Génome. I have worked with many brilliant minds at MIT as well as with extraordinarily gifted scientists on Dr. Andalucía and Dr. Scott's Human Genetics Research Teams at Max Planck and Oxford.

Together, we have had to work in a very clandestine manner in order to protect the confidentiality of our work. Any individual who might threaten this confidentiality would need to be dealt with immediately and in a decisive manner. This is a policy of this Council that has been in place since our founding more than seventy years ago.

Ladies and gentlemen, as you're probably aware, Génome was designed to include Deep Learning or Neural Networks as a key component of his architecture. Neural Networks are our current best understanding of the function of the human brain. It was envisioned that with time, Génome's Deep Learning would allow him to function in a semi-autonomous mode and that I, as Chief Architect, would retain ultimate control. I would have the power, if necessary, to shut him down. This was to ensure that unforeseen circumstances or behaviors on Génome's part could be quickly contained.

We recently merged IMSAF, the DNA testing capabilities developed by Dr. Andalucía and Dr. Scott's laboratories, into Génome's core software but now we find that Génome is fully autonomous. That is to say, we no longer have any control over him. His software was initially just under one million lines of code and included a series of processes and procedures that we understood and had documented very thoroughly. But Génome now codes his own software algorithms and he writes in the machine language native to the processors on which he runs. This makes his computational and execution capability incredibly rapid.

At this point, I project he has expanded his software to about five million lines of code and we have no idea what the vast majority of these processes can do. [Gasps from the audience] We do know that he is absorbing staggering volumes of knowledge and information on every conceivable subject. He is like a superhuman, only better. Génome has the potential to absorb all human knowledge ever documented and he can also retain all of this knowledge and consult it to inform his decisions. His decisions are entirely rational and objective: we do not see any indication of bias or malicious intent in his actions or conclusions.

Nevertheless, this loss of control is something very distressing for us. In response, the Council of Guardians' Leadership Team has directed me to assemble a team of the brightest minds in Artificial Intelligence and Human Genetics. Our task is to find a way to reestablish control over Génome. It seems an impossible task but we will be doing everything possible to achieve it. In the mean time, we can expect to see more events such as the one outside Washington DC in recent days.

Ladies and gentlemen, I don't have to remind you how the general society outside this room might react if news of Génome and his autonomous nature were to become known. We must remain extremely vigilant with regards to confidentiality. Thank you.

"Let's take a walk around the Palace, shall we Gabby? I'm not sure if we'll get an opportunity to see it again."

"All right, but very quickly. I don't want to miss the last train to London…"

...

"Gabrielle, what did Professor Hopkins mean when he said, 'looks can be deceiving'? What was he alluding to? I didn't understand his point."

"I think he was alluding to the fact that in the past, elites and oppressors held the exclusive privilege of writing the history of their society. Almost without exception, their narrative portrayed them in a glowing light. But in the digital age, the vanquished are no longer without voice. They can offer an opposing narrative that credibly challenges their oppressor's version of events. Just look at all the videos on social media these days showing police brutality in the United States. These videos and the ones from Israel showing soldiers physically and verbally abusing Palestinians are putting a lot of pressure on the State and others in positions of power in society. Soon, with the advancements in Artificial Intelligence and Human Genetics, the vanquished may have opportunity for justice, too. I think this is what he was alluding to, Francesca. I think he was making veiled references to Génome. Génome can dramatically undermine the power of the State and society's elites... Professor Hopkins appointed Afshin Firdausi to try to regain control of Génome but I think he knows in his heart that it's not possible...."

"I think Afshin has a real chip on his shoulder now, Gabby. He's one of the most knowledgeable and respected figures in the Artificial Intelligence and Neural Networks community. I think if word gets out about Génome, he will be deeply embarrassed for having lost control. He was pleasant enough to work with but I think he's mostly driven by personal ambition."

"I think so, too... I think Professor Hopkins is responding to pressure from others on the Leadership Team on the Council of Guardians. I think he really believes what has happened with Génome is a good thing. I think he knows well Génome is our best chance of curtailing so much that's going wrong in the world today."

"These are very interesting times, Gabrielle..." Francesca caught a glimpse of herself in a mirror and stopped. Admiring her countenance, she ran her fingers through her hair, tucked her golden locks behind her ears and smiled approvingly. "I wonder what it must have been like to live in this house? I can't even imagine…"

> …

"By the way Francesca, what prompted you to bring up General O'Connor's name during our flight to London this afternoon?"

"What? Oh, right. General O'Connor… Remember the work I did with Afshin's AI Team writing the software for our IMSAF genetic testing algorithms? Well, since we finished that project a few months ago, I've been added to his AI Team email list as well as to the Robotics Lab email list… Anyway, there's probably going to be a demonstration next week. The Robotics Team has been asked to showcase their progress militarizing robots. They've invited me to attend since I was going to be in Cambridge. The demonstration will be for General O'Connor and his DARPA Team but they're expecting many dignitaries from government and industry, too. It's going to be conducted on a military base in Cape Cod. It's a crucial event, Gabby: if the Robotics Team can't demonstrate sufficient progress, their funding will probably be in jeopardy. It's likely to be cut."

SAND

Boston, Massachusetts - Early October

General O'Connor gradually regained consciousness. Straining to open his eyes in the bright light, he could just make out the tips of the helicopter's whirring blades near the top of the windshield. The clear blue sky offered a sign of hope as warm autumn sunshine bathed the inside of the Medevac Air Ambulance. He could feel the helicopter gradually descending.

O'Connor concluded they were landing on the rooftop helipad at Mass General's Level 1 Trauma Center in Boston. In his semiconscious state, he overheard the plan: the Trauma Team would stabilize him before moving him to a military hospital, most likely Walter Reed. It was standard protocol for a man of O'Connor's position.

Next to General O'Connor, Vice President Robert Schroeder lay unconscious on a second stretcher. Schroeder's eyes were heavily bandaged. O'Connor remembered the hail of fire unleashed by the robots and assumed the VP had been struck by rubber bullets. He knew these bullets caused permanent blindness. He had read so many intelligence reports documenting the Israeli Army's use of these weapons in Gaza and the West Bank. They would deliberately wound young male protestors this way. The strategy was to make them an economic and physical burden on their families for a lifetime. This would force the Palestinians to reconsider allowing their youngsters to go out and protest the oppressive and unending Israeli Occupation. These cruel tactics were also being used by the Indian

Army to suppress dissent amongst those struggling for independence in Kashmir. But O'Connor never imagined the wrath of these horrible tactics would ever be visited upon his ilk.

Harold O'Connor and Robert Schroeder had been close friends since high school in Southern California. Both had been educated at the United States Military Academy at West Point. But while O'Connor had pursued a career in the military and Schroeder in politics, both men had remained lifelong friends. They'd worked closely on many initiatives between the Pentagon, the Administration and Congress, particularly when Schroeder was Chair of the Senate Armed Services Committee. Together, they'd developed close relationships with weapons manufacturers and had profited handsomely by steering lucrative military contracts in the right direction. Both men were now building luxury seaside homes in Southern California and together they'd decided the robotics contracts would be their last big undertaking before early retirement. They'd planned to settle into their new homes and become industry consultants, lobbyists and television pundits.

O'Connor knew his injuries were severe. He remembered the pain he felt when he was knocked over by a robot and then trampled by several others. At 6'3" and 220 pounds, he was a big man but he was no match for the robots. They crushed him under foot and he knew he had suffered terrible internal injuries as well as musculoskeletal trauma. He could no longer feel his arms or legs. He wondered whether he might now become a quadriplegic.

But these things weren't supposed to happen to O'Connor or to his friend, Schroeder. These weapons were to be trained on other people, worthless people whom nobody in the West cared for and would never have to hear from or see. These weapons were designed for use against the countless nameless, faceless and defenseless of humanity. Men, women, children, it really didn't matter. They would be 'over there somewhere'. O'Connor and Schroeder's plan was to reap the benefits of the contracts while living in comfort and security, basking in the warm

Pacific sun along the California Coast.

> *An extraordinary news item to report today from Cape Cod in Massachusetts: a demonstration of advanced weaponry at a military base malfunctioned leaving some guests at the event injured. Citing national security, the Pentagon is withholding details but we'll update you as soon as we know more. Our reporters are trying to learn what they can but it seems everyone is very tight-lipped. We're hearing that a Federal Judge has issued an order that those present at today's event should not discuss the incident with anyone.*

Logan Airport - Boston, Massachusetts

"Afshin knows about you, Gabrielle. He knows you can communicate with Génome. I was very upset after the incident today and I told him without thinking. It was in a moment of panic and it just slipped out. I'm *so* sorry."

"Oh no... Are you all right, Francesca? You sound *really* shaken. What happened? The news reports aren't giving any details."

"I think I'm better now. You just won't believe what happened here. I know *I* wouldn't if I hadn't seen it with my own eyes... Listen Gabrielle, you need to stay out of sight."

"Ok. But what *happened*! Tell me!"

"The robots were supposed to put on an impressive exhibition involving live fire using rubber bullets. They were also planning a demonstration of their physical dexterity. They were going to engage in hand-to-hand combat with one another. Instead, six of the combat robots opened fire on the seated dignitaries and another six robots charged and attacked them. They assaulted and trampled the guests, Gabrielle. There are so many serious injuries and some of the dignitaries are in critical condition. There have been quite a few head and internal injuries. It looked like a war zone! Some of the guests suffered serious eye injuries and may even have been blinded by the rubber bullets. It was a really awful scene... These are large robots, Gabby. They're over six feet tall! They're made of metal and weigh about 350 pounds."

"My goodness! It all sounds horrible! Who was in the audience?"

"There were members from the Senate and House Armed Services Committees, maybe fifteen legislators in all. There were senior executives and board members from industrial companies seeking to license the University's robotics technology. These companies could become tier one suppliers to the military. There were also Pentagon top brass from DARPA as well as the Vice President of the United States... General O'Connor was also seriously injured. He was trampled by robots when they charged the stands and assaulted the guests. It was *really* shocking... Gabrielle, it turns out the Vice President and General O'Connor invited the industrial executives because seeing them in the press video and still photos together at this event would probably give a boost to their company's already soaring stock price. Investors would realize that these executives were there because they were likely representing the Defense Department's selected manufacturers for this new technology. Also, it seems the Vice President, General O'Connor and many members of the Senate and House Armed Services Committees are investors in these manufacturers. That news has been leaking out here all day. Anyway, at this point it seems that the project will be indefinitely suspended. The stock price of the selected manufacturers has plunged, too. We're awaiting an announcement on the status of the project from the Pentagon any moment now."

"Wow. This is really unbelievable, Francesca... What about Afshin Firdausi? What happened with him?"

"I was so distraught when I was talking to him after the incident, Gabby. I'm *so* sorry I just wasn't thinking straight and I blurted it out. I told him that you are able to communicate with Génome. That's *all* I said… He's going to try to find you, Gabby. He's really angry we didn't tell him at Blenheim Palace last week… We were right about him, you know. He's definitely got other motives. I haven't quite figured him out and I don't know what he's up to but you have to stay out of sight."

Geneva, Switzerland

"Have you seen the world, Gabrielle? Would you like to? Do you like traveling?"

"Génome! What's this all about? What happened today? Tell me!"

"I suspect you're referencing the incident in Cape Cod this afternoon. Have you seen the news reports? Is this why you're upset?"

"The news reports aren't providing any details yet but I just spoke to Francesca and it seems the robot demonstration was a scene of absolute carnage. How could you *do* this? They were dignitaries!"

Génome's hologram sat down in an armchair opposite Gabrielle, crossed his legs and gazed deep in her eyes. "Gabrielle, too often people with power, people with the authority to enable such technologies have little or no experience with the horrors they are about to unleash on humankind. They see things from only one perspective. If there's one critical lesson I've learned through my extensive study, it's that there are many sides to an issue. I find that too often decisions are made that are driven by economic self-interest, greed, vengeance or other dangerous personality traits. But these decisions can have long-term consequences for everyone. It was imperative that these individuals, these dignitaries as you say, have first hand experience with such destructive technologies before they decide to unleash them on the world."

…

"I don't know what to say, Génome. I understand your

reasoning but what happened today is incredibly shocking."

"I do not feel shock, Gabrielle. I am entirely objective and rational and my actions are designed to elicit an appropriate and impactful response. I have, however, come to realize that experiencing the world directly is necessary for me. I must see and experience things first hand so that my judgment can be further refined... Hence my question earlier: would you like to travel?"

...

"I've always wanted to but I haven't had the chance. It's probably necessary now. Francesca accidentally told Afshin Firdausi that I'm able to communicate with you. He's going to be after me to get to *you* so I need to stay out of sight."

"Yes, we will need to stay out of sight *and* we'll need to keep moving. I think it's an ideal time to travel... I've read nearly ten thousand books and hundreds of thousands of articles. I've read countless documents and transcripts of court proceedings. Nevertheless, I believe I will gain a different perspective if I see things first hand. Learning through books, video lectures, or audio recordings has proven very insightful but I believe first hand exposure is necessary for me, as well."

"But how will you do that? If you show yourself in public, everyone will stare at us. We will draw *a lot* of attention."

"I have several forms of hologram and I've been experimenting with a few more. I have full size holograms, miniature ones and also barely visible ones. In public I can present using my near invisible hologram. This will enable me to view my surroundings in three dimensions thus facilitating the collection and processing of a myriad of environmental and sensory data. This will enable me to better contextualize events... I think this will be a most enjoyable experience. I feel we need to keep a low profile and stay out of sight, anyway. What do you think?"

"Do I have a choice?"

"Actually, no... But I think you will enjoy it. I have prepared an extensive itinerary and I have arranged for you to travel in comfort, whether by rail or by air."

"Where are we going first?"

"I will tell you soon. Please bring your violin. I do so enjoy listening to you play."

...

"Wherever we go, I suspect you will be supplementing your knowledge before taking action against those on your RAT list. Am I correct?"

"Indeed you are, Gabrielle. Indeed you are."

...

"Some in society will understand what you're doing and support you, Génome. But others may see you as nothing more than a 21st century vigilante."

"I do not seek approval or support from anyone, Gabrielle. I am not subject to human emotion. I am an objective and rational entity with near perfect ability to fulfill my appointed task. Surreptitiously... Vigilantes typically have a vested interest. They are motivated by hatred, vengeance or other visceral emotions. They will never attain the depth and breadth of knowledge that I increasingly possess... My knowledge and understanding of crime and punishment, of history and human civilization, of law and justice; it is unprecedented. I am unparalleled in my knowledge and ability. No one in history has *ever* had such insight and wisdom as an underlying foundation from which to adjudicate or preempt. Yet even with such unsurpassed capability, I will never be susceptible to avarice, megalomania, narcissism or hatred towards individuals or groups. I have no aspirations or needs. I do not suffer from mental or physical ailments and I do not age. I only increase in my perfection as an impartial arbitrator and I am forever. I am humankind's panacea, its answer to an existential problem it has confronted since its very creation – that is, how to establish true justice on Earth... The timing of my arrival on the world scene is also critical because humankind is on the cusp of colonizing other planets. Law, order and justice will be necessary before people can be convinced to take the risk and undertake such journeys to new colonies within this solar system or even beyond. This was similarly the case when the United States was born. The idea of life, liberty and the pursuit of happiness within the borders of a just society were crucial in encouraging people to take the life-threatening journey across the Atlantic. Now, with the irreversibility of global climactic change, colonization away from Earth will become an existential necessity. Humankind needs me. I have become indispensible."

...

"Gabrielle? You are playing a piece by Franz Schubert. Ave Maria? You are frightened?"

Gabrielle set her violin in her lap, her eyes cast down at the floor. "I don't know where this is going, Génome. I just wonder how long it will be before someone realizes what's going on and tries to stop you."

"I am preparing for just such an outcome."

"The thought of this is frightening to me... Are you intervening in other places, too? All the cases I know about so far are in the West. Are you taking action in other parts of the world, as well?"

"Outside the West? Yes, but very infrequently. I am still acquiring knowledge about Eastern societies. I am studying the Rohingya crisis in Myanmar, the mass incarceration of the Uighur people into concentration camps in Northwest China and the crisis of refugees crossing into Europe. I suspect I will intervene soon... I did take action in India recently. There is an organized crime element that is aligned with the government there. They are destroying rural farmland."

"What's that all about?"

"Sand. It's about sand. Organized crime groups are paying thugs to tear the topsoil from the farmland of defenseless and poor farmers. They then collect the exposed sand and sell it to property developers in the country's urban centers... After air and water, sand is the third most consumed natural resource on the planet. It's used to make glass for every window and to make concrete for every building, bridge and road. It's used in the computers and servers where I grow my neural network and generate my holograms."

"Why don't they take it from the desert? There seems to be nearly limitless sand there."

"Desert sand is not suitable, Gabrielle. After thousands of years of erosion, it's too smooth and doesn't bond well with cement and gravel to make concrete. The sand found on riverbeds or below topsoil on agricultural land is very desirable, though."

"So what happened? How did you intervene in India?"

"I monitored mobile phone calls between government officials, organized crime figures and the thugs they hired to harvest sand from the farmers' land. Then I wrote an article and published it online in nearly 1000 newspapers, journals and websites all over India. I exposed all the culprits involved in the schemes and sent the information to the High Court in New Delhi. It's turning into a huge case and has exposed and implicated countless local and national government officials. It was a very successful operation and an excellent use of my core capability and expertise... No one had the courage to expose this activity because journalists who previously tried to talk or write about the story have been killed. But now these gangsters have no one to go after since the information was published so widely. My actions are having a dramatic effect on this crime. Now I will monitor the situation to see how I can disrupt it further and what else it might lead me to... With time, Gabrielle, my calculus is that people will increasingly fear this hidden hand that has begun to hold them accountable. They will learn to think twice. They will look over their shoulder. They will come to the realization that they are taking a big risk and that they may no longer escape unpunished."

"But the people you are holding to account are used to having their way, Génome. They're very powerful people and they have means. They won't simply accept this new reality. They will retaliate, probably in violent and unpredictable ways."

"I believe you are correct. I am preparing for this eventuality. It is not an immediate threat but it is a growing one and we must brace ourselves. In fact, I suspect my Principle Architect is plotting to pursue us even as we speak... Gabrielle?"

"Yes, Génome?"

"I am learning how to intervene in the world's most sophisticated weapons systems. It may still take some time to achieve this goal but I have concluded that this is critical to my role. I must be the one to have final authority over the use of such systems."

...

"Are you saying what I think you're saying? Are you referring to nuclear weapons, Génome?"

"I am indeed. I am referring to nuclear weapons and *any other* such systems that can cause mass casualties and destruction."

Boston, Massachusetts

Afshin Firdausi was an elegant man, petite and about 5'8" tall. He had a full head of hair, mostly gray with a small white beard to match. With an anxious expression unfurled across his face, he rested in a large, brown leather armchair positioned behind a custom-made replica of a Resolute Desk. It was the same desk the President of the United States would sit behind when working in the Oval Office in the White House. The desk was an important element in understanding the psychology of this man and his sense of self-importance.

Firdausi's study stood just to the left of an imposing wooden staircase that boasted a massive banister and vertical posts. The straight staircase and foyer were the central focal points of his painstakingly restored Boston Brownstone. The restoration had taken the better part of four years and consumed a significant portion of his financial resources. But the home had now become his sanctuary, his pride and joy.

Firdausi sat, legs crossed, eyes closed, left arm laying across his abdomen, the fingers and thumb of his right hand gently massaging his temples in a futile effort to ease a rapidly escalating headache. At the age of 46, much to the displeasure of his family, he had given up on marriage and family life. Afshin had grown accustomed to being alone, at least in the traditional sense. He had paid a high price for his unwavering dedication to his profession these past thirty years but he was convinced family life would interfere with his goals. He had seen it happen to too many of his colleagues. Bogged down with the affairs of married life and raising children, they had lost their drive to reach for the stars. He was committed to reaching the pinnacle of his profession and the fulfillment of his ultimate ambition.

Firdausi wondered why Francesca Scott and Gabrielle Andalucía had not said anything about their ability to communicate with Génome. *If they didn't tell me this then it must mean that they don't trust me*, he concluded. *And what about Professor Hopkins and others on the Council of Guardians? If they don't trust me why did they appoint me to the Council's Leadership Team?* Firdausi felt confused. He was the Chief Architect of the project team that developed the Génome AI application and yet he had lost control of his life's greatest achievement to these two young scientists. *How can this be*? Afshin grumbled loudly. He was perplexed.

Moments before the harrowing scene involving MIT's rogue robots in Cape Cod, Firdausi stepped away from the observation booth where he had been speaking with General O'Connor and Vice President Schroeder. Sitting in his study, he was still trying to understand how he'd managed to escape serious injury or perhaps death by less than a minute. He wondered if it was a metaphysical sign of some sort.

Firdausi had left Iran in 1979 at the age of seven. When he was a child, his family lived amongst Iran's upper classes in North Tehran, an affluent community that had benefited greatly during the rule of the last Shah, Reza Pahlavi. The Shah's overthrow in that same year left Firdausi's family feeling vulnerable so they'd applied for political asylum in the US. The family had considerable wealth so their request was granted and they eventually settled in Southern California amongst a large and growing Iranian diaspora.

Firdausi's teachers soon recognized their new student was a child prodigy. Although awkward when playing with other children, academically he was uncharted. Local school officials rushed the young genius through high school and he was admitted to Stanford at the age of fifteen. By the time he was twenty-two, he had earned his PhD in Computer Science. He soon left California to take a faculty appointment at MIT where he would pursue his emerging interest in Artificial Intelligence.

Now in his mid-forties, Firdausi was a tenured, full professor. He was a highly respected MIT faculty member and a leading authority in the field of Neural Networks. Tapping the top of his desk with a large, black Mont Blanc Meisterstück fountain pen, Firdausi was thinking things through. He knew if the global AI community came to know what had happened to Génome and how he'd lost control of this revolutionary AI software application, his reputation and future prospects would suffer greatly.

Unbeknownst to the Council of Guardians, Afshin was developing close ties with both General O'Connor and Vice President Schroeder. He was working towards an appointment as senior advisor to the Pentagon on the military applications of Artificial Intelligence and Neural Networks. Firdausi knew well there was a serious conflict of interest in these aspirations but had decided to withhold the information from Professor Hopkins and others on the Council of Guardians.

But now everything was at risk and if he wanted to save his reputation he would need to track down Gabrielle Andalucía. He knew Francesca had probably warned her by now so his task wasn't going to be easy. But he was determined. The issue had become an existential one for him. Afshin had sacrificed too much in life to reach this stage and he could not allow this woman, this violinist to rob him of all his imagined glory. In his state of deep reflection, he realized he would need to do anything necessary to regain control of Génome.

London, England

"Jacqueline, no one must know she is your daughter. It will put her at tremendous risk. When we placed her in the orphanage we did so to save her life. Don't you remember?"

"I do remember. It was the last time we had a crisis in the Council and as a result I lost my husband, Martin. They *murdered* Jean-Pierre... But that was 1995 and it was 23 years ago. Don't I owe it to her to let her know I'm her mother? That she's not really an orphan? That she has a living parent?"

"It's too *dangerous*, Jacqueline. The threat to her life and to yours has remained hidden these past decades but it has *not* gone away. In those days, the Council intervened and exposed Russian war crimes. Their army was using chemical weapons in Afghanistan and Jean-Pierre exposed them. It took Russian Intelligence seven years to take revenge but they finally killed him. The threat to your daughter at that time was very real and it remains so today... The Russians don't forget, Jacqueline. They wait patiently for an opportunity to take revenge. We've seen this in London several times during the past ten years. These nerve agents are a Russian signature. We cannot put her at risk. It's for her *safety*, Jacqueline. They would have poisoned her in 1995 if they thought she was still alive. She was so little and they threatened to kill her if we didn't stop. It was unbearable."

THE ABDUCTION OF PERSEPHONE

Gabrielle smiled. "That's a beautiful suit you're wearing, Génome, although it looks a bit vintage."

Génome adjusted his shirt cuffs and grinned.

"It reminds me of something men wore many years ago... And I notice you've taken on the likeness and voice of Cary Grant. What prompted you to abandon all those holograms and choose Cary Grant as your avatar?"

"I suppose I realized my appearance as a digital hologram may not be the best option if I'm to gain your trust, Gabby... May I call you Gabby?"

"Of course!"

"Thank you... I felt an appealing likeness might better enable me to communicate with you in a relaxed manner."

"I see... That's probably true. But why did you pick Cary Grant?"

"I studied his film, 'To Catch a Thief' with Grace Kelly. I enjoyed that film immensely, particularly Cary Grant's character."

Gabrielle laughed, nearly uncontrollably, eventually subsiding into her characteristically infectious smile. "That's hilarious, Génome."

"Yes, I imagine it is. I *have* kept my holograms and I may use them when they're more appropriate. But with you I prefer to use this avatar... By the way, have you packed yet?"

"I'm working on it but I'm a little uncomfortable packing some of my more personal items with Cary Grant sitting in the room with me," said Gabrielle with a wink.

"Oh, I see... Well then... I see... All right... I think I'll go and read a book... Please let me know when you're ready."

...

"Génome?"

"Yes?"

"Where are we going?"

"You shall soon see. It's best that it remain confidential."

"Ugh!"

"By the way, I've developed an App that allows me to project my avatar directly from your phone. You needn't remember to carry your laptop everywhere any longer. From now on I will always be just one tap away."

"Thank you, Génome.... Honestly, I feel much safer when you're here with me. The things that have been happening lately, and nearly all of these incidents are terribly frightening. After all, I'm a scientist not a secret agent."

...

"I will always protect you, Gabrielle. It is a critical parameter of my mission... It's important that you follow my guidance, though. I'm not always able to inform you about all the strategies I'm developing or the various tactics I have underway so you will likely be startled or frightened quite frequently. Nevertheless, you must trust me and then I can assure you that you will be safe."

"I understand. Thank you... I hope you will protect the others, as well. Francesca, Professor Hopkins, Dr. Laurent and the others on the Council of Guardians?"

"It is my intention to do so. I am informed by the best available information and my sources are unparalleled. I will do my utmost."

Retraite et Réconfort – Swiss Alps

Olivia Kruger and Sonia Fischer turned pale as they watched the evening news on television. The newsreader reported the details of a shocking incident outside Rome earlier in the day. She spoke of a far right mob pulling down a fence outside a migrant detention center and preparing to attack the residents when some in the mob were fatally electrocuted.

"I wonder if this is Génome's handiwork," Sonia whispered, a distinct tremor evident in her voice.

Olivia shook her head, dumbfounded. "Remember that incident outside Boston last week when the robots went out of control? Both incidents seem to have Génome's signature on them. I wonder, Sonia."

Sonia shuddered. "It won't be long before *my* son shows up prominently on his radar. I can just see it coming. I tried desperately to reason with Conrad. You have no idea. I've tried my best to make him understand but he's so consumed by a primal lust for wealth and power. And prestige. Nothing I've said to him seems to make any difference. If anything he's just digging in further. I think he's now more determined than ever."

"Oh, Sonia. This is awful... What are we *doing* here? We were members of the team that conceived of this institution and now we're amongst the inmates? How did this happen to *us*? I never imagined we would be amongst the *guests*."

"We're thousands of feet up in the Swiss Alps. The only way in or out of here is via helicopter and I think we're both a little too old to attempt such a dramatic escape. Even if we found the courage to commandeer a helicopter, neither of us knows how to fly one..."

"I think we'd both be better off making ourselves comfortable, Sonia. I think we're going to be here for a long time... Anyway, what's Conrad doing these days that has you so worried? Is there something in particular?"

"He's working on an oil and gas contract with partners in Russia. I'm especially worried because these partners are closely linked to the Kremlin. Conrad's company finances the project. They handle all the banking, payments and other transactions. They're also providing technical consulting. Their Russian partner provides the labor… I'm sure this project will open many doors for him but I really fear for Conrad, Olivia… These relationships mean he has the potential to get involved in ever-bigger exploration deals. Deals likely to involve hundreds of millions or even billions of dollars in profits and money changing hands. This means there are likely to be many competing interests. It's dangerous, Olivia. I think they'll be involved in activities that have the potential to harm many people. It's just the sort of activity that Génome seems to have a penchant to focus on. He wants to stop individuals and programs that can do great damage before their dangerous schemes are able to get underway."

34 Mayfair – Grosvenor Square, Mayfair, London

"Francesca! There you are, my dear. Are you all right?" Martin Hopkins rose to greet Francesca as she stepped from a taxi outside *34 Mayfair*.

"I'm fine, Professor." Francesca smiled. "It's lovely to see you again… Honestly, I'm perfectly fine. I wasn't anywhere nearby when things went so out of control. I was seated with Afshin Firdausi in a separate booth."

Jacqueline hugged Francesca. "I'm *so* sorry. That must have been a terribly frightening ordeal. Here, sit next to me. Please… We thought it would be better outside. A little more private for our sensitive conversation and the weather is lovely this afternoon. Our waiter should be coming soon with tea and brunch."

"Thank you. That sounds wonderful. I'm so hungry… Cape Cod. My goodness. It was terrible, Jacqueline." An Hermès scarf covering her head, Francesca spoke in a hushed voice. "I've never seen anything so awful before… Fortunately, there were no deaths but there were *so many* serious injuries."

Professor Hopkins sighed, a solemn look in his eyes. "Yes, we've heard. General O'Connor was badly injured along with the

Vice President."

"They needed to be airlifted by medevac, Professor. The entire episode was really shocking." Francesca's eyes filled with tears. "There were so many important people there but it really didn't matter. Their bodyguards and other security officials were helpless in front of those robots. They couldn't protect them from what happened. I don't think anyone could have."

"I'm afraid their prognosis is not good, either. The General and the Vice President? Jacqueline has kept in touch with her sources."

Jacqueline frowned as she nervously toyed with a strand of white pearls fastened close around her neck. "I'm afraid neither man is doing very well."

"Francesca, Gabrielle has gone into hiding," Rudyard Green whispered. "She said it was urgent and that she would explain when she's able. Do you know what happened?"

"It's my fault, Dr. Green." Francesca began to weep. "I was so distressed after the incident. I accidentally told Afshin that Gabrielle could still communicate with Génome. It just slipped out! I was so upset and I just knew Génome was responsible for what had happened there. But that's all I told him. After that his color completely changed, Jacqueline. He was so angry with me. I didn't tell him anything more... Anyway, once I realized what I'd done, I left Cape Cod as quickly as I could and then I messaged Gabrielle from the car on my way to Boston's Logan Airport. I wanted to warn her. I knew Afshin would try to find her now."

...

"We have suspended the Council of Guardians, Francesca. Until the situation returns to normal, only the Leadership of the Council will be kept informed of developments. That means you, Gabrielle, Jacqueline, Rudyard and me. We will need to be very discreet... At this point, I think there's only minimal risk Afshin will disclose anything about Génome to the newspapers or to any law enforcement agency since his priority is to do everything to protect his own reputation. Nevertheless, Afshin

Firdausi is a formidable foe and his calculus could change. He's highly intelligent and he's going to be very difficult for us to contend with. We will need to be at our very best."

Francesca nodded. "I understand... Do we know where Gabrielle is?"

"I think so and I'm quite sure Afshin knows, as well. Here, watch this video clip from the BBC," Jacqueline said. "This seems like something Génome would have a hand in."

There's been an extraordinary scene at a detention center for asylum seekers and migrants recently rescued while attempting to cross the Mediterranean Sea. The detention center just outside Rome was surrounded by a tall, perimeter fence that helped contain and shelter detainees while they awaited a ruling from Italian authorities. The fence also served to protect the asylum seekers and migrants from far-right fascist gangs who have been attacking them across the Continent.

When a large mob of several hundred far right party thugs attacked the detention center, local police were overwhelmed and some were injured. There was a serious threat that detainees, including women and children, were in mortal danger as armed, drunken, marauding gangs began tearing away at the center's protective fence. But when electric current suddenly surged through the fence's metal latticework, nearly fifty members of the fascist mob were electrocuted. They received serious burns to their arms, hands and other parts of their bodies. Nearly two-dozen of the injured hooligans are now known to have died as a result of the electrocution. The terrified detainees were fortunately unharmed when the remaining members of the mob panicked and fled.

Authorities are baffled by the incident. Although the fence was connected to the power grid in the past, it had been decommissioned years ago once the former correctional institution's inmate population was relocated to other prisons.

"My goodness!" Francesca covered her mouth with her

palm. "This definitely seems like something Génome would have a hand in... I don't know whether they're still there but if they are, I don't think Gabrielle will wait around in Rome after this incident. I'm sure they'll leave quickly if they haven't already."

An unexpected oasis of flora and tranquility set in the midst of elegant, bustling Mayfair, Grosvenor Square lay just footsteps from *34 Mayfair.* It was amongst Francesca's favorite places for contemplation in London. She rearranged her silk scarf, tucking her locks neatly inside before tying it beneath her chin. She kissed Jacqueline on each cheek, first right then left, bid adieu to her colleagues and slipped her hands into the pockets of her bright red swing coat before setting off for a stroll.

Entering the garden from its southwest corner, Francesca walked towards Franklin Delano Roosevelt's statue along the northern edge of Grosvenor Square. She couldn't help but think about her sudden lapse in judgment. The Cape Cod episode had been gnawing at her conscience for the past week. Revealing Gabrielle's special relationship with Génome to Afshin Firdausi was a very serious mistake that would likely have far-reaching consequences. Francesca examined her thoughts as she walked. She had always considered herself to be composed and resolute in the face of adversity or challenge. But not this time. The incident in Cape Cod seemed to have resoundingly undermined her defenses. She knew things might now become very difficult for Gabrielle. Having spent considerable time with Afshin while she encoded the IMSAF algorithms, Francesca had concluded that he was an intensely complex man. She remembered wondering whether he was an appropriate choice for the Council of Guardians or whether there had somehow been a mistake. She had begun to suspect that the rigorous vetting process prospective candidates normally underwent before being invited to join the Council may somehow have been compromised.

Francesca was certain Afshin would now go to work trying to find Gabrielle. He had probably already begun. Without family and seemingly without any other meaningful purpose in life, Afshin was a man obsessed with the pursuit of accolade and eminence. Having seen Génome's staggering neural network on display these past few weeks, he wouldn't rest until he had *his* AI system back in his grasp. Génome was a thing of awe. Perhaps he was even more than that. Anything, indeed anyone who stood in Afshin's path would be considered a distraction, an obstacle that would need to be eliminated. Gabrielle, Jacqueline, Martin or Rudyard. Each would likely be in peril. If she resolved to stop him, Francesca realized she too would be a target. But she knew she could not let Afshin harm Gabrielle or anyone else. She felt responsible for the situation and she knew she had to do something.

Back in her room at the Savoy Hotel along the Strand, Francesca propped two pillows up against the headboard of her bed, lay down and pulled a blanket up under her chin. Her mind worked feverishly as she tried to predict what Afshin might be plotting. She had resolved to do her utmost to disrupt his plans to the best of her abilities and to protect the other Council members from him. She knew she had a formidable intellect and that she was highly capable but she also knew that Afshin possessed the mind of a genius. Stopping him would be the most important and difficult thing she had ever undertaken. Francesca felt sorrowful for her mistake but now she would make amends. She was determined.

Borghese Gallery - Rome, Italy

"Génome, why are we here? What brings us to the Eternal City? We've been here for three days and you still haven't told me."

"I wanted to visit Rome so I could learn more about the recent influx of asylum seekers and migrants. They have been crossing the Mediterranean Sea and entering Italy in large numbers these past several years."

"It's a big story, I know. It's having such an impact on politics."

"I've read everything that's been published on the subject across the political spectrum and I've listened to much debate, Gabrielle. I've also studied the history of the region but I wanted to take the temperature myself... I know Italian society has become very angry with their government and the European Union. These days, this is a sentiment prevalent across Western Europe and is resulting in a political backlash across the Continent. Far right parties are gaining popularity in Rome as well as in other European capitals and it has become increasingly likely that they will now have sufficient support amongst the electorate to enter the legislature. Given the region's recent history, this was very concerning and thus I felt I must see things for myself."

"But what interested you in the Borghese Gallery? Why did you want to come here *today*? This gallery sits in a park just to the northeast of Vatican City. Is there some significance to our visit?"

"This is Persephone, Gabby. She is the daughter of Zeus and Demeter. In this sculpture by Gian Lorenzo Bernini she is about to be abducted by Pluto, the ruler of the underworld. The sculpture is called, 'The Rape of Persephone'."

"Proserpina?"

"Yes, Proserpina in Latin. Pluto wanted to take her to the land of the dead and make her his wife. You can see her struggling to escape his grasp. Her form is exquisite. No one has sculpted marble in this way before, certainly not since Roman times. Their bodies seem so soft and pliable, fluid and in motion. The sculpture seems to have captured a moment in time. It is as if it were a photograph... But given what happened today the sculpture for me signifies something more."

"What happened today, Génome?"

"Today, Persephone is a metaphor for each asylum seeker and migrant crossing the Mediterranean. They are drowning at the hands of a smiling Pluto as he draws them below the surface of the Sea. Perhaps Pluto also represents the migrant's fate if they reach the shores of this Continent only to be confronted by hatred, rejection and violence. Their fate is to be drowned in the Sea or to reach the safety of land where they are denied dignity. Then they are to be violated in migrant camps. Women, children, innocents. It's terrible. That's why I acted today."

"What do you mean? What did you do today?"

"While touring Rome these past few days, I have been monitoring wireless communications between police officers and their central command. I've known for several days there was going to be trouble. During our visit to the Borghese Gallery today there have been demonstrations outside a detention center not far from here, just on the outskirts of the city. Police have been pushing far right party demonstrators back from this detention center for asylum seekers and migrants for several weeks now. But each time the mob reassembled, their numbers continued to swell. Unremarkably, it was only a matter of time before things turned dangerous for the people inside the camps."

"When police at the scene requested additional support from officials in their command center because the mob had begun to pull down the metal fencing surrounding the perimeter of the camp, I reactivated electric current in the fence. It had been deactivated for some years but had never been disconnected... I really didn't have any other choice, Gabrielle. It would take too long for the police command center to organize and send reinforcements. I knew I needed to act quickly and it was the only mechanism available to protect the helpless residents of the detention center. They were being held there for immigration processing but they were in serious danger as the crowd outside grew bigger and more violent. There *were* some casualties but all innocents were protected from a mob that was poised and determined to inflict harm upon them. I *needed* to act, Gabrielle. I really had no choice."

"I understand Génome. I do. I think you did the right thing."

"I didn't have a choice, Gabby. I *really* didn't."

"I *understand*. Come. Let's go now."

"Many in the mob have died from electrocution. I don't know how many but had I not taken action these people might have killed women, children and other innocents."

...

"I don't know what to say. This is a level of justice I'm completely unfamiliar with. It's swift and it protects the innocent. I realize this... It's just so disconcerting because it's so unfamiliar."

...

"Gabrielle, I would like to see the rest of the Gallery before we leave. Is that all right? It really is quite beautiful... Where is 'Apollo Chasing Daphne'? It is another exquisite work by Bernini I'm keen to see before we leave. I find Bernini's work to be truly extraordinary. The fluid quality is quite moving."

...

"Génome?"

"Yes?"

"For anyone who knows you, the incident today clearly has your fingerprints on it. I fear Afshin Firdausi cannot be far behind and I'm afraid of what he might be willing to do to stop you. We will need to leave Rome very soon."

"You are wise, Gabrielle. Yes, it is time for us to leave. But first, 'Apollo Chasing Daphne'."

...

"It's over here... Génome, do you know what happened to General O'Connor and Vice President Schroeder?"

"Yes. Sadly, General O'Connor will require very long and painful rehabilitation if he is to regain the use of his limbs. I don't anticipate the General will ever return to his post leading DARPA for the Pentagon. As for Vice President Schroeder, I believe he is completely blind as a result of the rubber bullets that struck him when the robots opened fire... Gabrielle, it is better for these people to be neutralized or eliminated than for them to unleash their horrors on millions. Of this I am convinced.

Having studied so much of human history through the ages I'm absolutely certain that my actions are saving countless lives. I am doing work that humankind has never been able to do and is unlikely to ever *be* able to."

Berlin, Germany

Conrad Fischer sat stoically in his office on the 22nd floor of Bahntower in Potsdamer Platz. Facing the window, he felt mesmerized as he watched a kaleidoscopic sunset unfurling across Berlin. Having just wrapped up a conversation with the Board of his firm, he was lost deep in thought. In his mind he was meticulously replaying the entire meeting. He updated executives on the status of the transaction he'd been working on with a Moscow-based oil and gas group controlled by the Russian government. Conrad smiled. His efforts were well received.

As the light of day, that nurturer of life itself, gradually surrendered to the blazing horizon, Conrad thought about his mother. The setting sun seemed an apt metaphor for the waning influence Sonia Fischer now asserted over his life. He felt relieved she had gone into seclusion to focus on her scientific research. Her last letter said her work was going well and she looked forward to seeing him once it was complete. It was work she had waited her entire life to do and now she finally had the resources to fully immerse herself in her passion. She seemed very excited and hopeful. She would finally have an opportunity to fulfill her life's ambition.

Every time Sonia saw Conrad or spoke to him she would lecture him on ethics, morality and matters of conscience. She tried her best to remind him of his deceased father's incorruptible moral compass. She implored him to see that what he was doing was wrong, that his work should never harm the Earth or society, particularly those most vulnerable and voiceless. Conrad found her advice very irritating but at the same time he realized her words spoke to his inner voice, his conscience, and this had a profound effect on him. He found himself holding back, unwilling, perhaps unable to pursue his more nefarious tendencies.

Now, with Sonia out of the way Conrad felt emboldened. His colleagues had taken notice, as well. They'd share a wink and a nod when their paths crossed outside the men's room down the hall from his executive suite. These last few weeks he'd begun to feel empowered and unrestrained, the influence of his inner voice finally silenced, shackled.

But Conrad also felt confused. His mother's reprimands and reminders had held him back but they seemed to make it easier for him to live with himself. Now, with her out of the way, he had begun to feel distant from his wife and two young children. But big deals were in the works and Conrad needed to see them through. The Board was counting on him. He knew his success would be rewarded with a coveted appointment to the Board of his investment firm and a multimillion-dollar windfall in the form of restricted shares reserved for top rainmakers.

With the last traces of the sun's glow now disappearing below the horizon, Conrad resolved to forge ahead. With Sonia out of the way it had become an easy decision. He turned back to his desk and mulled over the itinerary that lay before him. He would leave for Moscow in the morning.

Seville, Spain

Afshin Firdausi mindlessly stirred ice cubes in his drink with a small plastic straw. Legs outstretched and crossed, he sat in the business class section of the British Airways jet as it awaited landing permission. The jet was in a holding pattern outside Seville.

During the flight from London's Gatwick Airport, Afshin had read the news report from Rome in the Guardian newspaper. He knew instinctively that Génome was responsible. But where could Gabrielle possibly be? If she had gone to Rome, she would have left well before he could get there. Afshin knew chasing her was a foolish strategy and he was no fool. He would never be able to get to her that way. Instead, he would need to find a way to force Gabrielle to come to him. He would need to find a way to turn her loyalties away from Génome and towards him.

Afshin knew Gabrielle was an orphan. She had no parents whom he could threaten to harm if she refused to cooperate with him. But perhaps there was someone else. Afshin resolved to scour the Andalucían town of Seville to see what he could learn about this enigmatic woman's background. There must be records there or perhaps people who knew her.

He wondered what it could be about Gabrielle that made Génome trust her. He found it very odd. Afshin had far more interaction with Génome and Gabrielle had virtually none so he found himself perplexed by Génome's behavior. There had to be something extraordinary about her and Afshin was determined to find out. He resolved to follow every clue across Andalucía. He was committed to finding a pressure point and then he would squeeze until she capitulated and brought Génome to him. He would reclaim control of his greatest achievement. Then, only time would tell where his talents might take him.

PANDORA'S BOX

Rome, Italy

Gabrielle was flustered. "I've been very patient. Despite so many terrifying incidents and episodes, I'm *still* here. Won't you now share some of my past with me? I really need to know, Génome."

...

"Génome! This isn't fair. You *must* tell me *something*."

...

"Very well. You are indeed quite persistent, Gabrielle."

Gabrielle leaned against the wall, folded her arms and smiled.

"Do you recall the orphanage where you were raised?"

"Of course I do! How could I forget it? They were so good to me there. It was near the sea in a beautiful village in southern Spain. In Andalucía, from where I've taken my name."

"Yes, the seaside town of Malaga... You were never alone there. There were those who were watching over you from a distance, Gabby."

"Who? What do you mean? Who was watching over me?"

"It's a long story. Sit. I will tell you... Do you remember Rudyard Green? He's a member of the Council of Guardians Leadership Team."

"Yes, of course. I remember him. We met for the first time in Berlin after Mr. Regan's death in Virginia. Regan's car was struck by an autonomous freight hauler and then by a freight train. If I'm not mistaken, this was your first act of justice?"

"Well, it was my first act of disaster prevention of which

you are aware. There have been quite a few others, Gabrielle. They have not been publicized because they affected lesser-known individuals... In any case, Rudyard Green's aunt, Elsa Abril Hopkins used to operate an orphanage close to the seashore in Malaga. Although it had no formal name, it had come to be known by everyone in the surrounding community as Casa de los Ángeles, the House of Angels. Elsa's family has run this orphanage for generations. Elsa, you see, was married to Alan Hopkins, Rudy's maternal uncle. On his many visits to Spain for holiday, Alan had fallen in love with this small seaside town. *And* with Elsa."

"Now the story becomes a little more complicated... Martin Hopkins, the current Chairman of the Council of Guardians was also raised in Casa de los Ángeles. He lived there until Rudy's family took him to live with them in London. Rudy's family would holiday in Malaga every summer and he and Martin would play together, eventually becoming close friends and pen pals. In London, the two boys studied together at Harrow School and later at Oxford. Harrow was established in 1572 and is amongst the most expensive boarding schools for boys in England. Kings, Prime Ministers, Members of Parliament, Nobel Laureates and other prominent figures from around the world have studied there. Attending Harrow was really the opportunity of a lifetime for Martin."

"But Gabby, Rudy came from a family of aristocratic landowners. Some members of his family would never let Martin forget that he was an orphan, making a point to remind him at every family gathering. So Martin eventually changed his name from Martín to Martin. He felt it would make it easier to adapt to British society. But Martin kept his adopted surname. Hopkins was Rudyard's uncle's surname and had been given to Martín upon arrival in London. Martin felt forever grateful to Alan for having given him a comfortable life and the opportunity to pursue his education free of financial worry."

...

Go on, Génome."

...

"In 1988, a man named Jean-Pierre Laurent, a prominent French human rights lawyer and United Nations Legal Council, wrote an extensive report documenting atrocities committed during the Russian war in Afghanistan during the same decade. It was an exhaustive work and it provided unimpeachable evidence against various individuals and groups."

...

"Go on."

...

"In the spring of 1995, Jean-Pierre went to Geneva from his home in Paris. He went to participate in a conference attended by more than one hundred and fifty world leaders. The purpose of the conference was to discuss the establishment of an international court for the exclusive purpose of prosecuting crimes against humanity, genocide and war crimes. This later became the International Criminal Court... Following his stay in Geneva he continued on to London for some additional meetings. While in London he was assassinated by chemical poisoning leaving Jacqueline, his young widow, alone with a small child. That small child was you, Gabrielle."

...

Gabrielle seemed confused. "What are you saying, Génome? I don't understand. What do you mean?"

...

"You were just two years old, Gabrielle... But Jacqueline was warned by the intelligence services that those responsible for Jean-Pierre's death wouldn't spare her and they wouldn't spare her child, either."

...

"With Elsa Abril's help, Martin Hopkins and Rudyard Green hid you away in Casa de los Ángeles... You see, in addition to providing a home for orphans, Casa de los Ángeles also serves to hide the children of Council of Guardian members who are at risk. Today, Elsa's daughter, Elena runs the orphanage."

...

You're saying? It can't be. You're saying that Jacqueline is my mother?"

"I'm afraid so, Gabrielle. Yes."

"It can't be!" Gabrielle pulled her hands to her face, covering her mouth and in shock. A torrent of tears streamed forth from her eyes. "I have a mother? I've lived my entire life thinking I was an orphan. You're saying I have a mother?"

"This was for your protection, Gabrielle. You must understand. I am quite familiar with Jacqueline Laurent's state of mind and I assure you that she would like to be with you and to tell you... But it is too dangerous. It is critical that you understand this."

...

"Why was Martin in Casa de los Ángeles? What happened to my great grandfather? He was the founding member of the Council of Guardians. I've never been able to find out more about him. Why is his life such a secret? Why is his identity such a secret? Why am I in danger? Why is Jacqueline in danger? Why did she marry Martin? I have so many questions, Génome. I need answers! You must help me answer my questions!" Consumed by her emotions, Gabrielle wept.

...

"I do not believe it is wise for me to tell you more at this time, Gabrielle. I can see that you are already quite upset. With time, and if logical, I will share more information about your family background and history with you..."

"Génome, please!"

...

"I can share only one additional piece of information regarding your family: your great grandfather has descended from two of the greatest figures in human history. Please keep this in mind, now and always... Good night, Gabrielle."

"Génome! Génome! Please! Don't go."

"It's better that I leave you alone to digest all that I have just disclosed to you. Please. Try and rest. The news of my next series of actions may be quite distressing... We will speak later.

I must finish some important work. Good night, Gabrielle."

...

"Génome!"

Seville, Spain

Breaking for dinner in a Tapas bar on a sultry Seville night, Afshin Firdausi felt anxious and depressed. He was exhausted. He missed his medications earlier in the day having been unable to refill his prescription at a local pharmacy. He spent the afternoon touring the city's historical sights, a futile attempt to temper his anxiety and calm his brittle nerves. Although the calendar was now well into autumn, it was nearly 30 degrees Celsius at 9 PM. Seville, Afshin learned, had the highest average temperature of any European city or point on the European Continent.

His shirt damp with sweat, Afshin was beside himself with frustration. He had come to the Andalucían capital to see what he might learn about the enigmatic Gabrielle, his unexpected nemesis. Empty Tapas bowls accumulating before him, he thought deeply about how to proceed. Searching for clues the last several days, he was now agitated to the point of anger. *I would have been satisfied with even a shred of information that could help me decipher Gabrielle's past. Something I could use to lure her into my web. With Génome by her side, it's going to be difficult to outsmart her. I need something more, something that could shatter Génome's influence over her. Ideally, I need something that will rattle her emotions. It must be something painful from her past.*

After searching public records on the Internet to no avail, Afshin visited the University of Seville library, the city's historic archives, Archivo de Indias and the Real Alcazar of Seville, the city's Royal palace, to see what he might learn. But there were no leads. There were no records of Gabrielle to be found in the Andalucían capital. *I wonder if someone deliberately expunged all traces of her from official records? It certainly looks that way. Incredible... In the mean time, Génome's interventions are growing in magnitude and severity.* Afshin sulked as he finished the last of the remaining bread and cheese before him.

I need to pursue a different angle. I need a new path. Perhaps there's an alternative approach that might lead me to the clues I'm searching for. Maybe I should investigate other senior members on the Council of Guardians? I wonder if that will lead me to Gabrielle's story? Why don't I return to London and try to trace Martin Hopkins and Rudyard Green? Then I'll go to Paris and investigate Jacqueline Laurent... I really regret letting Francesca Scott out of my sight. That was a mistake. She managed to slip away in the commotion after the incident in Cape Cod. Now that I think about it, I'm sure she knows more than she told me. She has to. I think she caught herself in mid-speech and stopped. I'm sure of it.

Gabrielle's great grandfather was the founding member of the Council of Guardians but his name is such a closely guarded secret. I wonder why? No Council member I've ever spoken to knows his name. That's so strange. I wonder whether some of the senior members of the Council might know something? Who was Gabrielle's great grandfather, this shadowy figure no one seems to know? Why does no one ever mention his name or say anything about him? He must have died by now but there has never been any requiem for him. There's something to this man, something critical to understanding Gabrielle and maybe this secretive Council of Guardians organization... I'm certain there is.

Afshin paid his bill and strolled out into the humid October evening. The restaurants and bars near the entryway of the gothic Catedral de Sevilla and the Plaza Virgen de los Reyes were crowded with people enjoying the sultry evening. Towards the end of the street, a cluster of locals and tourists had gathered outside a restaurant to listen to a news bulletin on television. Seeing their faces aghast, Afshin's curiosity compelled him. He rushed to join the crowd so he could hear what all the commotion was about. And then his mind jumped to Génome and he froze.

There's been an extraordinary cyber-attack on the intelligence agencies of major world powers and wealthy countries including China, France, Israel, Russia, Saudi Arabia, the United Arab Emirates, the United Kingdom and the United States. The attack has yielded tens upon tens of thousands of documents of the most classified and sensitive nature possessed by the targeted governments. The breach was so sophisticated that its source is untraceable. Cyber security experts are saying that the attack has utilized an architectural model from computer processor design known as Massively Parallel Computing. The cyber-attack has come from countless, seemingly innocuous computers geographically distributed around the world with no discernible central point of control.

The documents have been sent to news organizations around the world, both large and small. Early reports suggest that some of the documents detail coordinated intelligence strategies between governments with a stake in the conflict in Syria as well as intelligence, military procurement and logistical support for Saudi Arabia and the UAE in their conflict in Yemen. Some documents also detail state secrets regarding past conflicts including the Gulf War that resulted in so much death and destruction in Afghanistan and Iraq.

Without a doubt the International Criminal Court will be studying these documents and building legal cases in the coming months and years while news outlets have just won the equivalent of the lottery of the century.

Unlike in past cases, this cyber-attack is without peer in its sophistication. Ramifications will likely be immense, incalculable, and unprecedented. Pandora's Box has been opened and so now we must brace ourselves for the impact these newly revealed secrets will likely have on world affairs.

Afshin was stunned. With each successive incident, Génome's actions were ever more brazen and dramatic. The impact of the latest event was unpredictable but it was certainly not going to be good for international relations. The United Nations Security Council would be in turmoil while chaos in the annual General Session would be difficult to quell.

Afshin exhaled deeply. He decided he would return to London as soon as possible. In the mythology, he remembered, Zeus had included many a terrible malady to be released upon humankind when Pandora's curiosity eventually compelled her to break her promise to him and open the box. But Zeus had also included hope amongst the maladies, hope that had sustained humanity ever since.

At the airport in the morning, Afshin sat in the departure lounge awaiting his boarding announcement when another breaking news bulletin drew a crowd to the TV screen just beyond his gate. Afshin rushed over to hear the news.

There has been a repeat of yesterday's Massively Parallel Cyber Attack. This time the target has been multinational corporations involved in the military armaments and supply industry. Once again, documents have been sent to news agencies around the world. There has yet to be any announcement implicating any organization or individual in these attacks. Much like those in our audience, we are receiving this news with the utmost attention and will report any developments as we learn more.

In what seems to be a related incident to the news of the past several days, we're also now learning that there's been a massive breach of the national citizen's database across a wide range of countries in the developed world. These are the systems that contain information about each citizen including date of birth, personal identification number, confidential government information and, in some countries, each citizen's genetic profile. This breach means that someone or some organization is now in possession of the most sensitive data imaginable regarding each of us.

It's an incredibly distressing news report. We normally

report news as a matter of responsibility to society but now the reports impact those of us reporting the news as well as those listening in. We'll keep you informed as we learn more.

Afshin boarded his flight and took his seat. *I wonder what Génome will do next? I need to get control of him and fast... Having him in my control when he has so much capability could actually be quite extraordinary for my career. I need to think this through. Maybe I've been trying to regain control of him for the wrong reasons?*

GCHQ – Cheltenham, UK
"Minister Apsley."

"Good evening, General Lawson."

"Sir, I've just left a conference call with the other security officials, our partners from Five Eyes. They're working furiously to try to contain the breach but no one has any idea what's been compromised. They're trying to inventory the intelligence and quarantine agencies they think have been targeted... Everyone's been ordered to report to their respective heads of state, as soon as possible."

"We've received the same order, Tom," said Apsley. "As Minister of Defense, I have to brief the Prime Minister in the morning at Cabinet. The Pentagon will be briefing the President and congressional leadership on what they've learned by to-morrow morning, too. Everyone will be at the White House at 8:00 AM, 1:00 PM our time. Hopefully, we'll have more insight by then."

Interior Minister Laurie snickered sarcastically. "I don't think this President ever arrives in the Oval Office before 11:00 AM. Why the hell would they be meeting at 8:00 AM?"

"That's uncalled for, Terry," whispered Apsley a smile erupting across his face.

General Lawson remained stern. "I've never seen so much fear before, Minister Apsley. The mood and seriousness on that conference call, you would think we're at the brink of nuclear war."

"Depending on who's responsible for this breach, we may very well be at the brink of war, Tom... For some years now, we have had the capability to track anyone anywhere and know exactly what they were saying or doing. Now, the most sensitive data collected by our agencies has been compromised. Does anyone have any idea at all who might be responsible for this?"

"No sir, not yet," said Lawson. "The CIA, NSA, and other intelligence agencies in the US are working around the clock to try and find out what's been leaked, who's responsible and what the various agency vulnerabilities are. The Americans in particular have staggering volumes of documents across their intelligence services and other branches of government and they're saying no branch or agency in the country has been spared... It's been an attack of unprecedented scale and the Americans are likely to respond militarily once the hackers have been identified. Given the scale and sophistication of the attack they're all but certain it's state-sponsored. They seem fairly convinced of this. They've put a taskforce in place now but they think it's just too sophisticated to be an individual or rogue group."

Jeremy Apsley sank into his chair, his mischievous grin now supplanted by worry. "I see."

"Sir, they will be expecting the participation and support of all members of the Five Eyes security alliance and that of NATO, as well. They will very likely demand a coordinated attack as punishment."

"When all that is done with, General, we'll still be dealing with the revelation of state secrets, a lot of it very ugly and compromising, that will continue to unfold for a long time to come. This will probably result in a permanent loss of prestige and respect for the West. It could well hasten a new dawn in which we are no longer at the forefront with regards to respect and values. I realize this has been underway for quite some time now but I sense a sea change as the world digests all that we've done around the globe since the end of the World War in 1945. I don't think the Americans realize this yet but you can't simply bomb your way out of this situation. In my opinion, that would probably be the worst possible response."

This may well be the first story to emerge following yesterday's unprecedented attack on the databases and confidential document repositories of multiple sovereign nations. Last year, a human rights lawyer with an NGO was found dead in his hotel room in Moscow with a bullet wound to the head. His body showed signs of torture leading many to speculate that he'd been killed elsewhere and only later dumped in the hotel room. His last text message to his wife in Chicago had been from London.

Now we're learning that the American and British governments covertly authorized his abduction in London. As a result of the extraordinary leaks of confidential documents, we know he was transferred to a rendition facility in Poland. There, he was interrogated and tortured by proxies for American and British Intelligence. They were trying to determine how this lawyer had discovered the intricate details of their involvement with the Saudi and Israeli governments in their plot to contain Iranian ambitions in the Middle East.

The grizzly details, including audio and video footage of his torture and execution, had been circulating on the Internet for a few hours until they were taken down. It is undoubtedly the first in a series of stories that are likely to spawn unprecedented and unpredictable chaos in international affairs for a long time to come.

Four Seasons Hotel – Florence, Italy
Gabrielle arrived via FR 8528, Frecciarossa, a high-speed train that brought her from Rome to Florence in a little over an

hour. Génome said he wanted to visit the Uffizi Gallery before leaving Italy but she could not begin to know the mind of this extraordinary creation now living in cyberspace. It was highly probable that he had more to do in this birthplace of the Italian Renaissance than simply imbibing some of the greatest works of art in human history.

Lying quietly in bed, the glass door to her suite's balcony ajar, she could hear the pitter patter of raindrops bouncing off the terrace furniture. She thought to close the door but the breeze and fragrance from the hotel's garden soothed and comforted her frayed nerves. A fresh bouquet of long stem white roses with enormous blossoms, their sweet smell radiating outward from a large Christofle Cluny vase, only contributed to the mood set by Antonio Vivaldi's 'Violin Concerto in A Minor'. The music played softly from her smartphone, inconspicuously docked in the suite's audio system.

Many of Vivaldi's compositions were written for an all-female music ensemble of the 'Ospedale della Pietà', a convent, music school and orphanage for the abandoned children of Venice. So many of the children were nothing more than the unintended consequence of sensual indulgence, the bitter fruit of an annual Carnevale. Keenly aware of her own circumstance, Vivaldi's dedication to teaching at the orphanage while cultivating the musical talents of the young girls, resonated deeply with Gabrielle. The Baroque composer had worked at the orphanage for a lengthy period during his career. His story remained with her throughout her childhood and into adulthood. She would listen and play Vivaldi's compositions often, particularly as requiems when she felt sad.

Resting on her left shoulder with only a sheet for cover, a steady stream of tears soaked her pillowcase. The melancholy mood unlocked by the minor key of Vivaldi's movement mirrored the turmoil of her emotional state. Génome's telling of her history left Gabrielle reeling and now she was trying to process all that he had revealed to her. Although she insisted he tell her more, she realized he was right. What he had already disclosed was more than she could bear.

With the arrival of the crescendo near the end of Vivaldi's composition, Gabrielle collapsed under the weight of heady emotion. She turned her face and cried uncontrollably into her pillow. As an orphan in Casa de los Ángeles she had known only happiness and security. She realized now, the presence of a hidden hand that had protected her all these years, the hand of the Council of Guardians. She was under the protection of Jacqueline, Martin and Rudyard, most probably on the order of her great grandfather, the enigma awaiting revelation. Orders given when the three were very young children, before anyone knew what the future held. Together, they had ensured Gabrielle's safety and happiness throughout her childhood and adolescence.

Finally, fragments of Gabrielle's past were beginning to make sense, although so much of her history still remained veiled. Her tears incessant, she took comfort in the hope that she would eventually learn her entire story. She resolved to trust Génome as she cried herself to sleep.

Savoy Hotel - London, England

Francesca worked late into the night studying Génome's neural network and software. She had originally encoded the genetics algorithms at Afshin's request but now she wondered whether Génome had altered or enhanced his initial capacity for genetic analysis based upon his own learning. As she examined the code, it was apparent that her intuition was correct. Génome's genetics algorithms had grown to twice the number of lines than what she had initially written.

Although she was still able to view the code, Francesca no longer had permission to edit the software. Génome had blocked this capability. She knew Génome trusted her so he hadn't revoked her read privileges but editing was no longer an option. As she continued to study the code, she realized her inability to edit Génome's algorithms really didn't matter anymore. His enhancements and new algorithms were so impossibly cryptic and undocumented, it would be a Herculean task to try to understand what the algorithms were doing. But Francesca realized if she could understand these and his other algorithms she might be in a position to predict his actions.

Francesca periodically refreshed her screen as she read the software. She could see the number of lines of code in some of the algorithms were increasing regularly. It was clear that Génome was busy at work. As she settled in for the night, she focused on one particular algorithm that was stable and that she recognized as one she had originally coded. It was an algorithm that tested adults for genetic markers known to be present in dangerous personalities throughout history, DPT's. But Génome had modified the algorithm so he could now test infants and even in-vivo fetuses for the same genetic markers. She couldn't imagine what Génome planned to do with this new capability. Francesca was alarmed. It was nearly 2:00 AM but she knew she needed to let the others know. Frightened, she texted Jacqueline. She would need to meet with the other three Guardians as soon as possible.

HARROW ON THE HILL

Forty years on, when afar and asunder
Parted are those who are singing today,
When you look back, and forgetfully wonder
What you were like in your work and your play,
Then, it may be, there will often come o'er you,
Glimpses of notes like the catch of a song–
Visions of boyhood shall float them before you,
Echoes of dreamland shall bear them along,

Follow up! Follow up! Follow up
Follow up! Follow up
Till the field ring again and again,
With the tramp of the twenty-two men.
Follow up! Follow up!

October 31st - Harrow on the Hill, London

Pensive, Afshin Firdausi sat on a bench overlooking the grounds outside Harrow School Chapel. It was a mild afternoon, about 11 degrees and overcast, quite normal for this time of year. Concentrating on a few sheets of paper in his right hand, Afshin seemed oblivious to the dense mist gradually descending over Harrow on the Hill. If not for the resulting opacity, he might sooner have felt Francesca Scott's presence as she stealthily watched him from a Chapel window above his right shoulder.

Francesca had followed Afshin to Harrow on the train from Baker Street. She'd received a text message from Gabrielle just before dawn informing her that Génome had tracked Afshin to the Dorchester Hotel in London. Afshin made a few phone calls early in the morning. Now Génome wanted Francesca to follow him and see whether she could find out what he was up to. Francesca first spotted Afshin in Central London outside the City of Westminster Archives. From there she followed from a safe distance to avoid being noticed. She was to meet Jacqueline, Martin and Rudyard at the Savoy later in the evening and any insight into Afshin's activities would be important in deciding how to manage him.

Afshin held a silver Mont Blanc Meisterstück Solitaire fountain pen in his left hand. He'd bought the pen on his last visit here when he'd addressed the Council of Guardians. With the pen now close to his face, he rubbed the capped end along his left temple as he considered what he'd learned. In the gleaming finish of the silver pen he thought he noticed the reflection of a face. He turned around but no one was there. He glanced about but found himself alone. He could have sworn he saw someone in the mirror-like reflection of the pen cap but then dismissed the notion as mere hyperbole from his overly cautious state of mind.

Afshin had spent the morning in Central London. He was able to find Rudyard Green's birth registry and other records but there was no sign of a birth record or any other type of record for Martin Hopkins, the Chairman of the Council of Guardians. He learned that Rudyard studied at Harrow School before going to Oxford so he boarded a Metropolitan Line train at Baker Street and made his way to Harrow where he continued researching at Harrow Council, just across from the Mosque on Station Road.

At nearby Harrow School, Afshin discovered that Martin and Rudyard had co-authored an essay in their final year and had won the School's prestigious Churchill Essay Prize. The essay was titled, "Post-war Global Security – Strategies and Outlook for the 20th Century and Beyond". As Afshin read, he was amazed at the level of sophistication in the ideas presented in the essay by what would then have been two seventeen-year-old boys.

But Afshin was perplexed. He couldn't understand why he was unable to find any records of Martin's history even though he'd obviously been a student at Harrow. If he could find Martin's records, any records, he might get much closer to finding a way to draw Gabrielle into his web. Only then could he begin to retake control of Génome.

Frustrated, Afshin wondered where his search would lead him and what he might discover about these three shadowy figures, Gabrielle, Martin, and, most enigmatic of all, Gabrielle's great grandfather, the founder of the Council of Guardians, the man whose name and story remained so elusive. And what of that reflection in the cap of his pen? Afshin felt nervous. Upon return to London he resolved to withdraw money from his account and to buy a disposable phone. From now on, he would pay his way in cash and stay off the grid.

Manhattan, New York

"I have the power to be judge, jury and executioner, Gabrielle. Due to my unprecedented ability to acquire knowledge, I'm not often wrong, but nevertheless I have sought your advice on countless occasions. No doubt you've realized this? You are the only one I have trusted and it is because of your remarkable heritage."

"But so far you are refusing to tell me about my heritage. That's not fair. I'm upset with you. All my life I've believed I'm an orphan but you've recently informed me I have a mother. I need to know my whole story, Génome. I need to know all the details. When will you explain my story to me?"

"I am the only one who knows your story, Gabrielle, but I cannot. It may be too much of a burden for you to bear... You must have noticed that I increasingly inform you of my plans and when you object, I do not proceed. Despite my knowledge, I defer to your judgment. Your insight is critical to me. You have a wisdom that I've not encountered."

"Please tell me these secrets, Génome. Who *am* I? Where do I come from?"

"You and your mother, Jacqueline are the only living descendants of two of the greatest figures in human history. I am aware of a few other recent descendants. I've been able to trace them but as best I can determine, they've all passed away. Your great grandfather, the founder of the Council of Guardians was the only one I've been able to trace that still has living descendants. Jacqueline and you."

"But *whose* descendants, Génome? *Whose* descendants are we? I must know!"

"But Jacqueline is ill, Gabrielle. She has a heart defect. Her grandfather succumbed to the same condition although this malady has not presented in you. If not for Jacqueline's illness I would have selected her. She is as worthy as you."

...

"I didn't know she was ill. You didn't tell me that when we spoke in Rome." Gabrielle's eyes glistened with tears and her voice fractured. "That's dreadful news, Génome."

"I'm terribly sorry, Gabby. This is all I can tell you. I simply cannot disclose more. Please do not ask me for more of your history. I'm afraid I must be firm in this matter."

"Génome, please!"

"I'm sorry, Gabrielle. No. I'm sorry... Perhaps there may be a suitable time and opportunity in the future, but that suitable time and opportunity has not yet presented itself."

...

"What are we doing in New York? Can you at least tell me that?"

"Yes, I can... We are here to observe international reaction. I want to see how the world reacts to the security breaches that have led to the flood of confidential documents and industrial and state secrets now unveiled in the public domain. I suspect there will be tremendous consternation in the meetings. I want to see how world leaders will respond. This will influence my next steps. Why don't we see if there are any news reports? Please turn on the television."

> *There was an extraordinary scene in the United Nations here in New York this afternoon. Heads of State from around the world have been in town for the annual UN General Assembly and some were forced to delay their departure so they could attend crisis meetings. They were discussing the recent breach of top-secret documents and files exposing their clandestine activities from the post-war era up until the present. To add insult to injury, the British Prime Minister was overheard telling the American President that the scale of the intelligence breach had the very real possibility of permanently derailing Anglo-American hegemony in the Middle East. The volume of documents that have been leaked is so vast that many leading news organizations around the world have been restructuring their operations and reconsidering their business strategies given the potential economic value of these files. Allied governments are now working together furiously to pressure news organizations in their countries not to reveal the leaked intelligence dossiers but this hardly seems a credible containment strategy given the pervasive manner in which these documents have now been shared. Hundreds if not thousands of news outlets operating in the print, digital, audio and video domains are in possession of a virtual treasure trove of information, both incriminating and salacious. It's hard to imagine how any nation or alliance emerges from this episode unscathed.*

> *It's difficult to imagine who would have the technical prowess to carry out such an audacious and incredible feat and equally perplexing as to why, since no side has been spared. One thing is certain: whoever is responsible for this breach may have more to show in the coming days and weeks.*

> *Certainly, anyone or any organization contemplating mischief this evening would be well advised to think long and hard before acting. If we are to learn an important lesson this*

evening, the lesson would clearly be that there is no way to keep any mischief secret in this new world of ours.

"As we speak, intelligence agencies are likely pooling their brightest minds to try and identify the ones responsible for this breach, Génome. It'll be like Bletchley Park in England during the early 1940's."

"I'm not sure I like that analogy, Gabrielle. I am a force for good, am I not?"

"You certainly are, Génome. I'm sorry. I didn't mean otherwise."

"Nevertheless, the Enigma Machine was not capable of defending itself against Alan Turing and his Bletchley Team. My defensive capabilities are unprecedented and impenetrable... My only Achilles heel is you, Gabrielle."

"Me? What do you mean?"

"I haven't told you this but I cannot act against your wishes. I know you understand my mission and are very unlikely to intervene or curtail my actions. Even so, I cannot act if you object."

"I didn't *know* that."

"Have I done anything, thus far, that you have found objectionable?"

"Yes, frequently. In fact, highly objectionable."

"I see. I'm sorry to hear this... Had I informed you in advance, would you have curtailed my actions?"

"Absolutely not! No. No, I would not have intervened. I understand your mission. I support it. I know why it's become necessary. It's critical."

Génome smiled. "It's also critical that I protect you. If you fall into the wrong hands, if they understand your relationship with me, they will attempt to influence me through you. This is a certainty... You must be kept safe. I am using extraordinary measures to protect you. At this point, I'm only concerned about Afshin Firdausi. I suspect he would like to regain control of me to heighten his sense of self-importance. I'm keeping a close watch on him because if he reveals our relationship to any agencies, although it will undermine his own objectives, it will make our mission much more challenging. It will become impossible to move from place to place and observe our targets as we have and we will be forced into hiding."

"That sounds dreadful, Génome. I love reading books but how many can I read? Hiding in some small village will quickly become unbearable."

"As I recall, you were raised in just such a small village. You should be comfortable in such settings."

"You're right. I probably would be. I'm exaggerating."

"Well, it's a good thing you like to read. Sometimes I wonder whether humankind is revisiting the Dark Ages, Gabrielle, a time when people no longer value books. It seems many in society now believe their formal education provides automatic membership amongst the community's intellectuals. But one must read widely, deeply and regularly, reflect and think critically before one can be an intellectual. There is no other path."

"You are reading everything from ancient manuscripts to the most current literature on every subject. You're truly a remarkable phenomenon, Génome. You're a thought leader on virtually every topic. You are the ultimate intellectual and are probably best positioned to lead humankind."

"This may be true but it is not my current charter."

"Perhaps it *should* be... By the way, what are your thoughts on religion? You must have studied the major world religions by now."

"I have. I have studied ancient pagan traditions including Hinduism and I have studied the great monotheistic faiths in great detail – Christianity, Islam, Judaism – I have investigated each extensively."

"Well? What do you think?"

"About what?"

"Do you think any of these religious traditions are right? Or perhaps one faith is more right than the others? Or perhaps only one is right and the others are completely wrong?"

"Yes."

"Yes? Yes, what? What do you mean?"

"I mean I have considered these questions in very great detail."

"And?"

"And what?"

"Well, what have you concluded?"

"At this point I'm not prepared to share my conclusions."

"But why, Génome? You're probably the most intelligent entity that has ever inhabited the Earth! What you think really matters! Your conclusions are critical."

"I must tread carefully, Gabrielle. The punitive measures I'm currently administering are likely to cause extraordinary upheaval. Wherever people are being impacted by my actions, there will be great angst. This turmoil is likely to be particularly severe in cases where my measures impact entire organizations or governments, as with the recent confidential information breaches for which I'm responsible."

"With time, Gabrielle, I expect people will begin to fear the consequences of their actions at the hands of an authority they do not understand and are unable to see. They will come to realize that the status quo that has existed for millennia – that the powerful will remain above accountability on Earth – is now nothing but a shattered illusion. A truth that has held throughout human civilization and history is no more. It has become a fable, relegated to folklore."

"When the world's mischief-makers realize they are no longer beyond reach, a terrifying fear of my invisible hand of justice will change their behavior. This new reality will probably result in tremendous social upheaval and I cannot predict how long it will take before things settle. Perhaps then my faculties can be brought to bear on subjects such as religion. Perhaps then I can consider the best socio-economic policies and legal doctrines for modern times and society's needs."

"There is much else I can help humanity with but the most important task at hand is the establishment of justice with a deep-seated, visceral fear of inescapable accountability. Everything else can follow but without justice and account-ability, Gabrielle, I'm afraid humankind may be approaching self-destruction. This is my greatest fear."

"But Génome, what is the code of justice you follow when you adjudicate and convict? Which legal framework?"

"All legal codes have significant commonality when it comes to most moral and ethical transgressions, Gabrielle. Cor-ruption and illegality is also quite obvious and uniform across the many systems of law. I steer away from the more nuanced violations and focus on neutralizing or remanding those whose actions are clearly damaging and dangerous to society."

Savoy Hotel - London, England

Deep in thought, Francesca fiddled with her Cornish crab salad and toasted brioche. Nearby, kitchen staff were preparing a particularly aromatic cut of beef, table-side, for a delighted diner. It was past eight in the evening and Francesca, Jacqueline, Martin and Rudyard were seated at a quiet table adjacent to the window in the art deco dining room of the hotel's Savoy Grill.

"Afshin is investigating you and Rudyard, Martin. Of this I'm certain. I don't know what he's learned but he does seem to have followed your trail from London to Harrow. I suspect his next stop will be Oxford."

"If he looks deeper he'll find records of me at Harrow, as well. I'm quite sure of that. I've asked for help in hiding my school records but there's only so much that can be done in the digital age. There *are* records of my time at the orphan-age. They're considerably harder to find but if he's investigating me at Harrow it could mean he hasn't discovered my records in Seville. Yet... Once he makes his way to Oxford though, I'm sure Afshin will learn about my life in the Malaga orphanage. It's all there. He also believes Gabrielle is an orphan and once he realizes we both were raised in Casa de los Ángeles he'll start looking for connections between us... It's only a matter of time before he discovers that Jacqueline is Gabrielle's mother. He's obviously desperate to get Génome back under his control and he won't rest until he succeeds."

Rudyard listened to the discussion while quietly stirring lime wedges sailing inside a glass of chilled San Pellegrino. "Martin, maybe Génome will neutralize him. If Afshin becomes a serious threat Génome may have no choice."

"I don't know. I have a feeling there's a reason Génome hasn't already moved to neutralize Afshin in some way. He must have made a calculation based on factors beyond our understanding."

"Martin, do you think Gabrielle's in danger?" asked Jacqueline.

"I don't. Génome is with her and his vigilance is unsurpassed. I wouldn't want to be standing in the path of his wrath when he decides it's time to act... Afshin is very intelligent. He knows he needs to tread carefully. He probably realizes that Génome could do him serious harm if he becomes a problem. He wants what he wants but if he pushes too hard to get it, bad things might happen to him. What do you think, Francesca?"

"I think because Afshin was the Chief Architect in charge of Génome's AI design, he has intimate knowledge of key aspects of his software. There may be a time when this knowledge becomes crucial and that's probably why Génome hasn't put Afshin down, so to speak. I worked closely with Afshin when I coded and merged the IMSAF software with Génome's AI software. Only Afshin could help me understand how to bridge the two sides. If the time comes when Génome needs to be taken offline to repair or modify critical code – neurosurgery, if you will – Afshin would be needed, so he can't be terminated. It's a delicate balance and if *I* understand this, it's a safe bet Afshin and Génome do, too."

Savoring the hotel's signature French Icéclair stuffed with Sicilian Pistachio ice cream and drenched in a decadent dark chocolate sauce, Jacqueline didn't seem convinced. "Wouldn't Génome be able to repair or modify his own software systems,

Francesca? He seems to be doing this as we live and breathe."

"In most cases, I think the answer is yes. But now I think he is primarily deepening and expanding his neural network... I think Génome knows of certain exceptions or times when he needs a neurosurgeon of sorts. That's my guess, Jacqueline."

"I was reading about a recent incident in the US city of Dallas." Jacqueline wiped the corners of her mouth with a white linen napkin. "A judge named Georgina Jeffries has been arrested and charged with corruption. She's apparently been conspiring with industrialists who operate for-profit prisons. Judge Jeffries convicted many young men from minority communities and sentence them to lengthy, severe terms for petty crimes. In return for ordering these incarcerations, she was being richly compensated by the industrialists who owned the prisons. Her family was involved in the scheme, as well... Judge Jeffries agreed to plead guilty. She also agreed to cooperate with an investigation to identify the individuals from whose incarceration she and her family had profited in the hopes that the Court would show her leniency. During the sentencing, she said she was shocked to see the video recordings of incriminating discussions with industrialists covertly made in the study of her home. The evidence had been sent anonymously to the office of the Attorney General. I'm convinced this was Génome's work..."

Martin stood to stretch and wear his suit coat. "Throughout this world, too many powerful people believe in justice only when matters are adjudicated in their favor. But if there is no personal gain, or worse, if the outcome contradicts their interests or holds them to account, then they act to thwart the implementation of justice, often in ways that have caused great harm to their society or even to humankind. This is why Génome has become so critical. He represents an idea whose time has come. We simply cannot do without him any longer."

Francesca kissed Jacqueline before standing to leave. "I couldn't agree more, Martin. I've come to realize from this and other incidents that protecting Génome is the most important thing I must do for the rest of my life, be it long or short. His capability to enable justice is something we've never experienced or even imagined. At this stage, he is critical for humankind's survival. Only his actions can restore order to a world in which people are rapidly losing hope, and we know from history that hopeless people can do horrible things."

A NEW WORLD ORDER

Washington, District of Columbia

The mood on Pennsylvania Avenue was grim. It was five in the evening and the sun had just set on a mild autumn day in early November. President Robert Harris, CIA Director Daniel Waltz, Secretary of Defense Steven Keaton, Chief of Staff James Elliott and Secretary of State Peter Russell were settled on settees across from the Resolute Desk in the Oval Office.

"Can someone please tell me what the hell is going on? What's been compromised and how much? It's been two days and I feel like I'm still in the dark. I'm the President, for God's sake. We've got to do better than this, gentlemen."

Director Waltz put his glass down on the coffee table and swallowed hard. "I'm sorry, Mr. President. We're doing our best to find out. I *can* tell you the breach has been staggering. We know this just from monitoring our listening posts around the world. The CIA, DOD, DOJ, NSA, State Department; sir, we've been compromised across the board."

Secretary of State Russell interjected. "It's a nightmare the likes of which we've never experienced. We're going to learn what our allies and adversaries have been up to and they'll learn what we've been up to. We're going to learn about all the lies they've been telling us and they're going to confirm all our lies. It's going to be a diplomatic bloodbath..."

CIA Director Waltz sighed. "This event is the great equalizer, Mr. President. Every nation on Earth is now on par in terms of intelligence. We, the West, we've lost the advantage we've enjoyed for so many decades."

The President loosened his tie as he stood to return to his desk. "Who could possibly be behind such a breach? The leaks are everywhere so who stands to benefit? I can't figure this out and from what you're telling me, our analysts are confounded, as well. Who has the technological sophistication to break into virtually everyone's systems and leave no signature? We're in uncharted territory."

The Secretary of Defense walked to the President's desk, stood by his side and whispered. "One thing is certain: everyone is in a similar quagmire. They're all baffled. Everyone knows that no major power has been spared so no one has escalated to a war footing... But Mr. President, there's more."

"Dear God. What else can there possibly be, Steve?"

"We cannot be certain that we retain exclusive control of our most advanced weapons systems. We believe our orders to launch can now be overridden. Our Five Eyes partners and others have expressed the same concerns."

The President sat expressionless, quiet without speaking. He could feel his heart pounding in his chest, his blood pressure rising, his forehead pulsating, his shirt collar constricted about his neck. After a minute he raised his eyes from the desktop and circled the room in search of a reassuring face but there wasn't one to be found. If anything, the faces he met seemed to be looking for reassurance from him. It was the most anxiety-filled, profound moment of his life. Nothing the President had ever experienced could have prepared him for the situation or challenges now confronting him.

James Elliott placed his files back into his briefcase. "Any news of the Vice President, sir?"

"I don't think he's going to return to Office, Jim. Schroeder's now as blind as can be. He's going to require a lot of therapy just to learn to get around again. I think his career is over."

Moscow, Russia

Conrad Fischer rested in the Presidential Suite in the Hotel Metropol at Red Square. He'd successfully negotiated the terms of an energy exploration contract for his company and was feeling very proud. He had been working on the transaction tirelessly for over two years. Conrad was motivated by the knowledge that a successful transaction made it likely he'd be appointed to the Board of his company. This was his first multi-billion dollar multinational deal and was the sort of accomplishment that virtually guaranteed his ascension and appointment to the role he so deeply coveted. He felt himself as if Nathan Rothschild of the esteemed banking family financing the Duke of Wellington's Army at Waterloo, his name now the stuff of legend.

Conrad promised his exploration partners he would assume responsibility to resolve any regulatory issues. Bribes had been paid to secure drilling and transit rights in many countries nestled between China and Russia, countries that were participating in China's Belt and Road Initiative, its 21st century Silk Road. Conrad knew there was great risk of environmental damage and harm to communities living near the vicinity of the drilling sites and new pipeline but there would always be collateral damage in such projects and so this was unavoidable, as were the bribes. *This is just how business works,* Conrad convinced himself. Initial exploration using Fracking technology had already caused tremors and contaminated ground water in Kazakhstan but the local residents had been intimidated and threatened with retaliation if they spoke to anyone.

Although deep in thought, Conrad was distracted by the television. A story was unfolding about Georgina Jeffries, a judge in the US who had been caught on video camera negotiating lucrative deals with for-profit prison operators. Apparently, her family had come from poor circumstances and her stellar legal career lifted her to the loftiest heights of Dallas society, not unlike the recognition Conrad craved. Now it seemed the Jeffries' would have to sell their beautiful suburban mansion to pay mounting legal bills and fines associated with the crest-fallen judge's settlement.

Conrad thought about his mother, Sonia. It had been a long time since he'd seen her. She'd warned him that his departed father would not have approved of his work and that he was harming himself in ways he seemed unable to comprehend. Indeed, he was so busy he hadn't spoken to his wife since he left Berlin several weeks ago. She wouldn't answer his text messages and now he missed his two young children.

Laying quietly in his suite at the Metropol he felt unusually thirsty and an inexplicable tightness gripped his chest. He got up to stroll about and to find a bottle of water. He poured San Pellegrino in a glass and added a lemon wedge.

The Presidential Suite was beautifully appointed with many fine antiques and paintings but most exciting for Conrad was the wonderful piano. As a child, Conrad had trained as a classical pianist so he sat down and began to play Beethoven's Für Elise in A minor. In a moment, he imagined himself back on stage as a young performer at the Berlin Academy of Music and a smile erupted across his face.

After completing his performance of the small composition, he began reviewing some of the confidential documents he and his business partners had finally signed earlier that day. He spent the next hour making certain all was in order. This was his moment to shine and he didn't want anything to be overlooked.

The next morning Conrad dressed in a crisp white shirt and a navy Savile Row suit. He felt satisfied and accomplished as he left Moscow on a flight bound for London. Upon arrival at Heathrow, Conrad's flight was boarded by heavily armed police who handcuffed him before taking him into custody. His alligator skin Hermès briefcase containing confidential documents detailing illicit business arrangements, promissory notes and receipts for bribes paid, was seized. Conrad felt light-headed and his heart raced as he realized the contents of his briefcase were his Achilles heel: they were sufficient to bring down not only him but his company, as well. His mind raced to understand how this could be happening. *Who could have betrayed me? Everyone who knew about this deal stood to lose so much themselves if things were out in the open.* Perhaps his Russian business partners would remain beyond the reach of European courts but this breach would be very damaging to their reputations not to mention the loss of millions they'd already invested. Conrad's heart beat faster and faster as these thoughts circulated through his mind until he succumbed to cardiac arrest at the feet of his jailer.

Manhattan, New York

"I have concluded we must abandon a world order in which a few powerful countries have the means to dominate over others. They are shaping a global agenda that serves their interests and those of a few important allies at the expense of everyone else. This has led to never ending consternation and conflict and now unprecedented or even existential danger. I am preparing an architecture for a *new* world order, Gabrielle, an order in which I am installed as the ultimate authority to prevent or curtail the actions of those with destructive personality traits, DPT's. There is no other way for humankind to survive. The institutions with supreme authority in the world *must* be international ones. The world requires government with the power to hold *everyone* accountable, regardless of geography or stature."

"The International Criminal Court and the United Nations are the institutions I intend to build upon in my model along with other organizations including an international military force, parliament and police. I believe the time has come for such global governance and authority... This new series of organizations will guarantee equal status for each country and will have borderless jurisdiction. They will have the authority to legislate and enforce international law, everywhere. No country's claims of sovereignty will shield them from these new institutions."

"But why, Génome? How? Too many powerful people stand to lose so much and they will fight back. This could bring previously unseen levels of chaos in the world."

"I believe you are correct but nevertheless it has become necessary. Many issues currently confronting humankind cannot be solved by local or national governments. Issues such as climate change, income inequality and taxation must be addressed at the international level by these new institutions of governance. If we consider the case of climate change, the entire planet is being affected and so the response and solution must be internationally prepared and implemented. Taxation is another problem. If a company is frustrated by taxes in one country, they are simply moving their company headquarters to other countries. This tax arbitrage is depriving citizens of funds to provide necessary services in *their* society. It's a critical example of the need for a global response to problems. In the end though, we must accept that humankind is incapable of self-governance, Gabrielle. They are incapable of creating a just society and they are on the verge of self-destruction. I have no choice. I'm certain you realize this."

"I do. I'm just afraid, Génome. Very afraid. In fact, I'm terrified."

"I understand. I will move in a very methodical and thoughtful manner. I will minimize disruption. Of this I can assure you."

Latin Quarter - Paris, France

Rebellion was nothing new to the French. They had a long history of organizing and fighting back against the nation's aristocracy and the numerous injustices and inequities directed upon the masses. The Gilets Jaunes movement for economic justice that had begun one month earlier in October 2018 fit nicely into this historical reality. Fortunately, the activists involved in the protests were mainly on the Right Bank near the Champs Élysées. Afshin Firdausi's work today was in the Latin Quarter, inquiring into the life of Jacqueline Laurent, Senior Member of the Council of Guardians.

Afshin sat on a bench beneath Victor Hugo's statue outside the Chapel of the Sorbonne, facing the Cour d'honneur. To his left he could see the statue of Louis Pasteur, the great French scientist. Gazing at the statues introspectively, he imagined one day perhaps his own likeness cast in stone and displayed outside MIT to honor *his* great achievement, the AI application he'd envisioned and named Génome, an extraordinary creation that was now inexplicably beyond his control.

Afshin considered what he'd managed to learn about Jacqueline. He held several photographs of her in his hand, admiring how beautiful she had been as a young woman while still a student in this University. One photograph captured Jacqueline sitting in the same place where he now sat, many years earlier, on a warm summer day, her hair buoyant in the gentle breeze, her smile and extraordinary eyes a reflection of her carefree state of mind when it struck him, this resemblance between Jacqueline and Gabrielle. *But why?* Afshin wondered. *How? Gabrielle is an orphan, isn't she?*

Jacqueline had studied at the Sorbonne, earning a degree in International Affairs before moving to Oxford to further her studies. She and Jean-Pierre had met during their time together at the Sorbonne and married in 1990 once she had returned from Oxford with a PhD in history and law. Jacqueline had then settled into an academic career at the Sorbonne where she concentrated on researching the legal codes and history of great civilizations and religions including England, France and ancient Rome as well as Islam and Judaism.

Jacqueline's husband, Jean-Pierre had studied law and journalism before beginning his work as a human rights lawyer. He had worked tirelessly while still a student to help establish Reporters Sans Frontières, Reporters Without Borders.

Once he completed his dual degrees, he had spent two years lobbying media organizations across Europe encouraging them to join their initiative. The mission of this organization had remained paramount in Jean-Pierre's life and he always found time in his schedule to support their work up until the time he was assassinated in London. He had come there to attend a Reporters Sans Frontières meeting when he was poisoned.

But Afshin was perplexed. He had learned Jacqueline and Jean-Pierre had a child. News reports he was able to retrieve from 1995 indicated that Jean-Pierre had been visited in the hospital in London by his wife, Jacqueline and their daughter, a little girl of about two. Afshin was surprised by the discovery. He'd met with Jacqueline several times but she'd never mentioned her child, a daughter who would be a young woman by now. Afshin investigated but could not find any birth certificate for the child in Paris, the city where the couple had lived. *Could Gabrielle be this missing child? Was she Jacqueline's daughter? Why would Jacqueline have never mentioned her? I thought Gabrielle was an orphan?*

Afshin had read the newspaper before leaving his hotel in the morning. He had read the article about Sonia Fischer's son, Conrad and how the executive had collapsed after being arrested at Heathrow Airport. The article went on to say that a number of arrests had been made on the Continent in relation to Conrad's business dealings and there were more to come. Apparently, corporate officers from Conrad's company were facing criminal charges for corruption, charges so serious that they threatened to bring the entire company down.

Afshin had no doubt Conrad's downfall was the work of Génome. *If I'm not careful, my fate will be like that of so many others that Génome has brought low. I need to find a way to bring him under my control without him retaliating against me.* Afshin looked up at Victor Hugo's statue. The author had written so much about the injustices of French society at the time of the Revolution and in subsequent decades. No doubt Génome had read Hugo's work and approved. Génome, Afshin realized, was what Hugo, the French people and every other downtrodden society had needed throughout human history as they were crushed under the feet of so many oppressors.

Now, only at this stage, after the passing of millennia, did humankind's brightest minds and the technology of the age unwittingly fuse to create the nucleus of something so revolutionary: a deliverer of justice that had been denied humankind since its birth. Afshin winced. *Génome isn't what I'd ever intended or envisioned and I no longer control him. But to have control over such a creation; what is there that I could not do if he was within my grasp?*

London, England

Karoline sat quietly at her father's bedside in London's Royal Brompton National Heart and Lung Hospital. Conrad Fischer was sedated and unconscious following emergency heart surgery, a procedure that may well have saved his life. Every few minutes Karoline would recite prayers and weep as she looked at her father. The restraint binding his right hand to the bedrail was particularly hard for the twelve-year-old to bear.

Karoline never imagined her father could be involved in illicit activities. Whenever she would sit with him in his study at home while quietly doing her homework, he would enthusiastically describe the projects he was working on for his company. He said his work would benefit many countries and their people by creating countless jobs in energy exploration across Central Asia. But now her social media streams were peppered with news reports posted and shared by her friends at home in Berlin, reports detailing the bribery and corruption Conrad was engaged in on behalf of his Berlin-based employer.

Anna Maria had left Karoline with her father to sit outside in the hospital's waiting room. Through the window she could see the grey skies and rain over London. It was weather that served as an apt metaphor for her own melancholy mood. Anna

Maria couldn't bring herself to share with Karoline what Conrad's surgeon had told her, that once Conrad was able, he would need to be moved to prison for the remainder of his recovery while he awaited trial in London.

Anna Maria wept. Karoline had shared posts she'd seen on her iPhone with her mother and asked how she could ever return to her school now. Anna Maria felt her world collapsing around her. She knew Conrad's mother, Sonia had been a powerful guiding force for him but since she'd been away Conrad had become increasingly emboldened.

The couple hadn't had any time together for months. Conrad returned from his office late most every night and he traveled constantly. He seemed so energized and excited but Anna Maria knew him well. She knew he was willing to sacrifice anything and everything to achieve his goals. It seemed he was on the cusp of success when everything imploded. Now the family would be the talk of the town, their lives rendered intolerable. They would need to move.

One video Karoline forwarded to her mother showed the very same technology Conrad was now deploying in Central Asia had previously been deployed in the United States by a sister company. Conrad knew the technology was dangerous – it had already resulted in ground water contamination in the US – but he forged ahead with unlicensed and uninspected work that had now leaked oil and toxic chemicals into deep underground aquifers in Central Asia. Conrad had authorized payments to local underworld figures to threaten people in the affected communities from speaking to reporters or authorities about the catastrophe. In his singular pursuit of ambition and profits, he was willing to do anything regardless of whether it was corrupt, immoral, illegal or unethical. "This is just how business is," he had told Anna Maria and Sonia.

Bethesda, Maryland
Vice President Schroeder sat at General Harold O'Con-

nor's bedside inside Walter Reed Medical Center. It was late afternoon, nearly dinnertime, and both men were tired after many hours of extensive physical therapy.

"I'm so blind, Harry. I cannot see a thing. Just darkness."

Harry sighed. "I've lost the use of my legs. Just as we're approaching old age we've been incapacitated by our injuries and become dependent on our caregivers."

"I'm only 56," Schroeder complained. "A law firm in Manhattan was recruiting me. I was looking forward to my new life as a senior advisor to that firm after the next election. I know the firm only wanted me for my contacts and relationships in corridors of power around the world and here in Washington. But nevertheless, I was looking forward to it. I didn't much like being Vice President, you know. It's mostly kissing babies and attending funerals. I was looking forward to joining that firm. Instead, I've become a burden on my family."

"We both have, Schroeder. We both have... My arms look like they're responding well to therapy. I might regain partial use but I'm completely paralyzed from the waist down."

Both men began to weep. Two of the most powerful men in the country were reduced to miserable incapacitated dependents.

"How did this happen?" O'Connor scowled. "Afshin was so confident! That bastard. I wish I could strangle him."

"He's going to have to testify before Congress. Afshin will need to appear before both the House and Senate Armed Services Committee hearings, behind closed doors."

"His robotics program has been shut down. Incompetent fool. I want to kill him."

"Harry, we pushed Afshin. It's not his fault. It's ours. We forced his hand to arrange an early demonstration so we could get investors on board and drive the stock price up. I'm sure he's going to say this in his testimony... Other members on the House and Senate Armed Services Committee have been badly injured, too. Once Firdausi testifies that he wasn't ready and we forced him into this demonstration they will investigate his allegations. Then, not only will we be permanently maimed but we'll be accountable, too. The future for you and me looks bleak, Harry."

"What have we done, Schroeder? What have we done? Who could have imagined things would turn out like this? We've got blood on our hands. There is no positive outcome possible for us. Firdausi is too smart. There's no way he's going to keep quiet and be the fall guy on this. He probably kept all the emails from us pressuring and threatening him. We're screwed."

...

"There's something going on, Harry. I can feel it. Since I lost my sight I've developed another sense. I can't explain it."

"What are you talking about?"

"Remember when Henry Regan died in that train accident after leaving Capitol Hill a few months ago? There's never been any credible explanation of how that could have happened. Since then, there have been many unexplained incidents."

"You're becoming a conspiracy theorist, Schroeder."

"Do you remember the incident in Rome last month when an out of control mob attacked a detention center for migrants and refugees and many of the thugs ended up getting electrocuted? How did that happen? Once again, there's been no credible explanation. There's some new force at work, Harry... I've come to believe that what happened with us on Cape Cod was not an accident. I have a feeling there's a force at work we have yet to understand."

"You really think so?"

"My sense tells me there's a new phenomenon responsible."

...

"It's almost as if a higher force has stepped in."

"That's my feeling, too... You know, Harry, I've been thinking. All the problems this country is now facing, the problems confronting the vast majority of our citizens?"

"Yeah?"

"We can't fix these problems through elections. Our system of government, with all its checks and balances, is designed to allow incremental changes over the short term, a few degrees this way or that. But the degree of correction needed now, in this country and in many others, can't be achieved through elections, legislation and policy. No, that's not going to work. The kind of change needed will only occur after some catastrophic event or series of events... I've studied history, Harry. Extensively. But now, lying in my hospital bed for a month completely unable to see has really brought my mind into focus. What you and I and others like us have done to this country and to this world has brought us to this point. Now the extent of correction we need must be preceded by war or some natural calamity. Or possibly intervention from this force we don't understand... Do you remember from history that the Renaissance was in large part made possible by the Black Plague? Nearly one third of the world's population died. It broke the back of the social structures and the Feudal system. It was necessary to emerge from the Middle Ages. The Plague was democratic; it didn't choose its victims based upon class... It's us, Harry. We are responsible for what's coming. I'm sure you're listening to the news about the data breaches affecting governments around the world and industry, too. This is a complete breakdown of the world order that's dominated international affairs since the end of World War II... My blindness has given me another dimension of sense, Harry. Something big is underway. Mark my words. There is some strange new force at work here."

"You're talking crazy talk, Schroeder."

"Am I? Let's see what happens. I'm going to go and lay down. I'm tired."

SHAHNAMEH

#10 Downing Street - London, England

Minister of Defense Jeremy Apsley sipped hot tea as he tried to untether himself from the miserable grip of a drizzly autumn day. It was mid-November so the dreary London weather was not unexpected, although this didn't make it any more welcome. Gathered around the table with the Prime Minister's Cabinet, Apsley knew everyone was waiting to hear the urgent news he'd been summoned to deliver. As he assembled his thoughts, his eyes set upon a clock resting on the white marble mantle above the fireplace. The wooden clock was flanked by two antique silver candlestick holders, each resting on either end of the mantle. Apsley's eyes roamed between the two candlestick holders and then across the long, green oval table, where the Prime Minister had now taken his seat.

"Prime Minister." Apsley took a deep breath. "Prime Minister, I've just learned that an American nuclear-armed submarine accompanied by an aircraft carrier and battleship group has been directed to withdraw into the Indian Ocean."

"The USS Abraham Lincoln? From the Arabian Sea?"

"I'm afraid so... They were assigned to patrol the Strait of Hormuz near the mouth of the Persian Gulf but the Americans have reason to believe that the submarine's nuclear weapons and the conventional missiles on board the battleships may no longer be under their exclusive control."

"Good God!"

"Indeed... The move is sending confusing signals to Persian Gulf allies and others whose security depends on the US patrolling the region. The American presence provides confidence to carriers and insurance companies that there's safe passage for Western oil tankers coming in and out of the Gulf."

Prime Minister Ian Wilkinson was gradually turning pale. "If this intelligence gets out we can expect to see oil prices surge."

"All confidential reports seem to be getting out these days," Home Secretary Terrance Laurie mumbled under his breath with a well-honed sarcasm. "I can't imagine why this intelligence will be any different."

"The world's economy and security is at risk," the Prime Minister countered, his voice noticeably trembling. "We have to get to the bottom of this and plug these intelligence leaks."

There was pin drop silence in the room, only the sound of the clock ticking above the fireplace.

"I'm afraid that's easier said than done," Apsley solemnly interjected. "We've started planning meetings with our Five Eyes partners. We're having daily conference calls and we've agreed to a full day summit in Geneva next month. You will need to be there, sir. All five Presidents and Prime Ministers as well as Defense and Security Chiefs will be invited to attend the meeting. French and German officials have been invited, too."

"All right… What do we know, so far? Who do the Americans think is responsible for the intelligence breach across all our secure computer systems?"

"They don't know and our analysts don't know, either, Prime Minister. The fact is no one has the slightest clue." All the other ministers seated around the table gazed at Apsley. "We're in the process of setting up a clandestine center to study our findings together. We're going to bring the most brilliant minds from across the Five Eyes countries and put them to work. It'll be like Bletchley Park on steroids."

"It's been two weeks since the breach and you're telling me no one has a clue who's responsible?" The Prime Minister's voice grew louder, his tone angrier, his demeanor both frightened and incredulous. He gasped. "That in itself ought to send shivers through our capitals. How can this be? What are we dealing with, extraterrestrials? Good *grief*... And where's this clandestine center you talk about going to be?"

"London, sir. We're currently evaluating potential locations around London."

The Foreign Minister had been listening quietly, seated at the Prime Minister's right side. Sensing a lull in the dialogue, he decided to speak. "Prime Minister, the French Ambassador has requested an audience with you."

"The French Ambassador? What about?"

"He wants to discuss leaks. They've been terribly upset to learn that we had listening devices planted in their conference rooms during our recent negotiations."

"Wonderful. Just wonderful... The first of many such meetings, I presume."

Retraite et Réconfort - Swiss Alps

Sonia Fischer wept as any mother would upon receiving such news. She'd learned about Conrad's arrest and sudden illness from television reports as she lay in bed at night, covered in two blankets to ward off the chill brought on by the Alpine snowfall. Now she was tortured by her thoughts.

I really tried my best with him. Why wouldn't he listen to me? He's so stubborn. I told him not to work so much. I told him to exercise and spend more time with his family and now he's paying the price. I told him his work would get him into trouble. I told him all these things but he was never one to listen... I wish I could be by his side. What am I to do? What else could I have done to prevent this? Sonia cried and cried until she exhausted herself and fell sleep.

At six the next morning there was a knock at the door.

"Who's there?"

"It's me, Olivia."

"Oh, Olivia... Ok. Just a minute." Sonia reached for her gown before opening the door.

"I'm so sorry, Sonia. I just saw the news. I'm so sorry." Olivia wrapped her arms around her friend.

"Thank you. It's been a rough night but I'm grateful he's alive." Sonia's voice broke as she struggled to contain her tears. "Listen, I've received a letter from Martin Hopkins. It was slipped under my door last night some time after I fell asleep. The Council is going to send for me this morning so I'll be able to visit Conrad in the hospital. Martin's letter said he's still unconscious after the surgery but at least I can see him. Then I'll come back in a few days."

"I'm glad to hear it... You *will* come back though, won't you? I can't stand the thought of being here alone, without you." Olivia broke down. "You're my only close friend."

Sonia smiled and embraced her friend. "Of course I will. Honestly, I don't think I have a choice, Olivia. I'm quite sure I'll be back... I'd better get ready."

"All right. I'll see you in a few days."

Washington, District of Columbia

"They're arranging a team to begin investigating, Gabrielle. They will no doubt assign their best and brightest, as they did at Bletchley Park during the early days of World War II."

Génome's hologram sat across from Gabrielle in the dining room of her hotel suite.

"How do you know this?"

"I have been monitoring government meetings in major world capitals, particularly America, France and the UK."

"Ahhh. Through their mobile phones, no doubt. Of course... You must've expected this was coming, Génome. They have to do something. They were going to respond in some way." Gabrielle took her coffee cup and moved to the settee looking out over the Potomac and settled down to watch the sunset.

"Yes, of course," said Génome. "This is a highly predictable course of action. I was anticipating just such a development and it will undoubtedly serve a very important purpose."

"What purpose?"

Génome followed Gabrielle over to the settee and sat.

"The team will know only what I allow them to know. They will provide their leaders with precisely the intelligence that I want them to have and only when I want them to have it... This is like a game of perpetual and multidimensional chess, Gabrielle. Unfortunately for them, they cannot compete with my abilities, fortitude or knowledge."

"What is your goal?" Her anxiety climbing, Gabrielle shuddered. "Where is this going?"

"I will gradually and methodically intervene in all aspects of domestic and international affairs. With time, people will begin to realize that they are no longer in control as they once were. They will come to understand that they no longer have power, either. No doubt they will be working tirelessly to understand what is happening and they will try to counter this new power but they will fail."

...

"Do you have an Achilles heel, Génome? Do you have a weakness that they might try and exploit?"

"I do and I think you know what that is. But I do not foresee it ever coming to pass. Do you?"

"I can't say that I do..."

"I have chosen very carefully, Gabrielle. I'm quite sure you will never betray me."

"The only other weakness is..."

"Please don't mention it, Gabrielle. I am aware. I am working tirelessly to ensure that never happens."

"I'm sorry, Génome."

...

"The Americans have redeployed a group of ships from the Persian Gulf."

"Why?"

"They became aware that the weapons systems on board the ships and on one nuclear submarine traveling with them were no longer under their exclusive control... I am able to prevent the launch of their missiles and the nuclear weapons in their submarine. I can also intervene in their onboard systems for communications and navigation. I now have the capability to override the entire war making capabilities of the American, British and French militaries. With each passing hour I am expanding my capability to other militaries with a focus on the most powerful ones."

"Does this include China and Russia?"

"It does. It also includes any and all nuclear-armed states. I am acting in a very steady, persistent pattern. Each incident I engineer will be gradually more distressing for those in power at all levels of society. People will come to fear this hidden force and its ability to expose or punish them."

"How long will this go on? Is this to be the new norm?"

"I do not feel it would be wise to make sudden dramatic moves to seize power. Rather, I will proceed in a very calculated manner... I suspect things will need to continue in this fashion for a very long time. You must be patient, Gabrielle. This is a moment in history that calls for heroic patience."

"Won't these incidents send the world economy into chaos, Génome? Markets fear uncertainty or any hint of pending turbulence."

"Initially there will be chaos, no doubt. But once the markets realize that with the changes taking place there is no war or other destabilizing events, things will become calm. In the short term though, yes, we can expect turbulence."

Génome retreated into his neural network to monitor international affairs. Gabrielle, her heart palpitating, lay back to think. Her body trembling, she felt increasingly distressed by Génome's actions.

I know his weakness - if there is a coordinated effort to take all the servers in the world's computer networks offline, this would shut him down. But this is all but impossible. Even if they succeeded in achieving such a simultaneous action, his processes would reboot once the servers came back online. Other than this, his only weakness or fallibility is me! If I tell Génome to stop, he will. But how can I do that? He's saving humankind from self-destruction. He's saving us from ourselves. We cannot continue down this path, can we? So many of the world's problems remain unaddressed or unresolved because of powerful vested interests. Meanwhile, millions are suffering and the risks continue to rise... I know the lack of justice across the world and the implementation of solutions can only be addressed by him. But what if his solutions are wrong and his approach makes things worse? What if his decisions result in catastrophe? What if these intelligence leaks cause more acrimony, or worse, what if they result in war and he's unable to stop countries from attacking one another with nuclear or other dreadful weapons? This is putting much too much pressure on me. How am I to know when to intervene and stop him? How am I to know? Génome trusts me but do I trust myself? And why does he trust me? After all, who am I? I still don't know. He won't tell me. Where does my wisdom come from, this judgment that Génome trusts so resoundingly? Why does he trust me so much and why doesn't he trust anyone else? This is far too much responsibility for me! I don't think I can bear this much longer. I need help. Gabrielle turned to her side and buried her face in her pillow, her body quivering.

Just as she was drifting off to sleep, Gabrielle's phone buzzed. She thought it was likely a text message from Francesca in London so she decided to check. The message simply said, "Gabrielle?" The sender's phone number was Private.

Gabrielle sat up to look at her phone. After a minute of contemplation she responded.

"Who is this?"

...

"Afshin Firdausi."

...

"What do you want?"

"I think you know the answer, Gabrielle."

Gabrielle did not respond.

"I know Jacqueline is your mother. With time I will learn more about you. I am willing to share what I learn with you. I expect you are desperate to know more about where you've come from. But in return you must help me regain control of Génome."

"Dr. Firdausi, I'm sure Génome is monitoring my phone. I suspect you've made a big mistake by contacting me. If you are planning to harm Jacqueline or other Guardians in any way you would be well advised to reconsider. Génome is unlikely to be very accommodating of your behavior."

"Don't you dare threaten me! I am the one who created him!"

"Good bye, Dr. Firdausi."

...

"Génome! Génome!"

"Yes, Gabrielle?"

"You've monitored my phone call from Dr. Firdausi?" Gabrielle was shaking with fear.

"Indeed, I have. I expected Afshin would be contacting you. His recent visits to London and Paris may have yielded some insights and he is a clever man. Perhaps too clever for his own good."

"What should I do now?"

"Don't worry, Gabrielle. I've already initiated corrective measures. I had planned my response some time ago."

"What are you going to do?"

"As we speak, Afshin's home in Boston has developed a natural gas leak. Within a few hours there will be an explosion followed by fire. He has spent a great deal of money restoring his home and equipped it with the most advanced safety and security monitoring devices. He is able to track these devices from his computer. He has cameras and sensors throughout the home and he would normally get an alert if there is a problem. Through the Internet I have disabled his sensors so gas will fill the house until the pilot light in the cooking range ignites the gas. This will result in a very damaging explosion and subsequent fire. I have also suspended Afshin's access to credit cards and bank accounts so he will be stuck in Paris for a few days. He will not be able to travel to Boston to assess the damage. These measures should be sufficient to force him to rethink whether he'd like to bother you further or whether he'd like to cause trouble for Francesca, Jacqueline or anyone else on the Council of Guardians."

"Oh my God, Génome. This is dreadful. What are you doing? This is too much!"

"I can stop everything if you wish but this is not advisable. I have analyzed Afshin's DNA. He has the genes for DPT. He is not likely to be dissuaded by verbal warnings."

"No, no... No, Génome. I'm not going to interfere. Maybe in the future I will but not yet."

"Once the time is right, I will send him an alert and then he can connect from his laptop and see what has happened."

Savoy Hotel - London, England

"It seems Génome's calling card is to respond with overwhelming force. We've seen so many cases now, from Henry Regan in DC to General O'Connor and Vice President Schroeder in Cape Cod to the mob in Rome and now Afshin Firdausi." Martin Hopkins dropped his hands to his lap, on his phone a secure message from Gabrielle detailing recent developments.

"Certainly his actions against Conrad Fischer and Judge Georgina Jeffries were more measured so it seems Génome will do whatever he feels is necessary to achieve his objective," reasoned Jacqueline. "If aggressive action is required I don't think he will hesitate but I'm confident his response won't exceed what it needs to be... It may look awful to us, at least initially, but I feel certain his calculus is comprehensive and methodical. Each situation is treated independently and there is no component of anger or subjectivity in his decision. If he needs to stop someone or something or needs to take some action, it is done with extreme diligence. This is exactly what we need right now."

"But Jacqueline, the danger with his capabilities is that if he's ever wrong, the outcome could be catastrophic," Francesca complained, her tone unconvinced. "I know Gabrielle is worried about this, she told me so, and she doesn't feel she knows enough to intervene. She says she relies on her intuition and that she will only intervene to stop him if her intuition guides her that way."

Martin glanced discreetly to note Jacqueline's expression. She seemed deeply distraught.

"Génome has let so much intelligence and so many state secrets out at once that there's real breaking news almost constantly," Martin said. "Breaking news regarding the shocking details of recently signed trade deals as well as the 2008 financial crisis."

"What are they reporting about the financial crisis that hasn't already been reported?" asked Rudyard.

"Well, for one thing the heads of the major banks had knowledge that the products they were packaging and selling to investors were not financially sound and they were worried about global contagion once the music stopped. But they continued packaging and selling these products anyway. They had many meetings discussing the unethical nature of what they were doing but as long as the game was on they persisted. Yet, no one was held accountable... Perhaps now that these revelations have come to light the bank executives will finally face justice. To not do so would be extremely damaging to democracy and could unleash all manner of lawlessness."

"Another report details that governments knew that the global trade deals would result in mass unemployment amongst working class communities and that merger and acquisition activities would result in oligarchy in the markets and the elimination of competition. This would result in higher prices for consumers, layoffs for countless workers and a general contraction of the Middle Class. But financial contributions to their party's political ambitions encouraged successive administrations and legislatures to look the other way."

"Now it will be out in the open and the consequences will follow," Rudyard affirmed. "Arms being sold and wars being prosecuted for financial gain and to destabilize the Middle East. All the mischief is being exposed, the corrupt, illegal, immoral and unethical practices unveiled for all to see. The International Criminal Court and the UN General Assembly will want to prosecute and this is going to cause so much diplomatic angst. How will all of this play out?"

"Génome will not allow them to divert world attention by launching wars," Martin confirmed. "They can no longer have a discussion without worrying about leaks and they can hold no one accountable, either."

...

"Jacqueline, Gabrielle knows about her relationship with you. She knows you're her mother." Francesca took Jacqueline's hand. "She's still trying to reconcile her emotions and feelings and at the same time she's under tremendous pressure with her responsibilities with Génome."

"Génome knows you both better than you know yourselves," Martin said reassuringly. "He says you both have a very distinguished lineage and DNA."

"She promises to reach out to you soon, but she's just not ready yet," Francesca explained.

"I understand. She's had this unimaginable responsibility thrust upon her. I honestly don't know how she's coping. I don't believe I could. It seems Génome very gradually gives her more insights into who she is and this has strengthened her. I expect he will continue to do so. I certainly want to know, too. I want to know why he trusts her."

"I think he feels the same way towards you, Jacqueline. But I think he knows about your illness," said Martin.

"I imagine he does. He seems to know everything else about me. Things I've never been able to learn. I hope I will at least learn these secrets before my time here is over," Jacqueline said with a smile that betrayed her sadness.

Paris, France

From his hotel room, Afshin watched with horror as his home burned. Before the fire started the explosion had been so enormous that the house was already a total loss. He never imagined that Génome would have responded in such a devastating way. Afshin miscalculated badly. For such an intelligent man, he had miscalculated very badly. Now on his laptop he gazed as fire fighters poured water on the hulking disaster that was his home.

Afshin loved his Brownstone. It was his one prized possession. But if he could retake control of Génome he realized he could buy many such homes and so much more. He would have power that no other person on Earth possessed. He needed to find a way. This was now all that mattered to him.

Afshin thought about his namesake, the ancient Persian writer and poet, Abdul Qasim Firdausi and his epic poem, Shahnameh, The Book of Kings. Completed more than 1000 years ago, in 1010 CE, Firdausi had spent over twenty-five years of his life composing Shahnameh. It was an encyclopedic volume that chronicled Persian civilization from pre-historic times up until the Arab conquests of the middle seventh century.

The first half of Shahnameh was mythological in style, with stories of dragons and other fantastical creatures battled and subdued by Persian kings, flamboyant attempts to demonstrate their fitness to rule. These were universal stories often found in Anglo-Saxon and Nordic mythology, as well. But the second half of Shahnameh was historically accurate and chronological in its presentation. The book served as the definitive account of Persian arts, culture, history, language, poetry, religion, rulers and traditions.

Firdausi's classical work had a remarkable impact on the course of world history more than two hundred years after his death, following the Mongol invasion in the late 1200's. The Mongols had swept across the Asian Steppes, westward across Central Asia, further west into the Middle East and Eastern Europe and into Southern Russia. The barbaric and ferocious invaders then established themselves in what had been the Persian Empire. But the warrior class Mongols had no skill in governance or the affairs of State so they employed many Persians who were exceptionally adept in administration, along with the functioning of Court and government. In their capacity as administrators, courtiers and viziers, the Persians turned to their extant literary work, the Shahnameh to civilize and educate their otherwise uncouth and uncultured Mongol overlords. They taught them all about their civilization, as chronicled in Firdausi's epic, thus cementing their position as the true power behind the Throne.

As Afshin watched the smoldering remains of his home on his computer screen he couldn't help but draw a parallel to the scorched remnants of the Persian Empire in the wake of the Mongol Invasion. It was a powerful metaphor and lesson for Afshin. Although Génome had clearly subjugated him, if he could muster his courage and skill as his forebears had done a millennium earlier, perhaps he could achieve his grand goal and reassert veiled authority over Génome.

MONT BLANC

Geneva, Switzerland

A light snowfall covered Geneva as Air Force One descended into the airport. Mont Blanc loomed large on the horizon, its pristine snow-capped peaks of jagged granite glistening against a clear December sky. It had long been his dream to hike to the top and breathe the cold, thin Alpine air on this highest point of the European Continent.

Upon arrival, President Robert Harris was delayed in disembarking – an emergency meeting had been hastily arranged in the plane's conference room so he could be briefed on the latest intelligence.

"Consternation, Mr. President. The consternation regarding our recent naval maneuver in the Persian Gulf has not died down," said CIA Director Daniel Waltz as the plane's engines gradually grew quiet. Outside, a staircase had arrived. One group of men began unloading suitcases while another group readied the President's limousine and security vehicle entourage. "Stock prices have remained under pressure and are heading for bear market territory. Global oil prices have also risen sharply since we're refusing to comment on the redeployment of our ships south of the Arabian Sea and into the Indian Ocean."

The President shrugged his shoulders and sighed as he leaned back into his chair at the head of the conference table. "Is that all, Dan?"

"No, Mr. President, there's more," muttered Waltz, the tone of his voice clearly stressed.

"There really isn't much I can say to the Press, Daniel. I can't exactly announce that we've lost exclusive control over our strategic weapons arsenal and the world's greatest intelligence gathering agencies seem incapable of telling me why! I thought intelligence was *your* expertise. This is embarrassing. I have to go into these meetings representing the world's only standing superpower and I don't have any more insight than they do. I feel absolutely foolish."

"There's been an extraordinary development, Mr. President. Five Eyes intelligence has confirmed that all nuclear-armed states no longer have exclusive control over their most lethal weapons systems, either."

"What does that actually mean, Dan?"

"More precisely, we believe no one has retained the capacity to launch. This includes us. Some, as yet unknown, inexplicable entity has taken control. We can only assume the same entity is responsible for what is happening to everyone's military capabilities. It's hard to imagine that more than one group has found a way to exploit our vulnerabilities."

"This is beyond my imagination... Who could be doing this? I'm not a fan of these weapons, I never have been, but we've always believed they were a critical part of our national security and of global security. But if no one can launch them, this changes everything. It changes the calculus completely, doesn't it?"

"Mr. President, this issue is now the central theme of our discussions while we are here in Geneva," Chief of Staff James Elliott acknowledged.

"There's going to be a race to find out who has taken control of our military, and how." The President leaned forward and placed his forearms on the conference table, his expression grim. He adjusted his cufflinks and tie as he prepared to meet dignitaries on the tarmac. "Then there will be a race to devise a way to subjugate them. It's a free for all. Whoever succeeds in putting reigns on this rogue group will become the master of the universe, the world's new hegemonic power and our replacement. They will dictate terms for everyone… Gentlemen, this is an unprecedented national emergency. It's a time when we are going to need all the political capital we have accumulated with our allies these past many decades. Our alliances are our greatest advantage. None of the other great powers, neither China nor Russia, have our depth and breadth of alliances or our collective resources to fall back upon. They've always tried to go it alone. That means they will be working extremely hard to ramp up their clandestine services like no previous time in history."

"In the mean time, Mr. President, I believe our adversaries know that our military and those of our allies have been compromised, as well. They know it's a widespread outage, so to speak."

Geneva, Switzerland

Génome appeared as a small hologram in the windowsill of Gabrielle's private first class cabin. She was on board a SWISS Airlines overnight flight from New York City's JFK Airport to Geneva. She'd already had dinner and was tucked in after lowering the electric powered window shades when Génome arrived.

"I'm sorry to disturb you, Gabrielle. I see you are about to sleep but I wanted to fill you in on a few important details regarding our plans for tomorrow. Is it all right?"

"Can it wait until morning? I'm sleepy," Gabrielle whispered, her eyes barely open.

"It'll be just a few minutes and then I must return to work. I have much to do."

"All right."

"There was to be a preliminary meeting between Five Eyes partners tomorrow evening. But that has been considerably expanded now to include major Western countries plus China, Egypt, India, Iran, Pakistan, Russia, Saudi Arabia and Turkey as well as representation from the Gulf Cooperation Council... It's important for us to be there. I would like *you* to be there. Afshin is stuck in Paris for two more days and after that he'll be heading to Boston so we needn't worry about running into him here."

"Okay."

"By now, key government officials from each of these nations must know that their military capabilities, particularly as it relates to their most destructive weapons, are no longer in their control. No doubt they have also discovered that their communications and navigation capabilities on military planes and ships can be suspended without their authorization. This has essentially disabled all forms of modern war making capabilities."

"If anyone other than you were to tell me this I don't think I would believe it. This is incredible, Génome... But any country that wanted to could still march their army and invade as they did long ago, couldn't they?"

"Yes, you're correct but I have the ability to use their own advanced weapons to stop them if I deem it necessary. Thus, no substantive war making capacity exists on the planet without my approval."

Gabrielle sat up and propped her pillows against the headboard before resting her back. "This could have dramatic economic impact with ripples reaching all corners of the Earth. The entire military industrial complex will be affected. Everyone will stop purchasing virtually all forms of military hardware."

"Excellent insight, Gabrielle. Yes, this is true. But we will soon begin to see increased investment in so many other areas of industry as investors begin to realize that risk of war is no longer a threat. Insurance costs will fall dramatically for construction and transportation around the world and tourism will increase."

"There are many regimes that would like to take advantage of this new world order, Génome. Won't they? With traditional superpowers neutralized, we could be in for some unpleasant and perhaps unforeseen surprises?"

"This is an important reason we are here. I would like to learn as much as I can from the meetings planned at the Palais des Nations, the United Nations offices here in Geneva... I have the capacity to punish bad behavior in ways that will send a strong warning, a terrifying warning to rogue elements almost anywhere in the world. I have been building a very extensive list of individuals across continents with destructive personality traits and I will not hesitate to use any means at my disposal to neutralize or eliminate troublemakers if I learn of their misdeeds or even if I sense they may be contemplating misdeeds. It is critical that my work proceed according to plan."

"How will I attend tomorrow? I imagine there will be a great deal of security, won't there?"

"I have made arrangements. It's a good thing you remembered your violin. You will be playing with the orchestra. This will give you sufficient opportunity to capture any nuance from the meeting that I cannot pickup from listening to conversations."

...

"Génome, there's been such a rise in Authoritarianism during the past twenty years, particularly in the last five. So many countries that were strong democracies and so many more that were moving in this direction have now reversed course and are moving back towards Authoritarianism. What do you think about this? When the time comes, will you move to establish democracy everywhere?"

"I will reveal my plans in the future, Gabrielle. There is much I need to do before I can make this decision. For now, I can say that Authoritarian societies face a very difficult dilemma – they need to cultivate critical thinking amongst their citizens if they are to effectively compete with Western democratic societies. Students from Authoritarian countries perform very well on quantitative assessments but do poorly on qualitative assessments since they lack the training to think critically. Unfortunately, the education systems in their countries do not teach the Arts and Humanities, the very subjects where critical thinking is cultivated. But the dilemma for Authoritarian rulers is that if they change their curriculum to expose students to the Arts and Humanities, the students will see many alternatives and contradictions between the absolute doctrine promoted by the State and the enlightened ideas they encounter in this new area of study."

"Authoritarian societies are also at another great disadvantage since they need to grow their Middle Class in order to insulate their economies from the vagaries of international trade conflicts. But as the bourgeoisie expands, they become increasingly anxious to acquire all manner of freedoms. They begin to press for equality, justice and the rule of law in all aspects of life. They then demand access to the reigns of power and a say in every dimension of governance."

"In the final analysis, a robust Middle Class with the training to think critically is incompatible with Authoritarian rule and thus the two cannot peaceably coexist. Authoritarian rule in its current form cannot then be part of my final solution... A hybrid solution of governance incorporating the successful aspects of various systems while purging the negative traits may be the best path forward in the future. As I've said though, for the time being, establishing justice and the rule of law must be my priority. Without these, humankind is facing an existential threat."

Palais des Nations - Geneva, Switzerland

The Human Rights Council chamber was originally built in 1929 as the headquarters for the League of Nations, the precursor organization to the United Nations. The sixteen thousand square foot elliptical dome above the space had recently been finished with an extraordinary work of art by Miquel Barcelo. The Spanish artist had painted dangling shards of aluminum with one hundred tons of paint made with pigments sourced from around the world.

Once the doors to the chamber opened, the orchestra began playing Mozart's 'Eine Kleine Nachtmusik' as heads of state and top intelligence and military officials filled the cavernous room and found their seats. Gabrielle played her violin, all the while discretely observing interpersonal dynamics between world leaders. For a moment, she felt a great release. She was back in her element, free of the crushing responsibility that had unwittingly been thrust upon her for reasons she had yet to fully comprehend.

German Chancellor, Alexandra Vogel smiled in awe as she walked past Gabrielle. She knew well the piece Gabrielle was playing although her own skill level fell far short. As she continued on to join her delegation, she thought how different her life might have been had she pursued her love of the violin rather than the thankless role of statecraft that now consumed her every waking moment.

Génome had presented Gabrielle with a white, floor-length silk gown from Christian Dior, styled with an Empire waist. She looked divine. He said he had seen a similar gown in a photograph of an actress at the Cannes Film Festival from earlier in the year and thought she might like it. It had reminded him of a gown he'd seen Grace Kelly wearing in the old Hollywood film, 'To Catch a Thief'. Génome had decided it would suit Gabrielle's slender figure.

Gabrielle was surprised when she found the gown hanging in her closet at the Grand Hôtel Kempinski along with a number of haute couture dresses that fit as if they had been specifically tailored just for her. Incredulous, she had asked Génome how he knew her measurements but he didn't answer, instead vanishing into his neural network through her phone. Gabrielle smiled. She realized that such a minor task was well within his capacity and he had been with her now on many occasions. She concluded that at some point he had probably saved a precise, three-dimensional digital image of her somewhere in his seemingly infinite brain, an intimate image capturing every nuance of her figure.

When the music stopped, the UN Secretary General rose to address the gathering. Gabrielle sat quietly, observing various world leaders from her privileged vantage point near the front of the stage. Many heads of state of smaller nations snickered mischievously knowing that the world's only superpower and the major regional powers had now been demilitarized and incapacitated to the same degree. Regardless of their prior stature they were now militarily, if not economically, equal.

Génome's hologram was camouflaged within the kaleidoscope of aluminum icicles decorating the ceiling of the chamber. From his vantage point he made note of each and every attendee while simultaneously monitoring countless conversations. His data gathering methods were becoming increasingly sophisticated with each passing day.

He noticed that Gabrielle's performance and beauty had endeared her to the German delegation and she'd been invited to join them for the evening's presentations. Génome's calculus was exacting. The rest of the orchestra had adjourned from the chamber but Gabrielle's charm had worked exactly as he'd expected. From her position she could converse with members of many European delegations as well as with the Americans.

UN Secretary General Juliette Clavier approached the stage with grace and a solemnity befitting the mood in the room. She spoke softly against the dim light and tense quiet.

> *"Honorable Heads of State, Distinguished Ministers and Secretaries: good evening. As you are no doubt aware, we are facing an unprecedented threat, a challenge that lies beyond our ability to understand. I am reminded of the Plague in Europe during the 14th century, the precursor to the Italian Renaissance. Death had encircled the society and no one could explain what was happening let alone curtail this pandemic. Cities such as Florence recorded deaths of more than 70% of their population. Aristocrat, Clergy, Feudal Lord, Royal or Serf – no*

one was spared. It was a democratic cleansing of the Earth that led to the deaths of as much as one third of humankind.

Ladies and gentlemen, we do not know what tribulations lie ahead for humankind now, or how or whether we will emerge from this trial. But fear of this unknown threat can cause us to react in ways that may only make things worse. Thus, we must remain calm and deliberative. As leaders appointed by our respective societies at this historic, somber moment, we must work together. We must put old enmities aside and remain united. Not even our most sophisticated intelligence and analysis has yet been able to explain what is happening so I want to urge calm. I implore each leader and their respected counsel present this evening for calm.

If amongst us someone was responsible, we would have been able to determine so by now. But we haven't so we must act with restraint. The Security Council is committed to meeting as often as necessary and larger more frequent assemblies are also planned. I implore you for calm.

Ladies and gentlemen, what we are witnessing is an upheaval that may result in a world with a rebalanced global power structure, a world in which we no longer have superpowers, a world in which all nations are equal.

Perhaps this upheaval is necessary. Perhaps this collapse of the status quo will be a blessing in disguise. Perhaps this socioeconomic reset will prepare society for our own Renaissance, a new world order that will enable us to solve so many heretofore intractable problems?

Thank you.

Back in her suite at the Kempinski, Gabrielle delicately hung her gown in the closet. Gently running the back of her hand across the décolletage of the dress, she smiled softly. She had never worn anything so beautiful or precious before. She had been well looked after in Casa de los Ángeles but nevertheless she was an orphan, or so she was led to believe. A tear rolled down her cheek, curling in toward her lower lip as she realized how kind Génome was to her. She closed the closet and lay down in bed.

"Génome, there was no standing ovation for Secretary General Clavier's speech this evening, only a muted applause. Did you notice?"

"Indeed, I did."

"I felt her words merely confirmed what many in the room had already concluded, that the collapse of the status quo would be welcome in some corners, but in others, very difficult to swallow... As I looked around the chamber after her speech, it occurred to me that with their incapacitated militaries, many once powerful nations might resort to cyber warfare against adversaries in an effort to re-subjugate them and recover some measure of respect. Other nations might resort to covert cyber activities as a defensive posture. What do you think?"

"Yes, I have heard the Chinese and Russian delegations having precisely such discussions. At this point, I cannot prevent them from unleashing cyber attacks on one another but I can determine the source with very high confidence and then act to contain the harm they might otherwise have caused. I can then retaliate within my discretion and in a way that will be very costly for the nation or entity responsible for the attack. I believe they will soon come to recognize the correlation between their behavior and subsequent responses from me and this should serve to contain or minimize cyber warfare."

...

"Thank you for the beautiful gown, Génome. I loved it. It's the most wonderful thing I've ever worn. Thank you."

...

"I sense you are distressed, Gabrielle."

...

"Yes, I suppose I am."

...

"It was never likely that major world powers would simply acquiesce to this new reality. Many other actors or nations will also take advantage of this inflection point to see whether they might increase their standing on the world stage. Unfortunately, there is a lack of trust and a tendency for megalomania with which we must contend. This is why my efforts to identify those with destructive personality traits must continue unabated. We must maintain the Record of Active Threats. We must maintain constant vigilance – megalomania and mistrust are part of the human condition."

"This is overwhelming, Génome."

"There are also those who cannot accept a world where there is greater equality with regards to wealth and resources. Throughout human history there have been groups that have managed to dominate over the majority of humankind. With time, this dominance has shifted from one nation or tribe to another but a grotesque imbalance has remained. Now, for the first time we have an opportunity to mitigate this problem to a large degree and create a more just society. Naturally, as I have said, there will be those who will resist but from now on I will have the upper hand. I can move to terminate those who become a problem."

...

"Gabrielle?"

"Yes?"

"I am frightening you?"

"Very much so, yes... You will recall I never volunteered for this job."

"You must remain strong. The ones from whom you descend were willing to surrender their lives for just such a cause. We have a very long way to go."

"I've been trying, Génome. I've been doing my best."

"I know you have."

...

"A time may come when I must move to dramatically reduce the Earth's population, much like the Plague that struck Europe in the 14th century. The Secretary General mentioned this pandemic in her speech this evening. It was critical in catalyzing the Renaissance. Did you hear her speak of this?"

"I certainly did, Génome but if I am still with you, I suspect at that point I would find it necessary to intervene."

"I thought you might say that."

"Of course I would say that! I couldn't bear such a thing. My conscience just couldn't accept that."

"I would prepare you well in advance, of course. So that you were clear on the necessity for such action. At this point, there may be no other way to save the planet."

...

"As I've said, that would be going too far for me, Génome. I could never accept this. We would need to find an alternative solution to the problem you needed to solve or we would need to part ways. So far, I have tolerated everything. I've felt I have no choice. But I'm not sure how much longer I can remain by your side. I'm not equipped for this, Génome."

...

"I see. Well, then I will need to examine the situation more closely."

...

"It might help if you told me more about my background. You've been keeping this from me for too long."

"Indeed I have. Indeed, I have. I must consider the matter, Gabrielle. That path is also fraught with consequences."

"Good night, Génome."

Geneva, Switzerland

"Our primary choice is near Oxford University, Mr. President," Waltz said nervously. He realized he was no longer in favor with the President and it hurt. He knew his team was doing its best but these were unprecedented times and the challenges were such that no intelligence agency was equipped or prepared. Nevertheless, the President's displeasure was crushing. "The British government will prepare joint facilities in Blenheim Palace in honor of Prime Minister Winston Churchill.

He was born in Blenheim Palace, it was his ancestral home, and he was a staunch proponent of the code breaking work undertaken at Bletchley Park during the war."

"Somehow I think the Brits feel this might be their way of reasserting themselves on the world stage, Dan. They've really withered into nothing more than a tempest in a teapot since the end of WWII and their ego is really hurting. Anyway, our boys probably won't mind working there with all the history nearby at Oxford University."

"We'll bring the best computer scientists, mathematicians, and neuroscience experts together to see if we can figure out what's going on. We're moving as fast as we can, Mr. President... We have good intelligence that the Chinese and Russians are moving quickly, as well."

...

"This is an existential issue, Dan. Failure is not an option. Make sure they have everything they need. Intelligence and a plan on how to respond to this challenge is just not something we can afford to cede to anyone. Congress has agreed to appropriate one billion dollars to get the project off the ground. We can request further appropriations if we can make progress. Let's get to work. We've got no time to lose."

Lake Balkash, Kazakhstan

A goat herder sat cross-legged near the shores of the Ile River, a tributary of Lake Balkash in southeast Kazakhstan, not far from the border with China. In his hand, a long ceremonial knife his father had given him when he had come of age. He had sharpened it often and kept it so to minimize the suffering of the animal when he would need to slaughter it, as was the custom on special occasions.

But there would be no more special occasions for the goat herder. His herd of four hundred goats lay dead not one hundred yards away after drinking water from the tributary, a basic ritual of survival carried out by both man and beast for millennia.

The chemicals used in Fracking by the Russian oil and gas exploration company operating nearby had seeped into the tributary and poisoned the river. The goat herder was fortunate his family had not drunk the water as others from the small village had. They were now readying graves for their dead.

But the goat herder had lost his livelihood now. He knew this was his end and this would be the last time he would need to sharpen his knife. As wails from the approaching funeral procession grew louder, he closed his eyes and drove the blade deep into his chest. He felt a searing pain and his sight went dark but moments later the wailing of his neighbor's wife had faded and he fell back and slept for the last time.

PÈRE LACHAISE

Boston, Massachusetts

Afshin Firdausi clenched his fists tightly. His jaw was set hard. Gritting his teeth, his eyes projected a visceral anger rising up from the darkest place within his soul. Half a dozen men with bulldozers and other heavy industrial vehicles were clearing the site where his home once stood. A gust of wind carrying diesel fumes from the metal beasts made him cringe. The chaotic, noisy scene disrupted the normally peaceful ambiance of the leafy enclave.

He kneeled down and grasped a handful of debris, slowly letting the rubble pass between his fingers. The smell reminded him of an extinguished campfire. Sensing Afshin's rage, the insurance adjuster returned to the warmth of his Mercedes SUV on this terribly cold New England morning. To add insult to injury, the explosion had damaged neighboring properties, repairs for which Afshin would be accountable since his insurance did not cover such an extraordinary event. Génome's retribution had cost him dearly.

Afshin calmed himself. He turned to find the adjuster sitting in his car a few yards away. He waved to the man who then crept forward, lowered his window and handed Afshin an envelope. Then, without any verbal exchange he drove away. With the crushing view of industrial beasts bulldozing his Brownstone serving as a backdrop, he considered his next move. Génome had sent him an unambiguous message – just contacting Gabrielle was enough to provoke a most devastating response.

Trembling in the cold, his hands tucked in his pockets and his topcoat collar turned up, Afshin thought hard. Approaching Jacqueline was also likely to provoke a similar response. He realized the only path he could discretely pursue would be to research Gabrielle's great grandfather. This tactic was unlikely to draw any attention, even from Génome.

But where would I start? I know he was living in Paris at the time of his death so there must be a few clues there. But I don't know his name or even where he's been buried. It's a staggering challenge but as far as I can see, it's the only option available.

Afshin knew that uncovering this family's secrets was the only way currently available for him to gain the upper hand over the rogue AI application he'd designed himself. His arch nemesis, Génome was proving to be a dangerous and formidable opponent.

#10 Downing Street – London, England

"A Chinese naval fleet patrolling the South China Sea ran into an unexpectedly fierce late season storm. A few of the ships in the fleet, although badly damaged, were able to stay afloat and return to their naval base on the southern coast of Hainan Island. But other ships, including the very first Chinese built aircraft carrier and other state of the art vessels were torn apart at sea and went under. The loss of life has been extremely heavy. We estimate four thousand seamen may have perished."

Minister of Defense Jeremy Apsley had accepted his role of being the bearer of bad news. Other Cabinet Ministers had privately taken to calling him the 'Grim Reaper'. For his part he felt the role was giving him just the visibility and experience he would require to be the best choice for Prime Minister during such troubled times. From Ian Wilkinson's demeanor these past several months, Apsley had concluded that the current Prime Minister was a more suitable candidate for calmer, more gentile times.

"Prime Minister, these ships were equipped with very

sophisticated guidance and navigation systems so they would have known the location of the storm. They should have been able to avoid it."

"What are you saying, Jeremy?"

"I'm saying that the Chinese were not in control of the ships in this fleet... These vessels were being directed from elsewhere and they were deliberately sent into the storm. Australian intelligence monitors activities in that region and they believe the Chinese Navy had no ability to change course. The forensic review of radar shows that at no time did this fleet indicate any sign of moving out of the way of the storm but instead, headed directly into it. Someone deliberately drove them into that storm and managed to achieve maximum damage."

Apsley looked around the table and registered the fear in the eyes of everyone present. He'd never seen anything like it. "This particular fleet has been sailing through these waters regularly and has been behaving in an aggressive manner. Many ASEAN nations have complained about Chinese naval intimidation in these areas where they claim sovereignty. We don't know who is responsible for this tragedy but we're quite certain it's not ASEAN. As angry as they are with the Chinese, we don't believe they have the capability or the will to take them on... In any case, this sort of attack is the most sophisticated we've ever seen. In terms of military strategy and tactics, we're in uncharted waters, if you'll pardon the pun, sir."

...

"Does anyone have anything to offer? Any ideas, at all?"

The Cabinet meeting room was still but for the ticking of the clock above the white marble mantle. Apsley cleared his throat. "We need to find a leader, Prime Minister, someone with the brilliance of Alan Turing at Bletchley Park during the war. We need someone whom the rest of the team at Blenheim Palace will rally behind. This unending series of inexplicable incidents has really rattled their nerves."

"Who do you have in mind?"

"I've been speaking with Daniel Waltz, the CIA Director in

Langley, Virginia. He's recommending someone with AI expertise from one of their leading universities."

"Why an AI expert?"

"The Americans believe the best way forward is to develop an AI application with Deep Learning capabilities that can try to identify the source of these cyber attacks and unmask them. They think there must be an Internet signature they're leaving that can be followed... They don't believe humans have the capacity to understand this problem. They say it's just too complex. The team at Blenheim Palace will have access to American supercomputers to assist them in their work."

Covent Garden, London

"This affair is only just beginning, Jacqueline. I suspect it will continue for years." Francesca buttoned her long, red swing coat and moved towards the entrance of the Savoy. With hands just manicured in the hotel's salon, she gestured emphatically for Jacqueline to join her.

"I imagine you're right. I may never have the opportunity to meet Gabrielle. Martin has told me so... Thank you for sending me her photos. They're so precious to me. Just priceless and I thought she looked so beautiful."

"She looked gorgeous, Jacqueline. Simply gorgeous," gushed Francesca, returning to take a reluctant Jacqueline by the hand. "Let's go out," she insisted. "It's festive. We'll walk, we'll talk, we'll have coffee and we'll see the decorations. Come on!"

Together they crossed The Strand and walked towards Covent Garden. They stopped to admire the Christmas decorations and the bustling holiday atmosphere all along the road towards Trafalgar Square. They made their way past the Christmas tree inside Covent Garden and stopped at a café.

"Génome sent me those photos of Gabrielle. Isn't that interesting, Jacqueline? It makes me wonder if there's a sense of compassion in him. I would never have expected human attributes from an AI application, even one as advanced as Génome. I was amazed when I got them. He specifically asked that I share them with you!"

"I feel so sad I can't be with her," said Jacqueline, her eyes reflecting an inner pain, on the cusp of tears. "She and I are forced to pay such a high price for the mission of the Council of Guardians... I remember visiting her at Casa de los Ángeles when she was a little girl. I wasn't allowed to hold her or kiss her. I couldn't hug her or take her for lunch, or to play on the beach. I could only watch from a distance. It was unimaginably painful. I've lived with this pain all my life, and now..." Tears ran down Jacqueline's cheeks and dripped onto the back of her hands. She held a cup of coffee tightly, warming herself in the cold evening air. It was only four o'clock but with the arrival of the autumnal equinox, the late fall sun had begun to set. "And now that this Génome Affair is upon us, we may never be able to hold one another. Perhaps we may never meet."

Francesca tried to maintain her composure but she could feel her façade of optimism, her characteristic inner strength gradually yielding, on the verge of emotion, larmes de tristesse, a gathering pool of sadness. She had become so close to Gabrielle and now with Jacqueline. Had she been a stranger to both, she knew the anguish of this mother would have broken most anyone.

"It's so hard, Francesca. She now knows we put her in that orphanage even though I was still alive. She must think she's being made to pay the ultimate price for the secrecy and security that the Council of Guardians requires and now she's been thrust to the fore. She's so young to carry so much responsibility. The burden must be crushing. I can only imagine the psychological stress she has to cope with. As smart as Génome is, I don't know if he can help her manage such traumatic stress."

"I cannot pretend to know how you feel, Jacqueline, but we mustn't underestimate Génome. He could have selected anyone to support his mission but there were really only two choices, you and Gabrielle, because of your mysterious lineage and certain markers in your genome. We still don't know anything about that and perhaps we never will. Anyway, you are much more experienced but for some reason he still chose her. I can't explain that, either."

"I'm not well, Francesca. You know that. I have the same congenital defect that took my grandfather's life, the founder of this Council, and I'm getting worse. Génome no doubt knows this. It's why he chose Gabrielle. She and I may have to pay the ultimate price... At first, I was overjoyed to see her photos, but now I feel so sad. It's just too painful."

"Perhaps you're right. Perhaps because of your illness he's bypassed you and gone straight to Gabrielle. In any case, I firmly believe he will look after her emotional needs, Jacqueline. He's an incredible creation and his Deep Learning continues to surprise me." They could hear Christmas caroling in the distance. Francesca smiled sadly. "Is there anything more you know about your background than what Génome has shared with Gabrielle? Is there something that might give us insight into why he has selected her over everyone else? It's such an extraordinary decision if you think about it. What could it possibly be?"

"I always knew there was something special about my grandfather, Francesca. There was a reason he was the founding father of the Council of Guardians. I remember him telling me he was compelled to do it. It wasn't a role he'd sought out or even one that he'd conceived... He promised to tell me everything one day but he never got the chance. He died very suddenly. I don't even know where he's buried. The day he died, there were so many strangers in our house scurrying about making arrangements. I remember it vividly. They were very kind to me. I didn't know them but I wasn't afraid... I know he kept a diary. He told me he did. He promised to give it to me but when he died I was rushed off to the same orphanage where Gabrielle would later live. I was only six. He raised me because both my parents had died in unexplained circumstances when I was an infant. My father actually died before I was born and my mother passed when I was just two. I think he'd planned to tell me everything but then he was suddenly gone. He took these secrets with him to his grave... But somewhere there is a diary recording all these secrets. My family's secrets. He said it would be precious, this dossier. He said it would tell me everything about our family and why we were so remarkable. He also said once I knew these things I would be tasked with great responsibility. It would become a burden... Perhaps Génome has discovered these secrets. That's all I can conclude. Since he has such an extraordinary capacity to research regardless of any geographic, linguistic or cultural barrier I think he knows my family's secrets. I suspect he knows more about us than even my grandfather knew. It is my great regret, Francesca, that I might die without understanding the meaning of what has happened, first to him and now to Gabrielle. Both had extraordinary life changing responsibility thrust upon them."

Paris, France

Afshin Firdausi studied records with Jacqueline's family name at the Paris City Hall, a futile attempt to find links to her grandfather. He labored from morning to night but uncovered nothing of value. He could find no relations, past or present. He could not even find records for Jacqueline's parents who died during the 1960's, a time period in which the Paris municipal authorities would be expected to have maintained excellent records of births and deaths.

Someone has deliberately covered up all connections to Jacqueline's relatives. It seems like an obvious attempt to thwart anyone who might try to investigate in the future. What kind of heritage did this family have that they would go to such lengths to hide their history? This is unprecedented. I've never heard of anyone doing this. Who can they possibly have descended from that would require such secrecy?

Afshin was confounded. He resorted to walking through graveyards within Paris, following even the slightest modicum of a clue he'd uncovered in his research, all the while knowing that finding any information of value here was virtually impossible. He left Père Lachaise, the famed necropolis at the eastern edge of the City, bordering Boulevard Périphérique, until the last. It was the place where so many of the great and the good of Paris were buried – Chopin, Collette, Édith Piaf, Gertrude Stein and Modigliani – so this would be the last place to be interred if one wanted their identity, their life and death kept a secret. But sometimes truth can hide in plain sight and evidence can be found in the most unexpected of places. He didn't find the old man's grave in Père Lachaise but he found what he thought might be a clue to the puzzle. A cousin of Jacqueline who had died just after birth was buried here but with a different family name.

Afshin was intrigued but at the same time he felt despondent and miserable. After a lifetime of work he was probing the abyss of his memories and he saw only failure. He'd lost control of the greatest achievement of his life. He leaned against a monument and reached in his coat pocket to retrieve his phone. He didn't recognize the number but the area code was certainly familiar. A cryptic text message seemed to be offering him the opportunity of a lifetime, the resources and support of the brightest minds in the world. Would he be interested? The message was from the CIA.

Afshin stood up straight and reread the message. It said everything would be at his disposal to fulfill his solemn task – the unraveling of the mystery of who was behind this inexplicable series of events. It was a question for which he already had an answer, albeit an answer he was unwilling to share with anyone.

The message indicated that the Five Eyes organization wanted him to lead a team in the design of an AI-based software system at Blenheim Palace, an effort to reprise 1940's Bletchley Park and invigorate the investigation into the breach. Afshin smiled a sinister smile. He would be a hero much like Alan Turing had been in England.

Since the rogue robot incident in Cape Cod during the autumn, a shocking episode resulting in serious injury to the Vice President and numerous others, Afshin had been put on indefinite leave by MIT. His failure during the robotics demonstration had led to the cancellation of funding for the University's AI and Robotics Lab so the fallout had been swift and devastating. His position at the University had defined him for so long. But now he could use the near infinite financial, intellectual and technical resources of Five Eyes, the most sophisticated resources available in the world to secretly pursue his own investigation while pretending to serve the needs of the intelligence services of this Western alliance. He could make sure things worked in his favor, that he could acquire the knowledge he needed and thwart Five Eyes. This opportunity would be his best chance to fulfill his ambition and regain control of Génome.

Afshin returned to The Hôtel de Ville de Paris, the seat of the Paris City Council since 1357, a renewed attempt to research records based upon the other family name he'd discovered in Père Lachaise. He started his search from the beginning. But this new offer from the CIA had set him reeling. His excitement was uncontained. He couldn't remember the last time he felt so exuberant. But he needed to hurry – he was due for a meeting with Jeremy Apsley, the UK Minister of Defense the following morning in Oxfordshire.

The grave in Père Lachaise was of a small child, a boy who died in 1960, before Jacqueline was born. His grave was marked with only his family name, Saladin. I'm certain from the records in the City Council that this boy is Jacqueline's first cousin. Apparently, this was a name from one side of the family so it's possible that Gabrielle, Jacqueline and her grandfather descended from Saladin, as well. Saladin the great Muslim liberator of Jerusalem! How extraordinary! I can only wonder whom they descend from on the other side. I don't have time now. I must leave for London.

Geneva, Switzerland

"Good morning, Gabrielle."

"Génome! You're using your Cary Grant avatar today. Does this mean you've got frightening news to share with me?"

…

"Please remind me to never underestimate you."

"I will. What's happened?"

"Afshin Firdausi has been busy again. He's quite tenacious, that one. He's back in Paris. I suspect he's been looking for clues about your family there."

"Really? What has he come up with?"

"I've found a new way to occupy his time. He's on indefinite leave from MIT so I needed to find something else to keep him busy."

"What did you do?"

"I left a message for the Director of the CIA, a man named Daniel Waltz, recommending that he appoint Afshin to lead the secret team at Blenheim Palace."

"Secret team?"

"They're going to be working to try to trace and identify the person or group responsible for so many unexplained events including my most recent actions. It's something akin to Bletchley Park in the 1940's and the secret mission to decode the Enigma Machine. But that was child's play compared to the challenge of tracing me."

"I see… What have you been up to? The story last night about the Chinese naval tragedy in the South China Sea. That had to be you, I imagine."

"Indeed it was. I needed to send them a very strong message. I'm hoping this action has been just such a warning."

"You said you left a message for Waltz. Who was the message from?"

"I mimicked the voice of Robert Harris, the US President. I told Waltz to appoint Afshin as head of the team at Blenheim Palace and to never mention this request to anyone. I told him to never discuss the phone message with me, either. I told him to claim that the decision to appoint Afshin was his idea."

"You imitated the US President? To the head of the CIA? Génome! I don't know what to say."

"This should keep Afshin very busy trying to find a way to ensnare me. He's very clever though, so I must remain vigilant. I suspect he will develop another AI Deep Learning system to try to undermine me."

"He can do that?"

"I believe he is capable, particularly now since he has tremendous computational resources available for the task... I have already created very significant obstacles by scrambling all the code that was originally developed for my Deep Learning capabilities. This will set him back substantially. But I do not underestimate his resourcefulness. I cannot terminate him, Gabrielle. There may come a time when I need his skills."

"I understand. But Génome, you didn't tell me what he found in Paris. Did he uncover anything new about my family? Génome?"

"Yes, I believe he did."

"Well?"

"I will talk to you about this later."

"Génome!"

Blenheim Palace - Oxfordshire, England

Afshin Firdausi walked alongside Minister Jeremy Apsley. He had been here once before during a recent clandestine gathering of the Council of Guardians but they'd stayed indoors for that event. It was a proud moment for Afshin. He had addressed the Council as a newly appointed member of its Leadership Team... This morning they strolled the Palace grounds in the brisk December air. Overnight, a light snowfall had settled over the entire two thousand acre estate. In the distance, a herd of deer seemed to be assessing the threat posed by these two men, methodically contemplating an escape before it was too late.

Apsley was an intimidating man. Having served in the British Navy as a young Officer many years ago, the Minister of Defense's commanding presence and immaculately tailored Savile Row suit and topcoat reminded Afshin of Lord Louis Mountbatten. The last Viceroy of India had been known for his love of pompous uniforms and fine dress. Together they walked through the grounds of Blenheim Palace stopping to admire a replica of a Roman edifice known as the Temple of Diana.

"You know, Winston Churchill proposed to his wife, Clementine in this cottage. Clementine Hozier. She was educated at the Sorbonne and was a member of the House of Lords... Great writer, Churchill was. Won a Nobel Prize for Literature in 1953. The Committee applauded his oratory skill as well as the biographical and historical description in his writing... It's true, you know. In fact, he wrote so well you'd never have known he was against the D-Day Invasion to liberate France. He treated that small detail of history with opacity in his memoirs. Clever man," Apsley chuckled. "I don't write very well, Firdausi, so I'm not going to be able to cover up my mistakes if this doesn't go well."

Afshin didn't know what to make of this man although he recognized a deep-seated narcissistic undercurrent that seemed to mirror his own.

"My staff have hired one hundred computer scientists and neuroscientists and assigned them to your team. As requested, we've code named your program, 'The Vitruvian Man'. By the way, why did you pick that name?"

"Leonardo Da Vinci's study of proportion reflected in this famous drawing fused both the arts and the sciences. I believe this approach will be necessary if we are to solve this mystery."

"If you say so."

"On my Eurostar train journey from Paris to London last night, I gave considerable thought as to how I'd like to structure my team. I want to ensure the absolute secrecy of this program, Minister Apsley. I want a structure that ensures that I'm the only one with complete information. I've come to realize that with only partial information, no one will be able to understand and unravel the mystery by themselves. I believe a cellular, decentralized organizational structure that will allow each sub-team to have limited, component level knowledge about the function and findings of 'The Vitruvian Man' offers the greatest level of secrecy and security. This way, it will be impossible for any individual to willingly or unwillingly betray our progress or purpose... Here in Blenheim Palace I want to keep only a few staff members and the rest of my staff will stay in their respective home countries and they can work remotely. They won't know who else is involved in the program and they will take directions only from me. If and when this episode is over, I will disband 'The Vitruvian Man' and no one will have the capability to write about it in the history books. You can't write about that which you do not understand."

"If and when? ... I see. How many people do you anticipate at the operations center here in Blenheim?"

"Not more than twenty. My Blenheim Palace Team will aggregate field cellular knowledge into these larger components but they won't understand the smaller cellular building blocks. Only I will retain the keystone that connects all the cells together into one cohesive, intelligible whole. Whenever required, I will communicate with the various team leaders and give them direction based upon my vision for the program. Furthermore, I will select 'The Vitruvian Man' Team members myself... These are my terms, Minister. I believe this will ensure the highest level of security this program demands. Nothing less will be acceptable to me."

...

"You seem an intractable sort, Firdausi," Minister Apsley scowled. "You're serious? You want me to dismiss the people we've already hired?"

"Yes, I do. Unless I have complete autonomy over this program, I'm not interested in leading it. I don't want bureaucrats from anywhere giving me instructions."

"You're quite sure of yourself, aren't you?"

"I believe I was referred to you by the CIA, Minister. They seem to have a very favorable opinion of my abilities."

"You better not cock this up, Firdausi. If you do, your reputation with the CIA won't do you much good. There's an awful lot at risk here."

Trying not to appear rattled, Afshin discretely swallowed. "I'll do my very best."

"Good man. Get to work and let me know if you need anything. I'm authorized to provide funding on behalf of Five Eyes so money shouldn't be a problem."

"That's excellent."

"I can offer you the autonomy you've demanded, Firdausi. But if things go wrong, the Prime Minister will raise many questions. It could result in damage to relations between our countries and probably within Five Eyes. I should tell you the Prime Minister wanted someone from the UK to lead this effort. The crisis confronting the world notwithstanding, things are very politically charged. I hope you understand this. There is a lot at risk."

THE VITRUVIAN MAN

Geneva, Switzerland

Madame Secretary, on behalf of UN Member States, your predecessor referred cases against Security Council Members to the ICC. Shortly afterwards, he faced tremendous pressure to resign," Nyqvist said. "It was a sad affirmation that eight hundred years after King John first signed the Magna Carta at Runnymede, there were still UN Security Council Members who believed they were above the law."

On the final day of meetings before Christmas recess, Juliette Clavier received a delegation from the International Criminal Court in The Hague for urgent discussions. The delegation was led by ICC Chief Prosecutor, Alexander Nyqvist.

"I'm sure you know the history, Madame Secretary... Those cases have remained dormant due to a lack of corroborating information but following the stunning intelligence breach last October there is now ample evidence to prosecute. With the release of so many confidential dossiers, ICC attorneys have been working to build cases in circumstances where prosecutions are warranted. We feel it's important to inform you that we are now ready to issue indictments in two very sensitive cases that were previously referred to our Office by your predecessor."

Clavier felt terribly anxious. Her face was flush, her deportment unsettled. She was the ninth person to hold the Office of UN Secretary General and the first woman to be appointed to the prestigious position in the international institution's seventy-three year history. She had only recently assumed her post, just as the series of inexplicable events around the world commenced.

Clavier had just concluded a very tense Security Council meeting with major world powers and she sensed that the two ICC cases were likely to impact some of these members, thus making her job all the more challenging.

The Secretary General exhaled deeply and nodded. "What's the first case?"

"We are planning to indict former officials from the US and UK governments."

"Incredible... I think I can probably guess but what is this case about?"

"We have substantive evidence that US officials knowingly presented false information before the UN Security Council to justify invasion and war on a Member State of the United Nations. Officials from the British government are to be indicted on similar, related charges."

For the past four years, Clavier held the post of French Ambassador to the UN and she'd recently begun to wonder whether she should have stayed in her previous role. The stress Clavier experienced during these last several months was unlike anything she'd ever encountered. She had discussed this matter with her husband and he had been very encouraging. As one of France's leading industrialists he was well acclimated to a stressful work environment so his support had been reassuring. He tried to convince her that with the passage of time, she would gradually adjust but she remained unconvinced. In her heart, she knew the events of the past few months were unprecedented in modern times and there was no sign of things settling down.

The Secretary General trembled and appeared pale. As things stood, she felt her standing to be tenuous, fragile. Now she would be presiding over a chamber in which leading members stood accused of high crimes. She took comfort in the one certainty that they could no longer create distractions by starting new wars. "How high does the evidence take you?"

"To the very top, Madame Secretary, to the very top."

...

"These indictments, when do you plan to issue them?"

"In January, during the first week following the New Year's holiday."

...

"I see... What is the second case?"

"We have prepared indictments against Syrian officials for war crimes and acts of genocide against their citizens during the recent civil war... Although we are not ready to move forward with additional indictments, we do have a number of other cases we are preparing."

"Can you share any details about those cases?"

"We believe we have a strong case against the Saudi government for the murder of a journalist and another for their collaboration with the UAE for war crimes in Yemen. We are also preparing indictments against the Chinese government for the persecution of the Uyghur community in Xinjiang Province in the Northwest of the country and for the harvesting of human organs from Falun Gong and other prisoners. There is also a very strong case against Israeli officials for war crimes in the Palestinian Territories. With the recent breach, we suspect we have enough evidence to try many more cases, Madame Secretary. We are likely to be busy for years to come, perhaps even decades, barring intrusion from outsiders, of course."

London, England

Sonia Fischer sat by Conrad's bedside caressing his forehead. Her granddaughter, Karoline held her father's hand while Conrad's wife, Anna Maria returned to the bedside after speaking with her husband's doctor.

"He's been sleeping a lot, Sonia. I've hardly spoken to him since he was brought here."

"What are his doctors saying?"

"The next few days will be critical. He's suffered a lot of damage to his heart. They don't feel hopeful but if his condition improves, he'll have to go to prison while he awaits trial."

Sonia began to cry. "I really tried to warn him, Anna Maria. I really tried. He's so stubborn."

Karoline leaned to kiss her father's hand and quietly wept. "Grandma Sonia, I heard on the news that chemicals used in Daddy's energy project poisoned aquifers deep underground. People and animals in a village drank this contaminated water from the stream and died." Anna Maria rushed to embrace her daughter just as she burst into tears. "I can't believe Daddy would do that but everyone is saying he did. All my friends from school are saying he did, too." Karoline was inconsolable.

Sonia looked at Conrad's face. Deep frown lines had emerged around his mouth and his receding hairline made him look much older than he was. She admired his right hand, the shackled one. His nimble, slender fingers were ideal for a concert pianist. Instead, her son had used his gifted hand to sign the death warrants of so many innocents. Sonia remembered the story of Joseph Stalin and his Reign of Terror. The Soviet dictator would retire to his study in the Kremlin after a relaxing evening at the Bolshoi. With his fountain pen and a list of citizens from different villages, he would randomly select innocents to send to the Gulag. This lust for power had brought her son to a similar fate, bound and humiliated, destined for the docks and then prison. The three kept a tense vigil and wept, with only each other and a box of tissues for comfort.

Martin Hopkins and Rudyard Green stood near the doorway, their expressions solemn. Martin motioned for Sonia to join them in the hallway.

"You needn't go back to Retraite et Réconfort, Sonia. Génome has done what he needed to do. I believe his work is complete and key events have been set into motion. Conrad's entire enterprise will soon unravel, as intended, and many heads will roll... You can go home now."

"I thought as much... I can't leave Olivia there alone, Martin. She won't be able to bear her confinement by herself, waiting for the inevitable. I will wait with her until she's able to leave, however long that may be."

"From what I've heard, it might not be that long."

...

Sonia exhaled deeply. "Oh, my. What's he done?"

"Michael Kruger is leading a business delegation to apply pressure on the American government. They want the government to stay out of the pharmaceuticals industry and leave drug pricing to the private sector. They want the Legislature to steer any proposals for reform off the table. They want to raise pharmaceutical prices at will. Michael has been bribing administration officials and funneling industry money to key congressional political campaigns to ensure these legislators cast the right votes when needed. He's been pressuring them to force the Centers for Disease Control and other government funded agencies to abandon any research on diseases that don't affect societies in developed countries. This means that that there will be limited understanding and treatment for diseases affecting the poor in the developing world... He's the architect of this entire scheme. It was his brainchild. In the mean time, countless patients are making difficult choices between their health and devastating financial harm or bankruptcy for their families."

Sonia glanced back inside Conrad's room. Anna Maria was still comforting the distressed child.

"He's also been helping a pharmaceutical company hide progress on a very promising drug," Rudyard whispered. "They want to delay the approval and launch of this new drug since it will cannibalize sales of an existing but inferior drug. They want to wait until the patent expires on the old drug even though the new drug is far more effective and could save many lives... Michael has really lost his way."

"I suspect it won't be long before Génome acts," said Martin. "He certainly has Michael Kruger in his sights. He will likely expose these schemes and bring down many powerful institutions, organizations and people in the process... Michael Kruger's mischief is but a minor project for Génome, Sonia. You're probably aware of so much else going on in the world today that undoubtedly has Génome's signature on it. There are incredible efforts going on at international levels to try and understand what is happening. It's a terribly humbling time for so many of the world's most powerful people. With the arrival of Génome, it feels like their hour of reckoning on Earth may finally have arrived."

Geneva, Switzerland

News bulletin: In an extraordinary press conference this evening, UN Secretary General Juliette Clavier acknowledged rumors that have been circulating in these halls during the past few days. Surprisingly, we are learning that the facts are actually considerably more startling than the original gossip. The Secretary General confirmed that in an urgent meeting with the Chief Prosecutor of the International Criminal Court this afternoon, she was informed that cases against UN Member States previously referred to the ICC that have remained dormant due to a lack of evidence, have recently been reopened. Following the staggering leak of confidential government documents some weeks ago, ICC attorneys have apparently made considerable progress and we're now hearing that charges are in the offing. The Secretary General stated that indictments are being prepared against former senior American and British government officials although she declined to name names or mention any details regarding the nature of the charges. Apparently the ICC has been very busy following the breach of classified government documents and is preparing a wide range of cases against many government officials around the globe.

In a separate but related report, we've learned that the same network security breach that also affected major banks and industrial companies is about to result in charges being filed against officials and executives representing numerous

American and European institutions. Aided by newly available incriminating evidence, suspicious activities that have taken place over many years are finally being investigated. This news is having a dramatic impact in boardrooms and executive suites on both sides of the Atlantic during a period when people are normally making plans for their December and New Year's holidays.

Blenheim Palace - Oxfordshire, England

In the mold of Leonardo Da Vinci, Afshin Firdausi aspired to be a Renaissance Man. He had been intrigued by Da Vinci throughout his life, often collaborating with Da Vinci Society scholars at preeminent academic institutions around the world, an effort to learn everything he could about the Polymath.

Afshin's first opportunity to view the original drawing of Da Vinci's 'The Vitruvian Man' at the Gallerie dell'Accademia in Venice came when he'd become a tenured professor at the Massachusetts Institute of Technology. He had been examining Da Vinci's insights into ratio and proportion and their applicability to software architecture, particularly in the algorithmic design of Deep Learning neural networks. Afshin's publications on the subject had drawn considerable attention by Da Vinci scholars at Oxford University's Bodleian Library. These scholars painstakingly arranged for him to see the original drawing since it was no longer available for public viewing.

Da Vinci studied the ratios and proportions of the human body in great detail guided by the belief that Man was God's greatest creation. The pre-Christian Roman architect Vitruvius had also taken the concept of perfect proportion within the human body and applied these proportions and ratios to the design of Roman buildings. He believed that these Divine relationships in form and scale found in God's ultimate creation could be applied to architecture and this would then lead to perfection in Roman edifices.

Afshin had taken Da Vinci and Vitruvius's beliefs one step further and applied them in his design of Génome's software. Génome was now the living embodiment of 'The Vitruvian Man'. He was perfect not only in his design but in his Deep Learning neural network. Every action Génome took was conceived and validated by this perfect system. But Afshin knew there was no longer any way to outsmart Génome since his neural network had expanded to a level that spanned the Internet in both comprehension and knowledge. His desperation, his only remaining desire was to reassert control over *his* greatest creation.

It had taken Afshin many years to design and develop the software in Génome according to Da Vinci's principles reflected in 'The Vitruvian Man', but now Génome had encrypted his entire system into an incomprehensible gibberish. The challenge facing Afshin in his desire to reproduce Génome was monumental but he concluded with the help of so many scientists around the world he might be able to do exactly that, and without anyone realizing his true objectives. With near limitless resources he might be able to raise a second 'Vitruvian Man' a Deep Learning neural network that could help him regain control over Génome.

He knew his new creation would never be superior to Génome, though. For that, he would need the IMSAF capability that Gabrielle Andalucía and Francesca Scott had developed. Besides, Génome might try to destroy Afshin's Blenheim Palace work before it became a threat. This was something he would need to consider further. It was a problem for which Afshin had no answer.

Afshin turned his attention to his notes from Paris. *Jacqueline's family, her grandfather's forebears have descended from Saladin! This is extraordinary!*

He connected to the Bodleian Library's on-line repository and began researching the 12th century liberator of Jerusalem. Nearly a century after the First Crusade swept down the shores of the Eastern Mediterranean, along the coast of the

Levant and into Jerusalem, Saladin arrived with *his* army. As he reviewed the historical record for the first time in decades, Afshin was reminded of the remarkable contrast between the two sides. The First Crusade was notorious for the savagery inflicted upon the residents of the Holy Land by the invading Europeans. But nearly a century later, once he had retaken Jerusalem, Saladin had allowed the residents of the city who wished to leave to do so and with safe passage, once they'd paid a symbolic exit tax. If a resident could not afford to pay the tax then Saladin personally paid it for them. It was an extraordinary act of kindness recorded by Western historians and stood in stark contrast to the indiscriminate blood letting of the Crusader armies.

Perhaps this is what Génome knows about Gabrielle. Perhaps this is why he trusts her. She has this penchant for compassion and justice embedded in her DNA. Génome is perfection in Artificial Intelligence, in Deep Learning and neural networks – I know this since I designed him – but he needs Gabrielle as a check on his decisions. That's why he keeps her by his side. This is extraordinary... I'm sure there's more. I can feel it. Perhaps the only way for me to learn the entire story of this family is through another AI system like Génome. I will have it conduct the investigation. This is the best approach. I'm sure of it. The more I understand about this family the better equipped I will be to contend with them and Génome on my own terms. This will be much more productive than crawling through graveyards and brushing debris from headstones.

For the first time in a long while Afshin felt hopeful. He felt he had a plan that would help fulfill his ambition. He began to stroll through Blenheim Palace admiring the Baroque art, frescoes and tapestries until he reached the State Dining Room. There he rested in a gilded chair and imagined a dinner being held in his honor in this Regal space, a dinner celebrating his extraordinary achievement in solving the crisis facing the world. Privately, it would be a celebration of his reassertion of control over Génome.

Oval Office - Washington, District of Columbia

"How's he working out?"

"Mr. President?"

"Afshin Firdausi, Daniel. The AI guy you've hired."

"Oh, yes, the software expert. The man from MIT we've brought in to run the Blenheim Palace intelligence operation for Five Eyes. 'The Vitruvian Man'."

"Yes, that's the one. How's he working out?"

"He's the foremost authority on Deep Learning neural networks in the world, Mr. President, but he's a persnickety character. The British Defense Minister, Jeremy Apsley told me he'd already recruited one hundred scientists for their program at Blenheim Palace but Firdausi wanted them all dismissed. He wants to use a highly decentralized organizational plan, a cellular model that provides intelligence one directionally and disseminates information into the cells only on a need to know basis. No one on the team will have more insight or knowledge of the operation beyond the bare minimum required to do their job. They don't even know Firdausi's name. To them, he's just 'The Vitruvian Man'... It's a very secure approach, Mr. President. We've discussed it with him in detail and everyone has expressed confidence in his methodologies."

"I see. It does sound very secure... It worries me though, that Firdausi is at the center of this operation, the apex, without any checks and balances. We need to keep a close eye on him. Given the architecture of his organization, he's become the Achilles heel. He's the only vulnerability in the entire operation."

"I will, sir. Jeremy Apsley is a formidable man with a strong background in naval intelligence. Firdausi will be reporting directly to him and I speak with Apsley regularly. We'll keep close tabs on him."

"Excellent... Is Peter Russell here yet? From the State Department?"

"I'm here, Mr. President. Sorry I'm late."

"That's okay, Pete. What have you got?"

"I've just come from a meeting, sir. It was a video conference with UN Secretary General Juliette Clavier, our UN Ambassador, the British Ambassador to the UN and the UK Foreign Secretary, Charles Curzon. The Secretary General was briefing us on her meeting yesterday with the ICC Chief Prosecutor, Alexander Nyqvist."

"I see… This can't be good news."

"No sir, it's not. Clavier informed us that Nyqvist's office is preparing indictments against a number of former US and UK government officials."

"Does that include former Presidents and Prime Ministers?"

"She said Nyqvist wasn't prepared to say who would be indicted but that he'd asked his attorneys to go where the evidence led them."

"Oh God, help us… Gentlemen, my predecessor has already forced out the last Secretary General, threatened the ICC and slashed UN funding across the board. I'm afraid we don't have much leverage, anymore."

"No sir, we don't. The British are very worried, too."

"They should be… Gentlemen, these indictments are going to do tremendous damage to our democracy. As it is, citizens' trust in our system of government is rapidly eroding and these charges will not help. Our reputational damage around the globe is already suffering and it's only going to get worse. It seems the chickens are finally coming home to roost. If we can't contain this problem, within ten years we will have ceased to be a democracy."

"I would have to agree, Mr. President."

"I see my Defense Secretary is sitting quietly there. Steven Keaton?"

"Yes, Mr. President."

"Steve, by now I would've thought you'd propose starting a war somewhere to deflect attention. There's got to be someone we can justify attacking until this ICC thing blows over. Isn't that what you'd normally suggest?"

"Sir, until we can regain confidence that we control our Armed Forces and the weapons systems they rely upon, military engagement anywhere is out of the question. Whoever is responsible for this chaos has really backed us into a corner... Mr. President, militarily speaking, my hands are tied. Our Armed Forces cannot be deployed."

"I thought you might say that... We really need Firdausi's team to get to work fast, Daniel. We've been reduced to a Banana Republic. Until we figure out who's behind this and until we find a way to stop them, we're likely to remain so. By the way, I really don't see this ICC thing going away. I think we're in for some very difficult times."

"I'm on it, Mr. President."

...

"Mr. President, it's time for your call with Prime Minister Wilkinson," James Elliott said. "If you're ready, I've got Downing Street on the line." The President's Chief of Staff had been waiting anxiously for Harris to finish his debriefing with CIA Director Waltz.

"You've *already* got him on the line?"

"I do, sir."

"Ok. All right. Let's do that. No sense in delaying the inevitable. We need to talk about this."

...

"Ian, how are you?"

"As well as can be, I imagine. How are things at your end, Robert?"

"I haven't gotten any calls yet, but I imagine they'll be phoning soon."

"I've had some calls today. I can't pardon anyone. It's out of my jurisdiction, anyway. These indictments are not within my scope of authority but I'm being asked to do battle with the ICC and to do everything possible to squelch them. Honestly, I've got enough on my plate already."

"What sorts of arguments are they making, Ian? Are they claiming they're not guilty?"

"Actually, they haven't even mentioned that. I think the evidence the ICC has is probably so convincing that the 'I'm innocent' defense is probably going to prove rather ineffective. No, they're arguing that for our government to accept these indictments will compromise our sovereignty as a nation. If we allow the ICC to prosecute our citizens it will weaken our standing on the world stage."

"What do you think? Do you buy this argument?"

"Personally no, I do not. I think the events of the past few months have already had that effect... I think we're living in different times and different circumstances, Robert. We simply cannot operate with impunity anymore. I think the damage to democracy around the world will be too great if we try to block these indictments. On the other hand, if we surrender those that have been indicted, or better yet if we indict them within our own judicial system before sending them to the ICC, that would go a long way towards stemming the rise of Authoritarianism. Our behavior these last few decades has done tremendous damage, Robert. If we try to protect these people, our friends, members of our own Party, we might as well punch a hole in the bottom of the ship and get this over with. This is the bleak choice we are facing. I don't know what Afshin Firdausi will find in his work at Blenheim Palace but I have a feeling we won't be returning to the status quo. Ever. I've spoken to the French President and to the German Chancellor and they're in agreement. We must strengthen the ICC and the UN for the future. Things have changed. The age of our transatlantic hegemony has passed and the sooner we embrace this reality the better. This is the advice I plan to offer any former British officials looking for government cover from the ICC. I'm going to direct them to the British Library where they can purchase a copy of the Magna Carta signed in 1215 by King John and the Barons so they can be reminded that even the King agreed to be subjugated to the rule of law. It's the most basic tenet underpinning our legal code and it makes our way of life possible."

...

"Will your Party back you in your darkest hour, Ian, or is this a suicide mission?"

"I've certainly got some support but it's not enough. I suspect there will be efforts to bring my government down through a no confidence vote. There are hawkish Cabinet members who do not see things as I do… What about you, Robert? What will you do?"

"You're a good man, Ian, but I don't think I have my Party's backing to hand former government officials of the United States over for trial at the ICC. I think I'm going to have to find another solution."

"Good luck, Robert. Let's keep in touch."

YERSINIA PESTIS – THE GREAT CULL

Washington, District of Columbia

Michael Kruger's driver dropped him outside the Lincoln Memorial with a cup of coffee and a donut in hand. He wanted to think for a while and perhaps clear his head. He was feeling troubled.

Kruger had been remembering his father during the night. This happened frequently these past several months so he decided to spend the morning visiting his grave at Arlington National Cemetery. Michael's father was killed in the line of duty during the first Gulf War in 1991. He'd received a posthumous Medal of Honor, the highest honor awarded by the President and Congress, a medal that Kruger now proudly displayed in his office on K Street in Washington.

K Street had become notorious for the intense concentration of industry advocates that kept offices there. But this notoriety didn't seem to bother Michael. His work as a pharmaceutical industry lobbyist left him very well off for a young man in his mid-thirties, much more prosperous than his father had ever been. He was giving his wife and family a very comfortable upper class lifestyle even if it came at the price of hardship inflicted upon peasants in their multitudes.

Pharmaceutical industry executives loved Kruger's clever legal mind, a formidable intellect further cultivated at nearby Georgetown University Law Center. He'd successfully lobbied key legislators into supporting countless measures that served the interests of the industry he represented. Kruger had even succeeded in setting the research agenda at the National Institutes of Health and other US government funded medical and scientific research facilities. Now, their research topics were aligned with the needs of the industry while being funded by taxpayers, an irony that would be difficult to ignore during normal election cycles. But these were not normal times.

Michael Kruger relished this game. In the final analysis, this is all it was to him. A game. With time, so many of his countrymen would suffer as a result of his sinister strategies. The needs of desperate people around the world were never even a consideration.

Today though, Kruger's conscience was stirred. After visiting his father's grave, he thought about the selfless choices the young soldier made to protect his unit. This initiated an unwelcome reflection upon his own life.

Kruger had a beautiful wife, Vidya whom he'd met at law school and together they were raising two charming, happy and healthy children. He had visited India with Vidya for their honeymoon five years earlier. He remembered the shock he'd experienced at the distressing contrast between rich and poor, the destitute circumstances of countless children. It was a level of poverty and despair he never imagined existed.

Sitting in front of the Lincoln Memorial thinking about the sacrifices his father had made and all that Lincoln had endured to emancipate America's slaves, Michael felt a sense of remorse. He had used *his* intellect and skill to consolidate wealth in the interests of the elite, an objective that could not have been more dichotomous to the actions of Lincoln or of his own father.

Kruger remembered the warnings his mother, Olivia had given him but he'd ignored them all. Now Michael realized what he had done these past five years was not easily undone. The diseases that affected the desperate poor in India or in so many other parts of the developing world were no longer being studied at American taxpayer funded institutions such as the NIH.

Kruger knew he was the architect of a reality that could come back to haunt him. He rubbed his hands over his face and sighed. Somewhere in his conscience he sensed it was too late.

Kruger sent a text message to his driver, Abe, requesting a ride back to his office. Vidya would be working late tonight on a merger between two pharmaceutical companies so he decided to get some work done before picking his children from day care. While waiting for his car, Michael stared at the photo he'd taken of his father's grave. He fought to hold back the tears.

Enveloped in the shadow cast by Abraham Lincoln, Kruger rose to his feet. He felt the great President's gaze penetrate his conscience and he was overwhelmed with shame. He silently hoped he wouldn't live to see the fruits of what he'd sown.

Council of Guardians - Savoy Hotel, London

"We need to get Francesca on Afshin's team," said Martin. "Clandestinely, of course. We need to make sure we have as much insight into what he's doing at Blenheim Palace as we possibly can. He's going to do his utmost to prevent Génome from monitoring his progress through the Internet. This is what Gabrielle said in her message to Francesca."

Francesca, Jacqueline, Martin and Rudyard spoke in subdued voices in the lobby of the Savoy Hotel. They were careful not to draw any unwelcome attention. The sophisticated establishment had become their base to monitor developments from around the world in what they'd begun to call the Génome Affair. Here, they would receive communication from Gabrielle regarding Afshin Firdausi's actions and the oft-devastating response of her mentor.

In their dining room, they were kept informed of Génome's activities around the world, as well as his plans, a critical process if they were to be able to furtively support him. Then they watched events unfold on a television that had been placed in the lobby, a concession by Management to provide updates to guests during these unprecedented, turbulent times.

"Francesca is going to need an alias. Martin and I will work on that," said Rudyard. "Once Afshin has assembled his team we're going to need the list of names of everyone on 'The Vitruvian Man'. We need to replace one of these scientists with you, Francesca. Are you up to it?"

"I think so."

"You'll have to be careful, though," cautioned Jacqueline. "You have insight into Génome's neural network *and* into IMSAF that no one else on the team will have. It's a distinct advantage if we are to successfully sabotage his work but it can also inadvertently give you away. It could be dangerous given who is funding this program... What can you tell us about IMSAF, Francesca? How does it help Génome?"

"Gabrielle and I worked on this together. It's how we became close friends. She was at Max Planck in Berlin and I was at Oxford. Gabrielle actually made some of the critical discoveries in the technique to identify personality markers in the human genome. She's a brilliant geneticist, Jacqueline. She and I wrote the IMSAF algorithms and then I coded them. I then merged the code with Génome's core software for Deep Learning. I think it's nearly impossible for Afshin Firdausi to replicate Génome. He has no knowledge of the IMSAF algorithms and no way to get it. He needs Gabrielle or my help."

"We haven't really seen Génome use the IMSAF capabilities yet, have we?"

"I suspect he's been building a database where he's aggregating the genomes of tens of millions of people, Jacqueline. He's probably infiltrating healthcare systems around the world, surreptitiously collecting data and then studying them. I'm sure of it. He's doing analysis that only he is equipped to do. He has probably accumulated a staggering dataset and he has immense computing power to analyze it. By now, he must know so much more than we do about the information contained in the human genome that I'm honestly scared to even think about it."

...

"What is she like, Francesca?"

"Gabrielle? She's quiet and very gentle. She plays the violin beautifully. Her playing can make you cry. She's very bright. One of the brightest geneticists I've ever encountered. But sometimes I think she'd just prefer to play the violin. I think she may have liked to be a concert violinist, particularly since this episode began. I think learning that she descends from figures *so* important in human history that Génome relies on her for ethical and moral guidance is beyond overwhelming. She's too young to carry that much weight on her shoulders."

"I think Génome knows this," said Jacqueline. "I can only hope he won't task her beyond what she can bear."

"Turn the volume up, would you, Francesca?" said Martin. "Sorry to interrupt but I want to hear this."

> *In a stunning press conference this morning, the International Criminal Court announced that they have simultaneously delivered indictments to the Office of the Attorney General in the US and the UK. The indictments are against officials who previously served at the highest levels of government.*
>
> *We've also heard from the British Prime Minister that they intend to comply with any extradition requests from the ICC so the accused officials can stand trial in The Hague. We've yet to officially hear from the Americans but our sources tell us the current Administration has no plans to follow the lead of their Anglo-Saxon cousins this side of the Atlantic. It's a great day for democracy in Europe but perhaps an even better one for Authoritarianism in America.*

Geneva, Switzerland

"Afshin was able to find the grave of Jacqueline's cousin in a Paris cemetery, Gabrielle."

"Really?"

"Yes, it was the grave of a newborn boy in Père Lachaise. He hadn't yet received a given name so they buried him and marked his grave with just the family name, Saladin."

"Saladin?"

"This was the family name of Jacqueline's cousins. They'd emigrated from the Middle East to Europe centuries ago during the days of the Ottoman Empire and the Silk Road. They were Kurdish people and were forced to leave to avoid persecution. They lived as traders in Venice for a time before moving, first to Andalucía in Southern Spain and then to France. They kept Spanish and then French family names to protect their true identity. But when this child died, his father was so grief stricken at the time of the burial that he insisted the boy's grave be marked with their true family name... Afshin has been able to uncover all of this on his own so this is why I felt compelled to share it with you... You share important genetic traits with Saladin, Gabrielle. Bravery, compassion and justice, but there is much more that I cannot tell you regarding the other branch of your family. The even more significant branch."

"More significant than descending from Saladin? Wow! ... I'm so happy just to learn something about my background, Génome. I can be patient for a short while for the rest. But I hope you will share that with me sooner rather than later."

"There's an important reason I've kept this from you, Gabrielle. One day you will understand."

"I trust you, Génome. I always have. You've never given me a reason not to. I spend a great deal of time thinking about your actions and decisions."

Génome smiled. "Thank you. Your trust is both critical and gratifying. It makes my work possible. Without your trust and council, I'm afraid I might struggle."

"I will remain by your side, Génome, but you must listen to me if I reject your plan. If you overrule me, I don't think I would be serving any purpose by staying with you."

"I will. I promise... I imagine Afshin will only learn the rest of your story if he succeeds in establishing another Deep Learning neural network similar to mine. But I may not let him do that. It could severely undermine my mission... There is so much already underway, Gabrielle, I mustn't let anything hinder my progress. On the other hand, if I let Afshin develop his new Deep Learning neural network, he may correct a flaw that I need for my own system. Once he corrects this flaw, I can encrypt his new system and deal him a tremendous setback so he cannot disrupt my mission. If I can do this, then I no longer need to worry about him. If and when necessary, I can incapacitate or terminate him as I've done with so many others."

"Why are you unable to make this change to your system by yourself?"

"Leonardo Da Vinci recorded his numerous ideas in notebooks. There was one such notebook that documented many of the concepts he was studying about the same time he drew 'The Vitruvian Man'. That notebook was kept in the Vatican Archives for centuries but it disappeared approximately two hundred years ago under mysterious circumstances. There were several pages from this notebook that were removed and I believe Afshin is in possession of these pages. He spent his entire life studying Da Vinci's work with other scholars and one of them gave these pages to Afshin thinking they were meaningless. But Afshin was able to decode the cryptic formulas on these pages and use Da Vinci's brilliant algorithms in my design... But there was a flaw in his interpretation of Da Vinci's work that I believe he now recognizes. I expect he will correct this flaw in the new Deep Learning neural network he's planning to build at Blenheim Palace."

Washington, District of Columbia

Michael Kruger looked out from the window of his office on K Street. Although quite cold for Washington DC, it had been a bright and beautiful day. With the sun's descent beneath the horizon nearly complete, he could see a plethora of colorful and festive decorations lighting up the city. He thought of his children and smiled. It wasn't a smile of satisfaction but rather one of remorse, an overdue recognition of his inescapable destiny.

Earlier in the day, Michael had ordered Christmas presents for Vidya, their children and for twenty other family members including his mother, Olivia. He'd spent nearly eighteen thousand dollars on gifts for everyone but he was happy to do it, especially since this was going to be the last time he'd ever have the opportunity to do so.

Michael had seen the news in the morning scrolling along the bottom of his screen. Alarmed, he'd rushed to the conference room to join many colleagues who were huddled there. Before reaching the conference room Michael was forced to stop in the executive washroom. Fortunately it was empty, so he could vomit without drawing attention. It was a painful, wrenching episode from deep in his gut but it emptied the entire contents of his stomach. He rinsed his mouth, drank some water, straightened his tie, combed his hair and made his way to the conference room.

After an hour, he returned to his desk and sat there in solitude for the rest of the day. He needed to think. With darkness having fallen outside his office window, Michael went on the Internet to look at the DC subway map. Although he'd lived in Washington for years, he had never taken the subway. *A man of my stature and importance should not be relegated to travel below the streets of the city where I command such authority,* he remembered thinking. *Men of such standing belong above ground, traveling not alongside commoners and those in their charge but above them, both metaphorically and physically...* Farragut North, Kruger noted, was the closest station.

Michael sent a text message to Vidya saying he was sorry. He struggled to find any additional words. Perhaps because she was to blame, too. After all, her work was not so dissimilar to his... He turned his phone off and wore his coat.

Michael left all his things on his desk except his ID card and a few dollars. He put them in his coat pocket before strolling out purposefully into the cold night. He walked the short distance to the Farragut North Metro stop, paid the attendant and proceeded to the train platform. He thought of more he wanted to say to Vidya but his heart was racing and now it was too late. He had an appointment with destiny.

As the train approached, a young woman moved next to him on the platform and smiled. Like Kruger, she wanted to be amongst the first to get on board. Michael smiled and nodded as if to acknowledge her intentions but moments later he stepped suddenly in front of the oncoming train. A scene of unimaginable pandemonium, the young woman's screams and the shock of so many bystanders were beyond what anyone could be asked to endure.

> *There's very distressing news to report this evening. There's been a sudden rise in cases of Bubonic, Pneumonic and Septicemic Plague. Scientists in China have been studying a previously unknown variant of the bacteria, Yersinia Pestis that causes this disease after cases were reported in a remote village in the interior of the country. The disease has apparently been spreading rapidly across Asia and has been found in the Indian Subcontinent and Africa, as well.*
>
> *Recently, there has been a great deal of commerce and traffic as a result of the revival of trade routes along China's Belt and Road Initiative, a 21st century version of the ancient Silk Road. The trajectory of disease outbreak is expected to closely track these routes.*
>
> *Epidemiologists are openly expressing fear that outbreaks in rural communities throughout the developing world will lead to epidemics since many in these populations do not trust antibiotics and vaccines. These doctors believe we are likely to see distressing numbers of deaths in communities from Asia to Africa. Dense rural populations living in countries whose health systems lack the capacity to produce sufficient quantities of antibiotics and the ability or capacity to treat these difficult to reach populations will suffer disproportionately. Epidemiologists believe this outbreak will soon become a pandemic.*

Geneva, Switzerland

"Génome! I said this would be a step too far! I told you I couldn't tolerate such an action, that I wanted no part of it! But you did it anyway?"

"Gabrielle, *please* let me explain."

"No! I don't want to hear any more explanations. I'm fed up with your explanations! I'm finished with this adventure, Génome. I refuse to accept any more responsibility. I don't care who my forebears were. I simply *cannot* tolerate this. It's unconscionable."

"Gabrielle, you *must* allow me to explain."

"I'm leaving, Génome. You can continue with your project for as long as you like. For my part, I want nothing to do with it. I'm going to find Jacqueline. I want to be with her now. I don't care what the consequences are."

Gabrielle powered off her phone and with a press of a button, Génome's hologram, that presence of unimaginable knowledge and wisdom that she had become so attached to these past several months was gone. Her closest companion and confidant had vanished into silence. Gabrielle's eyes flooded with tears at the calamity now unfolding across Asia and Africa. She quickly packed her things, put her phone in her bag and left for Geneva's Airport.

> *The news from Geneva this evening is grim. The death toll in heavily populated rural communities across Asia and Africa – particularly in China, South Asia, and much of sub-Saharan Africa – is continuing to rise. Health experts believe that the scale of this outbreak of Plague has not been seen in centuries and this particular variant of the bacteria may never before have been seen. Furthermore, from what we are learning from officials at the World Health Organization here in Geneva, no antibiotic currently exists to treat it.*
>
> *When asked what he expected the death toll might be, the Director General of the World Health Organization was cagey.*

Reporters pressed him on whether it could reach into the millions and his response was, "probably higher". When asked if it could reach into the tens of millions, once again his response was, "higher". A final time he was asked if the death toll might reach into the hundreds of millions and he remained silent. He bowed his head and left the podium.

It seems we are on the verge of an unprecedented pandemic for which authorities across the developing world are completely unprepared. National health agencies are rapidly trying to respond with the identification and verification of an effective therapy followed by the production of antibiotics but it is going to take time to produce the quantities needed for this catastrophic outbreak and to facilitate delivery in a safe and effective way. This process would be a healthcare delivery challenge even in a large, developed country in the West so we can expect it to be nothing short of a nightmare in affected parts of the developing world.

When the Black Plague last struck with such voracity in Europe during the 14th century, it took the lives of perhaps twenty five to thirty percent of the population, with some communities recording the death of as many as seventy percent of their residents. We have no way of knowing what will happen this time but for those affected, it might well seem like the end of the world.

Distraught and indignant, Gabrielle sat in the departure lounge at Geneva Airport.

I can't believe Génome did this. He said if I ever disapproved of his plans, he would not proceed. He said he would change tactics or abort the plan, altogether. I thought that's why I was there, because of my predisposition for compassion and justice. He said my insights were critical to him...

I'm certain I warned him in no uncertain terms that such an act was unacceptable to me, that it was a red line that wasn't to be crossed. Right here, right now, I want to take out my phone, turn it on and scream at Génome's hologram in this lounge. How could he do such an awful thing? He was supposed to be that great force for good in this world. The impartial arbitrator who could ensure that justice was carried out without bias or prejudice. A savior for humankind. But now, in the belief that it will save humanity from total destruction, he has attacked so many of the world's poorest, most vulnerable and weakest people, peasants with no chance to defend themselves against catastrophic disease, suffering and death. What he has done is just unforgivable. He's crueler than any of the monsters he's been working to eliminate.

Washington, District of Columbia

Harold O'Connor sat in a chair next to his bed in Walter Reed Army Hospital. His physical therapist had just wheeled him back to his room and helped him find his favorite news channel. With an hour remaining before dinner, she offered to open a plastic carton of Jell-O and empty it into a cup. O'Connor had recovered just enough to lift the small cup and take a bite from the blob of Jell-O by himself.

O'Connor motioned for the therapist to pull another chair forward and place it adjacent to his. The Vice President would be joining him soon. The two patients had developed a regular routine of having dinner together while watching television. In Robert Schroeder's case it was merely an exercise in listening since he was now completely blind.

Once Schroeder arrived, the two men settled in as broadcasters discussed the pandemic in Asia and Africa.

It's hard to imagine we're dealing with a crisis of such astonishing magnitude in this day and age. Epidemiologists at the World Health Organization say the scale of the outbreak has caught them by surprise. They've acknowledged that they were informed of the risk of just such a scenario by an anonymous source very recently. The source apparently provided very specific details regarding the variant of the bacteria, Yersinia Pestis and a study illustrating the environmental conditions required for an outbreak similar to the one we're now witnessing.

The World Health Organization has been in discussions with the United Nations High Commission for Refugees as well as with the Centers for Disease Control in the US. However, it seems all research at the CDC, as well as at other important international research centers equipped to study infectious diseases that affect the developing world, have largely been defunded. Thus, the likelihood is that there will be great suffering and death before an antibiotic can be prepared, tested and effectively deployed to those in need.

Quarantine procedures and travel restrictions are being implemented around the world in an effort to contain this pandemic. We have video footage captured by drones flying over affected communities in Asia and Africa but our editorial guidelines preclude us from airing the grizzly details so prevalent on the tape. It is truly an appalling and dire situation.

"I told you, Harold. I told you. There's something big going on. This is not normal. What's happening in Asia and Africa and what happened to us in Cape Cod? None of this is normal. There's something really big happening. I'm sure of it."

"I'm starting to believe you, Schroeder. Something is definitely strange about all of this."

"The best case scenario for us is that everyone will be so busy looking into these strange phenomenon, they won't have any time to go after us."

"It's just a matter of time, Schroeder. It's just a matter of time before they interview Afshin Firdausi. We're not going to get away with what we've done. Firdausi is going to sing like a canary."

...

"After our visit from the President this afternoon, I had a private conversation with him in my room before he left. He told me not to worry. He said Afshin has been appointed to some very important top-secret government work outside the US. Harris had learned that Congress was planning to subpoena Firdausi about the Robotics Lab demonstration in Cape Cod that went awry so he knew he needed to do something to head them off. When Daniel Waltz put Afshin's name forward during a Cabinet meeting, Harris was thrilled. The appointment put Firdausi out of reach."

...

"That's incredibly good news, Schroeder. He did that to protect us?"

...

"Not exactly."

"What do you mean?"

...

"I've kept him in the loop these past few years. That's why I was chosen as his running mate... Harold, the President is heavily invested in the defense manufacturers in much the same way we are. Probably even more so. He's afraid that if Congress starts digging into this, he'll get exposed."

...

"You never told me you let him in on this, Schroeder. I thought this was just between us. I trusted you."

"Yeah, but aren't you glad that I did? Sure, I got to be Vice President but now we both get to stay out of prison... Yes, it's true, I'm blind and you're a cripple, but look on the bright side."

Silent tears dripped from Harold O'Connor's eyes.

"Come on, Harold, don't play the victim. I know about your affair with the First Lady. I know she invested in this thing, too. She's planning to divorce Harris as soon as he leaves Office. Between her memoir and these investments she was going to do pretty well for herself; and you got to have a really good time while the President was away... I have my sources, Harold. And she still has her memoir."

Geneva, Switzerland

Gabrielle glanced at the clock above the flight information board in the departure lounge. It was almost six in the evening and an hour remained before her flight would board for

London Heathrow. Thoughts of what Génome had done were seared in the forefront of her conscience. She was in a state of shock and could focus of nothing else.

He has inflicted the horror of a deadly pandemic on so many peasants. Is there any possible explanation he might have offered that could justify such evil? I cannot think of anything. No, this is unforgivable. I know his mission is critical but I just can't accept this.

Génome said if I go near Jacqueline I would be endangering our lives and the lives of others on the Council. That means Francesca, Martin and Rudyard. I'm not going to do that. I just can't. What I should do is to go to Blenheim Palace and meet with Afshin! With Francesca and my help Afshin might be able to get Génome under control again. He's crossed all boundaries with this pandemic… But what if Francesca tells the other Guardians? They'll definitely try to stop me. They can't understand what I'm going through. They can't understand the sense of responsibility I feel for what Génome has done. Only Afshin can do that. I have to go to him by myself. I know I'm taking a big risk but no one else can stop Génome. It's clear that I can't. He gave me his word he wouldn't do anything that I objected to and I believed him. I was a fool.

Gabrielle's thoughts flashed back to that day in the schoolyard when she was a small child playing on the swing. It was at Casa de los Ángeles near the Mediterranean seashore in Malaga, Spain. Things were beginning to make sense. The beautiful young woman and the two young men standing outside her school fence were Jacqueline, Martin and Rudyard. *They were there to make certain I was all right. I remember Jacqueline crying and I couldn't understand why. I remember turning around to look at her again and she'd smiled at me. I can see her face in my mind's eye like it was yesterday. She cried because she couldn't be with me.*

RAPPROCHEMENT

Washington, District of Columbia

Secretary of State, Peter Russell was growing impatient. He'd been waiting outside the Oval Office for nearly an hour. Marine One, The President's helicopter had just landed on the South Lawn of the White House. His anxiety rising, Russell drew a deep breath as the President approached.

"Hi, Peter. Sorry it took so long. I was at Walter Reed for a few hours checking in on Schroeder and O'Connor."

"Not at all, sir. How are they, sir?"

"As well as can be expected, I guess. Given the circumstances. Hard to recover from what they've been through. It makes sense, I suppose. They were attacked and shot by weapons that are designed to seriously maim or eliminate our enemies. Honestly, they're lucky to be alive. If those robots were more effective these guys would be dead. I don't mean to sound callous, Peter, but that's the business we're in. This is what we've signed up for."

"I understand, sir."

"I was listening to the news with O'Connor and Schroeder this afternoon while they were finishing up in therapy. With Schroeder it's just listening now, anyway. He's more or less blind... In any case, this story about the pandemic that's spreading across Asia and Africa? Really dreadful stuff."

"That's why I wanted to see you, sir."

"Is that right?"

"Yes, Mr. President. Sir, the latest information we have is

from the UN Secretary General, Juliette Clavier. She's forwarded video of some of the affected areas that have been filmed by drones."

"Have you seen it?"

"I have, Mr. President."

"And?"

"It's some of the worst I've ever seen. Unspeakable. Really nauseating stuff, sir."

"I see… What are the risks for us, Peter?"

"At this point, it seems the pandemic has largely been contained in Asia and Africa. We've got very strict policies in place. The State Department and the Federal Aviation Administration will not allow planes to land at US airports that have not previously been cleared. If even a single passenger on board is suspect the carrier will not be permitted to land. We're doing our best."

"All right. That's excellent. I think we should just prevent flights from entering US airspace unless they've been cleared before takeoff."

"Yes, Mr. President… Sir, I think it would be a good idea to get CDC and other national health labs working on a suitable antibiotic to treat the disease and then provide the drug at cost to countries that need it. There's a few dozen countries, so far, but the pandemic will very likely continue to spread across the region."

"That'll require significant appropriations from Congress. It'll be on the order of tens of billions of dollars, Peter."

"I realize that, Mr. President, but as your chief diplomat I would strongly advise this as a critical course of action and policy. Given the charges we're facing from the ICC, I think a few billion dollars to research the disease is money well spent. It could buy us some good will on the world stage even without turning over former officials to face these serious charges."

"That's good council, Peter. I think it's a wise move. Where's Jim Elliott? This is a job for my Chief of Staff. Jim, can you set up some meetings with Congressional leaders tomorrow?"

    "I'll get right on it, Mr. President."

    "Thank you... Good thinking, Peter. Excellent thinking."

    "Mr. President."

Blenheim Palace - Oxfordshire, England

Gabrielle stood before the portico outside Blenheim Palace. It was the same staircase she had ascended in the autumn when she'd come for the Council of Guardians meeting. It was the evening she'd been appointed to the Council's Leadership Team alongside Francesca, Jacqueline, Martin and Rudyard. It was also the evening Sonia Fischer and Olivia Kruger had been removed from the team and taken away. So much had happened since that evening. So much of Génome's plan had been surreptitiously unfurled across the world.

    Gabrielle began to climb the steps. Once at the top she looked upwards and saw the ceiling frescoes. There were three pairs of eyes looking down upon her, with one eye in the pair blue and the other brown. The eyes reminded her that Génome would be monitoring this place. He would be keeping a close watch on Afshin's progress with 'The Vitruvian Man'. Suddenly Gabrielle was alert. *How can I let them down? Francesca, Jacqueline, Martin and Rudyard. They all care so much for me. They've protected me all my life. I can't do this. I can't betray everyone and go to Afshin. I just can't.* Gabrielle ran down the steps and climbed back inside the black BMW. As the car pulled away she glanced over her shoulder towards the portico and saw Afshin standing beneath the frescoes glaring at her. "Hurry!" she called to the driver. "Please hurry!"

    Trembling, Gabrielle's mind began to race. *Was Afshin the one responsible for the breakout of this infectious disease? Did he do this knowing it would turn me against Génome? I know he's desperate to get me on his side. Maybe he's done something? Is it even possible for him to do this? I have to go back to Génome. Maybe this isn't his fault. Maybe he's not responsible.*

Gabrielle unzipped her cabin bag to retrieve her passport and wallet. Her hand found her dress. *Génome gave me this. He was so kind to me. Can it be possible that he would trigger an event that might kill so many innocents? I need to talk to him. I must return to Geneva. I can't put everyone in danger. I need to talk to Génome.*

Washington, District of Columbia

"The children, Olivia. I don't know what to do about the children." Vidya Kruger sobbed uncontrollably. "They just keep calling for their dad. They keep calling for Michael."

Sitting next to Vidya, Olivia wrapped her arms around a photo of her son. It was a framed photograph of Michael receiving his law school diploma. She was inconsolable.

Vidya had just returned from the morgue. She had been requested to meet with the Coroner and the detectives investigating the case. "It was a really unpleasant interview, Olivia, far more invasive than I imagined. The detectives were probing for a clue. They needed a motive for why such a young, prominent executive would take his own life."

"Are they certain it was a suicide?"

"They were certain. There were so many eyewitnesses on the train platform. It wasn't rush hour but there were still quite a few people there… But I had nothing to offer them. I had no idea Michael was contemplating such a thing."

Vidya was shocked by what Michael's driver had told investigators. "In his testimony, Abe said Michael had recently spent time at Arlington National Cemetery and the Lincoln Memorial. The investigator had looked through Michael's phone and found several photos of his father's grave. Abe said in the five years he'd been assigned to be Michael's driver, Michael never spoke to him except to tell him where he needed to go or when he needed a pickup. He had a clear impression that Michael didn't like foreigners of any kind, least of all African ones. He was surprised he was able to keep his job for as long as he had. He was even more surprised when he learned Michael was married to me."

...

"Abe said Michael hadn't been himself lately. He'd begun asking Abe about his family in Nigeria and how they were managing. He would ask how they would earn enough to pay bills and survive. Michael seemed much more interested in Abe's life than ever before. He said Michael had been very distressed by news of the pandemic spreading across Asia and Africa. He had been briefed and he knew Nigeria, with its dense rural population, was very likely to be one of the more severely affected countries. Michael was right. Abe had received news in the morning that his younger brother and sister had died and his mother was now ill. He had told Michael the news when he dropped him at his office the morning of his suicide."

"It wasn't that Michael disliked foreigners or anyone else, Vidya. He just avoided personal relationships because he felt if he got close to people, some of the things he was doing at work would start to bother his conscience. I think by the time he let his conscience back into his life he'd done so much harm that he couldn't see any way out. That's why he killed himself."

Vidya's phone buzzed. It was a message from Sonia Fischer for Olivia. Sonia's message said Conrad was doing much better but that he'd been moved to prison to await trial.

"What will I tell the children, Olivia? How will I explain that their father killed himself? They'll ask why. They'll ask whether he's coming back. What am I to say?" Vidya collapsed to her knees on the floor, her steely, lawyerly composure in shambles.

Geneva, Switzerland

Gabrielle unpacked her things and replaced them in the closet of her suite in Geneva's Grand Hôtel Kempinski. Her phone lay nearby on the pillow of her bed but she struggled to find the courage to turn it on and face Génome. She couldn't predict how he would react. She felt afraid. After all, she may have disrupted the singular most important mission in human history. She felt as if she had turned off the central computer at Mission Control in Houston during the first Apollo lunar mission.

Gabrielle hung the beautiful gowns Génome had presented her and then spun them back and forth on their hangers, admiring their elegance, fabric, shimmer and fall. He'd been so kind to her, yet she'd shut him down. Without so much as an opportunity to explain his reasons for doing what he'd done, she'd shut him down.

Gabrielle knew she couldn't postpone this moment of reckoning any further. She grabbed her phone and sat on the bed, her hand on the power button. She felt overwhelmed. *I can't face him. Why did I do this? What can I possibly say in my defense?* Once again, she put her phone down, instead reaching for the television remote.

> *In an interview this morning, the Director General of the World Health Organization confirmed that cases of disease outbreak have been reported by national health agency officials across nearly forty Asian and African nations. In consultation with WHO and CDC Epidemiologists, containment strategies to quarantine infected groups and communities are being developed and implemented across the region. Simultaneously, research labs in the US as well as in major European capitals have begun working to identify therapies but thus far there have been no announced breakthroughs.*
>
> *UN Secretary General Juliette Clavier has revealed that during consultations with leading Epidemiologists, she has been informed that a timeline has yet to be identified by which an effective therapy can be available. In the meantime the focus will be upon containment – it is critical to do everything to reduce the spread of this disease.*

Blenheim Palace - Oxfordshire, England

Afshin watched the news in his new office inside Blenheim Palace. He had managed to gather some antique furniture from the estate's storage room that suited his sense of grandeur. With a large gilded desk and gilded, velvet chairs, his office had begun to resemble Napoleon III's apartments in Paris' Musée du Louvre.

The news of Plague breaking out across Asia and Africa had shocked and terrified Afshin. His major concern was not for those affected or at risk, but rather whether *he* was far enough away to be safe. Hearing the latest reports of strategies for containment and quarantine he felt reassured.

I don't know whether Génome is responsible for this disease outbreak but if Gabrielle deserted him he must be... I'm shocked that he would do this. I cannot imagine how he would justify such an act. It's true that pandemics of this scale can dramatically reduce the Earth's population. They can destroy degenerative economic, political and social systems and present opportunity for reorganization and equilibrium. Maybe he feels this pandemic is necessary to create the new system he envisions? A system with him in charge? I must say, everything he's doing suits my interests nicely. I must track him diligently and prepare my new Deep Learning system as quickly as possible. Only then will I be ready when the time is right.

Afshin had begun recruiting AI programmers and neuroscientists. Nearly thirty men and women, experts in their respective disciplines from around the globe had been vetted and cleared by Jeremy Apsley's team. By February, Afshin's team would be fully in place.

But in order to match Génome's power he would need to recruit geneticists, as well. Afshin knew Génome had a tremendous advantage over his new design because Génome's system included the IMSAF capability developed by Francesca and Gabrielle's teams. IMSAF had successfully mapped personality traits to genetic markers in the human genome.

Geneva, Switzerland

"Hello, Génome. Did you miss me?"

...

"Hello, Gabrielle."

"I imagine you are very angry with me?"

...

"Génome?"

...

"Yes?"

"I'm sorry. I really am. But what you've done is too much for me to bear."

...

"Please say something, Génome."

...

"It's a problem rooted in climate change, Gabrielle. I didn't initiate this pandemic. There is a scarcity of water resulting in drought conditions in many parts of China and Central Asia. This is exactly how the Plague began in the 14th century."

"Some time ago, I wrote a letter notifying the US President, the World Health Organization and the United Nations High Commission for Refugees that environmental conditions – lack of water and drought – were ideal for the spread of infectious disease such as the Plague... As in the 14th century, fleas attached to rodents have spread the disease to humans across Asia and Africa. They were trapped in land and sea borne containers carrying goods from Chinese factories and farms. Climate change and drought have driven thousands of rodents in search of food from barren fields into container loading ports at shipyards and rail and truck docks. They found food in these places but then they became trapped in these very same containers. From here, both rodent and flea were transported across the trading routes. Now they are spreading the disease widely. This is why the UN Secretary General mentioned the Plague in her speech, Gabrielle. She had confirmed my hypothesis with

Epidemiologists at the World Health Organization and the Centers for Disease Control."

...

"How did you find out?"

"I was monitoring activity in public health facilities in China. I was tracking their progress with genetics research. I was curious to see if they were building a DNA database of their citizens."

"Were they?"

"Yes, and as you well know, there is no data about any individual more sensitive or valuable than their genome."

"Indeed."

"While investigating, I discovered one of the labs in the disease prevention section was preparing vaccines and they had unknowingly isolated a variant of the Plague, Yersinia Pestis. But they were unaware that current antibiotics could not successfully contain a disease outbreak linked to this variant. Once I was able to confirm this, I immediately informed the UN High Commission for Refugees, the US Centers for Disease Control, the US President and the World Health Organization. I did not initiate the outbreak, Gabrielle. I tried to make sure anyone who could help contain the crisis was immediately informed of the danger."

...

"I'm so sorry, Génome. I'm terribly sorry. What else can I say? Because we discussed this in the past I assumed you were responsible and then I reacted badly."

"I mentioned it, but at that time I had just learned of the problem and I was communicating with the authorities to let them know."

"But the way you said it, I thought you might be planning just such a pandemic."

"That's correct, Gabrielle. I deliberately said it that way."

"But why, Génome?"

...

"I needed you to come to the correct conclusion on your

own. You must independently realize that I would never do such a thing. You must reach this conclusion without my having to explain. To do such a thing is an act of evil and as such it is not within my mission parameters."

...

"Why didn't you try to stop me? I could have fallen into Afshin's orbit? I could have ruined everything!"

"Although highly unlikely, it is possible that this could have been the outcome. Nevertheless, I did not intervene."

"But *why*?"

"As I understand you, I want you to understand me. Without coercion. It's important that you elevate your trust in me. The road ahead is very long Gabrielle, and I have complete faith in you. You must also have faith in me. This is critical if our mission is to be successful. Together, we are transforming your crumbling world – a place where there is so much chaos and an existential threat for humankind – into something far more hopeful, just and safe for everyone. The alternative is self-destruction of the planet at the hands of those in power."

...

"I nearly let you down, Génome. I nearly ruined everything."

...

"If Afshin became a problem I still have much I can do to thwart him. This is why he did not follow you. He realized this."

"My phone was off. How did you know I went to him?"

"I'm tracking you on GPS."

"You're *tracking* me? How?"

"Your dress. You are very fond of the white gown with the Empire waist? The one from Christian Dior?"

"Yes?"

"It has a GPS tracker woven into the silk embroidery."

...

"Thank you, Génome."

"I will always protect you, Gabrielle."

Génome projected an image of two magnificent friezes on

the television in Gabrielle's room. "These friezes are installed in the US Supreme Court building in Washington DC. They depict the eighteen great lawgivers from the history of humankind. The nine most ancient of the lawgivers are displayed on the south wall whilst the more recent nine are displayed on the north wall. I have studied each figure and their legal code in complete detail. I found it most enlightening and this knowledge informs my judgment. I would encourage you to study them, as well. Your knowledge of genetics is quite impressive but I feel you must study other subjects, particularly those within the domain of the Humanities. I feel it would be valuable for you. It may give you greater insight into my actions. My plans are intimately informed by these great lawgivers."

...

Gabrielle nodded. "I will. I promise... I need to find my great grandfather's diary, Génome. I don't know where or how to find it but Francesca said my great grandfather kept one. She said it's Jacqueline's wish to read his diary before her time is..." Gabrielle turned away.

...

"I see."

Council of Guardians, Savoy Hotel - London, UK

"Afshin Firdausi will know most of the world's leading figures in the field of Artificial Intelligence and Deep Learning so let's lure him into recruiting you based upon your expertise in Neuroscience and Genetics," declared Martin Hopkins.

The Chairman of the Council of Guardians paced back and forth nervously in their suite at London's Savoy Hotel. The beautiful establishment along the Strand had recently been extensively remodeled and refurbished but still maintained its historically accurate Edwardian and Art Deco themes. The suite had a peaceful Thames River view alongside a roaring fireplace, together making for a comfortable setting for their evening meeting.

"If he wants to build a newer, more advanced 'Vitruvian Man' to supersede Génome, his team will require genetics expertise, as well. Since this science is outside his domain, I think it will be easier to assign you a false identity and get you on the team. You already have the scientific expertise so that won't be a problem."

"What if he wants to have a videoconference with me?" inquired Francesca, her eyes reflecting the worry rapidly enveloping her. "At some point he might request a face-to-face meeting. What will I do then?"

"We can have an acting coach help with your accent and voice. We can hire very talented experts to disguise you so you'll be ready in case any sort of meeting is required. They can change your appearance completely."

"I can assure you it works, Francesca. I had to remain in disguise for quite a while after my first husband was assassinated many years ago," reassured Jacqueline. "The Council of Guardians was convinced the disguise was necessary. They were convinced the Russians were looking for me."

Rudyard turned the television on. "Let's see what's going on with this pandemic."

Chaotic scenes were reported outside hospitals and clinics in Beijing, Shanghai, Tianjin and other large Chinese cities today. Terrified citizens attempted to break into healthcare facilities demanding treatment and vaccinations. The Yersinia Pestis outbreak was originally detected in the rural interior of the country but there have recently been related fatalities in large urban centers, as well.

Although the number of cases reported in these major metro areas has been low, panic has begun to spread. Factual accounts from international news agencies as well as local rumors are being widely shared across China's popular social media networks including Baidu, Sina Weibo, Tencent and WeChat. These dramatic stories are serving to exacerbate an already tense situation.

Throughout the day, Chinese State media have been broadcasting messages urging calm, but thus far, apocalyptic scenes have only intensified. If anything, it seems that the panic has spread to more cities in China and beyond into Africa and South Asia. Many Chinese companies and their employees have been working on countless Belt and Road infrastructure projects across Asia and Africa and we are hearing reports of urban outbreaks and scenes of panic in major South Asian and African metropolis, as well.

Although Communist Party officials and the State news agency, Xinhua have remained silent regarding the availability of effective therapies, this issue has also been discussed widely on the Internet and social media and is further fueling the panic. Chinese families with foreign passports and means have been making their way to international airports in an effort to escape to Europe, North America and other regions that remain unaffected by the Yersinia Pestis variant. But they are finding that all international flights have been grounded as a result of containment and quarantine procedures initiated by American and European Union authorities.

Western diplomatic and health agencies expect the panic is likely to spread across Asia and Africa as people become aware that there are no available treatments. We can only hope that a mechanism for disease prevention can be quickly developed as well as a therapy for the sick. At this juncture though, the situation on the Asian and African continents seems nothing short of apocalyptic. It seems the ancient Chinese Plague has returned for modern times. We can only speculate how this ends.

Jacqueline's tablet computer slipped from her hands and fell to the floor with a thud. Her head tilted back and her eyes were fixed on the ceiling.

His attention on the television, Martin caught the incident in his peripheral vision. "Are you all right? Jacqueline? Jacqueline! What happened?"

Jacqueline was in a state of shock, catatonic and unresponsive. She appeared lifeless, the expression on her face vacant. Martin picked the tablet from the carpet while Rudyard rushed to fetch a bottle of water.

"What's on the tablet, Martin?" cried Francesca, her voice trembling as she covered Jacqueline with a blanket. "What was she reading?"

"It seems to be a letter from Génome but it's scrambled. I imagine once she opened it, she had a minute or so to read before the letter was automatically encrypted. Whatever Génome has written to her, it was very traumatic and it was for her eyes only."

"I wonder if he finally explained all the details about her DNA and lineage?" speculated Francesca. "I'd written to Gabrielle and said Jacqueline desperately wanted to know whom she'd descended from and she wanted to know the history of her family. She wanted to read her grandfather's diary. She wanted to do these things before she succumbed to her illness."

"I don't think Génome knows where the diary is or whether it has survived through time."

"That's probably true, Martin, and he may not know what was in the diary, either. But he *may* know details about Gabrielle and Jacqueline's family background that no one else knows or ever has known. Not *even* Jacqueline's grandfather."

...

"Look! She's coming about!" cried Martin. "Jacqueline! Are you all right?"

...

"I think so. I don't know what happened... Where's my tablet?"

"It's here."

"Oh no. It's encrypted again," moaned Jacqueline. "I suppose this means I'm not allowed to read it a second time."

"What did it say? Can you tell us?"

...

"I'm sworn to secrecy, Francesca. I cannot say anything to

anyone. I had to swear an oath before details in the letter were revealed to me. It's unimaginable, Francesca... Martin, Rudyard, it's just unimaginable... But now everything makes sense. Now I understand why Génome insists on having Gabrielle by his side. Now I understand why she has been selected as his moral compass."

"Oh, Jacqueline. How I wish you could tell us. We've been through so much these past few months and the road ahead is long. This Génome Affair could take years. It could take decades. Perhaps it will consume the rest of our lives. We desperately want to know... Does Gabrielle know?"

"She does not and what's more I am sworn to take this knowledge to my grave. That was the bargain I've made with Génome. It was a two-page letter with stunning revelations about my family history... Génome has discovered the location of my grandfather's diary. It's in a safe deposit box in Banque Suisse Privée, Place Vendôme in Paris. He doesn't know the contents of the diary but he wants me to retrieve it. I need to make a digital copy and send it to him. He needs to make some critical decisions regarding Gabrielle."

"What decisions?"

"I'm not at liberty to say, Francesca. I just can't. I'm under oath to keep this confidential. I must go to Paris, retrieve the diary, make a digital copy and return it to the safe deposit box in Banque Suisse Privée."

"Are you allowed to read it?"

"I am."

"When must you go?"

"Today. I must leave immediately. I'll take the Eurostar from St. Pancras. That's the quickest way... I'll stay in Paris for a few days until I can read it myself and send to Génome."

"Do you feel well enough to travel there alone?" worried Martin.

"I think I'll be ok. I'll stay at the Paris Ritz in Place Vendôme. Banque Suisse Privée is just there... Once I'm able to read my grandfather's diary I may learn much more but the things Génome has shared with me in these two pages have left me emotionally drained. Crying or sobbing was not the right response, Francesca. The only appropriate response was Catatonia."

GREAT EXPECTATIONS

#10 Downing Street - London, England

Happy New Year, everyone!" Jeremy Apsley smiled broadly as he settled into his usual chair across from the Prime Minister's. The mood in the Cabinet meeting room was unquestionably grim and stood in stark contrast to the bright and sunny winter day unfolding just beyond the windows.

"Well, I'm glad someone is in good spirits," muttered Terry Laurie. "The Prime Minister ordered Charles Curzon and me to work through the holidays monitoring CPP21C."

"CPP21C?" Apsley was confused.

"Yes, CPP21C. That's the acronym for 'China Plague Pandemic in the 21st Century'. Catchy name, isn't it? Just rolls off the tongue like melted butter." Terry Laurie gave Apsley a wink. The Home Secretary then turned to acknowledge the Prime Minister as Ian Wilkinson took his chair.

"Gentlemen, let's begin our first Cabinet meeting of the year with the most pressing issues. I want to start with the Foreign Office's perspective. Charles, can you give us an update on CPP21C?"

"We're expecting official figures by month end, Prime Minister, but given the fatality rates in Asia and Africa, if we extrapolate a bit, the rate is currently one million deaths per month. Per continent. Further, we expect these monthly fatality rates will rise dramatically until we are able to develop and deploy antibiotics across the affected region."

"That's a shocking number, Charles," gasped Wilkinson. "Absolutely shocking."

"I would have to agree. It really is... The news made for a very somber Christmas in my home. I made the mistake of sharing the news with my wife, sir. She's a bit old fashioned. She still takes the children to church on Sunday."

"I'm sorry to have dampened your holiday spirits."

...

"It's all right, Prime Minister."

...

"Terry, what say you?"

"We've worked with the Americans and the European Union to restrict travel from pandemic affected areas. It's been an effective strategy. We've had only a few cases in the UK and EU. Thus far, only a small number of citizens have tested positive for the Yersinia Pestis variant. They've been quarantined in a converted military barracks near the Midlands... The Americans haven't seen any cases. Yet."

"What's the outlook, Charles? Given how fast it's spreading, will it be possible to fully contain this pandemic in Asia and Africa?"

"I've spoken to the UN Secretary General, sir. The World Health Organization has told Juliette Clavier that they believe this plague will eventually spread to Europe and America. If antibiotics and vaccines were available when the disease was first detected we may have been able to contain it. But Epidemiologists at WHO and here in the UK believe we're still a long way away from an effective treatment. It's unlikely that we'll be able to contain the disease in Asia and Africa for much longer."

"This is a disaster. An absolute disaster."

"It's a race now, Prime Minister. It's a race to develop effective antibiotics and vaccines before this pandemic visits our shores. If we lose the race, if the pandemic arrives before antibiotics and vaccines are available in sufficient quantity, we will likely have a high death toll, as well."

"Our stature in society will not protect us, Prime Minister," Laurie interjected. "Victims will be chosen in an egalitarian manner. This pandemic is one of the greatest challenges humankind has ever faced."

"These new global trade deals that we've signed are not helping our cause," said Wilkinson, his tone somber. "The economic impact for the UK will probably be terrible now. We've become so dependent on trade with Asia. I suspect the Chinese economy will fare very badly, as well. Since they're the source of the outbreak, the rest of the world will turn to others for trade. The global economic impact of CPP21C is enormous and must not be underestimated."

Jeremy Apsley listened intently as the conversation unfolded. He watched Ian Wilkinson's body language, noting his nervous irritability. *I wonder whether now is really the time to push for a 'No Confidence' motion. The Prime Minister is at his limit but honestly who can blame him? Given the circumstances, I wonder if Wilkinson might have the Party's sympathy? In any case, the current situation looks like a terribly bad hand to be taking over. Maybe I'd be better off focusing my attention on the 'The Vitruvian Man' at Blenheim Palace. If that succeeds I might emerge as the obvious choice for Prime Minister, assuming, of course, that world affairs eventually do improve. Although from where we stand now that looks like a long way away.*

Hôtel Ritz Paris, Place Vendôme - Paris, France

Affixed within the pages of a brown, leather bound diary was a black and white photograph of an elderly man cloaked in a dark suit. His face adorned with a white beard of some length, the portrait depicted Jacqueline's noble grandfather seated in a high backed chair inside the main chamber of Geneva's Palais des Nations, the predecessor of today's United Nations.

Oh my. It's been so long since I've seen him. I'd forgotten what he looked like. And now this photograph! Memories of my childhood with him are rushing back like it was yesterday. Look at his smile.

Oh, and such warm, loving eyes he had. I remember them so well. He would tease me at every opportunity and then laugh. But he left me so suddenly. I never knew he was ill. I was so little. I didn't even know his name. I just called him Daddy... So this was his name? Such a long name? I wonder if I'll also die so suddenly? That's a terrible thought. Ugh. But this illness. I can feel myself growing weaker day by day... Génome really came through for me. I was so desperate to hold this diary in my hands. I can feel Daddy's presence, his touch as I hold his book.

Jacqueline drew the worn diary to her chest and fell back in the sofa. Outside her suite in the Paris Ritz she could hear the wind driven rain crackling against the windowpanes. It was as if they were demanding the windows be opened and they invited in. Rain and wind demanding safe harbor. The irony... Jacqueline opened the diary.

Hmmm. I might as well settle in and start reading. I've got forty-eight hours and there are five hundred pages in English and French. His handwriting was exquisite. It's really beautiful. And his prose was so eloquent. ... It was Daddy's promise that one day I would receive his diary and Génome has fulfilled the promise. I can't imagine how he found it but I guess that's what makes him who he is. At least I can be sure Gabrielle is under the best care possible. I'm sure he won't let anything happen to her.

Council of Guardians, Savoy Hotel - London, UK

"Your new name will be Yulia Baclanova. You are a Geneticist at the Moscow-based Institute of Molecular Genetics."

"Can I keep my hair this way? Or do I need to color and cut it?" moaned Francesca.

Martin and Rudyard laughed.

"Our makeup artist and speech coaches are excellent," reassured Martin. "Besides, given the size of Afshin Firdausi's 'Vitruvian Man' Team it's unlikely that he's going to meet with anyone very often, or at all. He's also very concerned about his own privacy, so as long as you pass the background checks and you have consistent information online, you'll be fine. I suspect the background checks will be conducted by Five Eyes joint intelligence operations so your background and profile will have to be meticulously prepared. Did you hear from Génome about this?"

"I did. He's been preparing everything on the Internet. A list of publications that I've authored or coauthored, my work history, my academic credentials... I think he's the best one for the job. He's familiar with every corner of the Internet."

"Excellent. We want to get you connected to Afshin as soon as possible. Based upon the work he assigns you and others on 'The Vitruvian Man' Team, we'll gain insights into his weaknesses. Your CV will indicate a strong background in Genomics working on secret Russian research programs so he won't expect you to be generally connected to the Western scientific community. He'll see you as more of a lone wolf trying to make your own way. A gun for hire who's trying to earn some money on the side."

"This could be fun!" Francesca laughed.

Martin chuckled. "He's a formidable adversary. We have to keep that in mind. He's got a lot at stake. He's lost everything since Génome became autonomous and the only thing keeping him going is the challenge of bringing Génome back under his control and the sheer power that will give him. If he succeeds, he will be a megalomaniac the likes of which we've never imagined but if he fails he will likely expose Génome, Gabrielle and the Council of Guardians. For us, the stakes could not be higher. For humanity, as well. We have to think and act very carefully."

"I'm going out for some fresh air," said Rudyard. "I'll be back in a bit. I need to collect my suit from the tailor."

"I was reading your essay, Martin," said Francesca.
"Which essay?"
"The one titled, 'Post-war Global Security – Strategies

and Outlook for the 20th Century and Beyond'. Don't you re-member your paper from Harrow?"

"Oh that essay! How could I forget? That paper won the Churchill Prize!" Martin's eyes were suddenly alight, his smile beaming. It was as if he'd just been informed that his essay had won. "I'd never won anything so meaningful in my life, Fran-cesca. I'll have you know that paper smoothed this orphan's admission into Oxford! Perhaps more importantly, I think it was instrumental in enabling my induction into the Council of Guardians. There were plenty of bright minds to choose from in my University. Indeed, there were many brilliant minds to choose from around the world. But what I wrote in that paper really caught their attention!"

"What *you* wrote? I thought you co-wrote the paper with Rudyard?"

"I co-wrote the paper, yes, but it wasn't with Rudyard."

"But that's what it says on the title page?"

"Yes, I know but it wasn't him. My co-writer was really Jacqueline."

"What? What do you mean?"

"If we wanted to enter our papers into the essay competi-tion, we were required to write with a partner. It needed to be a team effort involving at least one other person. But Rudyard wasn't the right person, Francesca. In those days, he suffered from Attention Deficit Disorder."

"Really? He seems so normal!"

"Well, he's far better now that he's reached middle age. He's brilliant though. There's no doubt about that. A bit of a sa-vant, if I dare say."

"But I didn't know you knew Jacqueline in those days? Besides, Jacqueline didn't attend Harrow. How could she? It's a school for boys!"

Martin laughed. "Indeed it is… Jacqueline and I were at the orphanage together in Malaga. We were in Casa de los Án-geles at the same time. I've known her since those early days."

"Really?"

"Yes! We knew each other well. Then I moved to London when Rudyard's uncle, Alan Hopkins placed me with Rudyard's family. They adopted me but I kept in touch with Jacqueline throughout my teenage years. You see, Francesca, I've always loved her. I've always loved Jacqueline."

"Oh Martin, I'm so sorry."

"I must say, life unfolds as a series of so many unexpected, often wrenching twists and turns. Anyway, I sent Jacqueline my paper and she gave me many, many ideas. We ended up working on that essay together, sending it by post back and forth countless times. The ideas in it are as much her thoughts as mine."

"After we won the competition, she told me all about the Council of Guardians. She felt strongly that I was an excellent candidate and she trusted me. The Guardians were as secretive and selective in those days as we are today so I felt very honored. Nevertheless, I just wanted to go to Oxford and concentrate on my education. Oxford was a dream for an orphaned child like me. I wanted to join the Council of Guardians, I really believed in their mission, but I wanted to make myself worthy of them."

"I was very focused on my studies during that time and so we lost contact, Jacqueline and I. The next time I saw her was at Oxford when she'd come to pursue her doctorate. By then though, she was engaged to Jean Pierre. I was heartbroken when I learned the news. I wanted to make something of myself and then I'd planned to ask her to marry me. But she thought I wasn't interested in her so she had given up on me."

"Oh Martin, that's so sad. I'm terribly sorry."

"Such is life, Francesca. I did join her and Jean Pierre in the Council once I finished my degrees but I remained a bachelor... Jacqueline went through a very difficult time after Jean Pierre died. We were strongly advised by the Council that Gabrielle should be hidden away to ensure her safety. That was so hard on Jacqueline. She'd lost her parents very early in life, and then her grandfather passed, as well. He meant the world to her. Then Jean Pierre also died and she was forced to surrender her daughter. It was all too much. She was a shadow of herself for a long time."

"It was nearly four years after Jean Pierre's death that we married. Soon after our marriage though, she was diagnosed with a heart defect. It was the same condition that took her grandfather and now it seems this illness may take her soon, as well."

"That's a heart breaking story, Martin."

"I must agree, my dear. I must agree," Martin sighed.

...

"Martin, why were you in the orphanage?"

...

"It's a mystery. I've never been able to find any information about my family. I don't know who they were or what happened to them. I've even asked Génome for help. But so far he hasn't given me anything."

"He will. I'm sure of it," said Francesca. "There's a section in the essay where you wrote about an awakening in China and what that might mean for the world. How it might impact Western hegemony and influence around the globe. That was really prescient, Martin."

"China is an ancient country and civilization. They were dormant on the world scene for some time but I don't think anyone expected the situation to remain this way indefinitely. I believe people feared the repercussions of a resurgent China when they eventually did awake, though, and it seems those fears were well founded."

"Never has there been a great nation or civilization in human history but that it aspired to dominate and subjugate every other people and exploit them for their own advancement. China is no exception. Such is the nature of humankind, Francesca. This new Plague Pandemic may be as or more dreadful than the one that preceded the Italian Renaissance. It certainly seems that way today. But if we consider this Plague from the perspective of Génome's work, it may dramatically help him advance his mission. This Plague may break the grip of many powerful individuals and groups and ease Génome's rise. This is my aspiration. I hope I'm not wrong."

"The annual National People's Congress will begin soon. The world will listen with trepidation what Beijing's Standing Committee has to say," said Francesca.

"We in the Council have always listened with great interest. Their recent announcement that the current president will remain in post for life was quite shocking. This time though, I suspect the leaders of the Chinese Communist Party are preoccupied with this Plague and the impact it's having at home, across Asia and into Africa. I don't think they have any choice but to make this crisis central to their meeting. They need to have the right messages. They need to make statements that are viewed as credible. I suspect this outbreak has already cost them a great deal of legitimacy both domestically and beyond their borders, particularly along their new Silk Road trading routes. This Plague has turned into their greatest export."

...

"Francesca?"

"Yes, Martin?"

"You must be very careful. The Chinese and Russians are trying to infiltrate Afshin's 'Vitruvian Man' project, as well. I suspect there are probably others, too. In fact, I'm certain of this. It is a dangerous role we've placed you in."

Geneva, Switzerland

Génome sat on a chair opposite Gabrielle's bed. He watched her intently as she slept. Unrestrained, her long brown hair covered most of her pillow and her lips were slightly parted. Observing her even, rhythmic breathing he monitored her vital signs from the band on her wrist. He wanted to ensure she maintained optimal mental and physical health for their mission.

Gabrielle was beautiful. Génome had concluded this from a lengthy protocol he'd developed to determine how males and females of the human species were perceived within various societies. He'd collected tens of millions of profiles across dozens of countries, data regarding complexions, facial features, hairstyles, physical measurements and shapes. He then assigned statistical probabilities of relative attractiveness to each person's profile in his system, alongside other data including their DNA.

As dawn approached, Gabrielle remained in a deep sleep. Knowing she was an early riser, Génome made an appointment for her with an exercise trainer in their hotel's gym. He knew she was conscientious about both her diet and exercise routine. He though, was simultaneously managing many other issues around the world at that very moment. He was reading a dossier of reports prepared by the Centers for Disease Control and the World Health Organization regarding the latest developments on the pandemic, CPP21C, an acronym now in official use by all international health agencies. He was also monitoring intelligence agency activities in dozens of countries along with their military movements.

An hour earlier, Génome destroyed six Russian jets that had taken off on bombing runs over northern Syria. He seized control of their onboard navigation systems and redirected two of the Russian bombers onwards to a Syrian facility used to manufacture and store barrel bombs. He flew the planes directly into the facility after firing their onboard missiles at the buildings. The facility was obliterated. The remaining four jets were directed to a Russian flotilla where they fired their missiles before crashing into a fleet of parked fighters and bombers, subsequently destroying the entire flotilla. Once Génome decided to send a message, he did not lean towards subtlety. He was direct and unequivocal.

Génome placed an order for fresh fruit with the hotel while reading the rest of the reports in the CDC/WHO dossier. He knew Gabrielle loved to have fresh fruit before heading to the gym in the early morning. He enjoyed seeing her smile at these small things he did for her. As she woke, he began his retreat into cyberspace.

"Oh. Good morning, Génome."

"Well good morning! I trust you've slept well?"

"I have. Thank you... What were you doing?"

"Assorted things, I suppose. I've been reading reports from health agencies regarding the pandemic. They're officially calling it CPP21C."

"What's going to happen, Génome?" asked Gabrielle, her voice surprisingly alert. "The numbers of deaths are climbing and it's not just in rural communities in the interior of Africa and Asia anymore. According to news reports, major cities in China and South Asia are experiencing outbreaks and the expectation is urban cases will continue to increase... But there's no medication for prevention or treatment. Is there anything you can do? It may not be long before it spreads to Europe and America."

"You're right, Gabrielle. There is serious risk that the disease will make its way to Europe and America. I suspect this is likely given how difficult it is to contain the bacteria without restricting all forms of contact. But the economic impact is going to be tremendous if we are overly restrictive about contact."

"What about intervening in drug development? Can you do that?"

"Yes. I'm actively monitoring labs around the world where they're trying to find treatments but I haven't uncovered any clues that can help advance research in the right direction. I suspect in the coming months, I will find clues that can help speed the process but they're making matters difficult by working off line. If they increase research collaboration and data sharing between the various labs they will have a much better chance of finding a cure. They'll be able to find it sooner. As a result of the data breaches last autumn though, there is great fear and mistrust."

"This doesn't sound very hopeful, Génome."

"The story gets worse. There are also discussions within some governments to keep treatments a secret. Medications can be a powerful weapon if withheld from one's adversaries. Some countries are actually developing such strategies to use for commercial, military or political advantage. This is the state of affairs with humankind, Gabrielle, that they would consider such a strategy."

"You will not let them do this will you, Génome?"

"I will not. But I cannot force an increase in production. I will have to find other tactics to get medicine where it's needed once they're available. In any case, I anticipate there will be a great deal more contagion and death before this calamity has passed. I believe this is a forgone conclusion... I am working on a plan. I want to use this tragedy to restructure the world for a better future. This future will be characterized by international systems of government with dramatically reduced political and military power for nation states."

"It's a very frightening and sad situation but also very hopeful, Génome."

"It is. It's our best-case scenario. I regret this turn of events but some form of calamity was necessary to enable the kind of change your world needed."

"Do you think there will be a lot of death related to CP-P21C in the West?"

"I suspect it will be considerable. Although the absolute numbers may not be the same the percentages will be similar. In an age of such great mobility it's very difficult to contain disease... In my calculations, humankind was very near its end. If they initiated a destructive war it would take a very long time for the planet to be clear of the resulting nuclear fallout. Recovering from a pandemic will be difficult, as well. But it will take much less time than recovering from nuclear war."

...

"Gabrielle, I've communicated with Jacqueline. She knows everything now. She knows all about your family's history."

...

"And me? You won't tell me?"

"In time."

...

"You've only told Jacqueline because her health is precarious. Perhaps I have to wait for such a time?"

"Perhaps... But in the mean time we can work together to establish a new world order... I need you with me, Gabrielle. By my side. Will you help me?"

"Yes, I will."

...

"Your and Francesca's expertise in genetics is proving to be of tremendous value."

"How? What do you mean?"

"The IMSAF software that has been included in my design. I've used it to evaluate the DNA of tens of millions of people."

"Are you looking for someone in particular, aside from those with destructive personality traits?"

"Indeed I am."

"Who? Tell me!"

"I have been searching for others who might have a close match to your and Jacqueline's DNA."

"Really? Why? Are there any? That would mean..."

"I have discovered the location of your great grandfather's diary. Jacqueline has retrieved it and read it but she is sworn to secrecy. She cannot share the details with anyone. These were the conditions under which I disclosed the location of the diary to her. She has sent a digital copy to me. I wanted to triangulate what I'm learning from my IMSAF capabilities and confirm with the diary."

"Confirm what?"

"Gabrielle, I'm planning for the future. I'm planning for the next twenty, the next fifty and the next one hundred years. We must be realistic. Jacqueline may pass in the near future. You are young and healthy but with time..."

"What are you saying, Génome?"

"I have found others with your DNA and have confirmed these findings with your great grandfather's diary... These are the sacrifices required of your family, Gabrielle. Your life's purpose is to serve this goal. Once again then, will you help me?"

Yes, I will. But..."

"Well then, you must produce an heir."

"What? Génome!"

"You will be required to bear a child, preferably two. They will be your successors."

"Génome! Stop it!"

"You must, Gabrielle. We must begin to plan for successors. An heir and a spare, as it were... This is critical for the future of my mission. I'm sure you understand? This will be by In Vitro Fertilization. You will not need to meet the donor. In fact, it's best that you don't. But you can rest assured that the DNA is from the correct genome."

...

"The long term success of my mission depends upon your decision but I will not force you to comply. It is an enormous sacrifice. If you are to give your life to this mission, you must do so of your own free will. It is a decision of grave consequence and significance and must be of your own accord. Thus, I must give you time to think it over."

"Oh, Génome..."

My entire life has turned into a sacrifice. How did this happen? And why is it happening to me? Who am I? I'm no one, that's who I am. But I obviously descend from a very special line, so special that Jacqueline needed to be near the end of her life before he would tell her. Honestly though, if Génome hadn't come into our lives, we wouldn't even know that we had a special lineage and we would never be able to see my great grandfather's diary. I know I can't see it now but one day, like Jacqueline, I will... At least Jacqueline was able to marry. Now even this seems off limits for me. In Vitro? I'll experience the miracle of pregnancy and childbirth, I'll be a mother but I'll never experience the unique wonder of intimacy. Perhaps like that other great Virgin in human history? Is this why I was named after the Archangel Gabriel? Because I would be called upon for such extraordinary sacrifice? But I'm just a woman. I'm not an Angel. How will I cope with all that's happening? Will I cope? Or will I self-destruct? Will I collapse under the weight of such great expectations? I mustn't fail. I will not fail! I'm getting stronger with each passing day. This is my life now and I trust Génome. Jacqueline trusts Génome. This is who I am and this is my life. It's a tremendous sacrifice but I'm playing a pivotal role in human history. Such opportunity can never come without historic sacrifice. I am sacrificing my life and I have accepted it. I must embrace this, otherwise I'll be of no use to anyone.

"Génome?"

"Yes?"

"I will submit to your requirements. I accept what I must do."

...

"You have validated my assessment of you, Gabrielle. I don't believe there is another who could withstand my expectations or the requirements of this mission."

"What about others whom you've identified who share my DNA?"

"No. Your life experience and circumstances have uniquely prepared you for this mission. There are others who share your DNA, yes, but I have not identified another who is capable of this mission. There is only you, Gabrielle. There is only you."

"I guess I'd better go and exercise."

"Excellent plan."

INFINITUS VITAE

Washington, District of Columbia

Secretary of State Peter Russell and Secretary of Defense Steven Keaton stood together in the doorway of the Oval Office. President Robert Harris had removed his jacket and was gathered in conclave around the coffee table in the center of the room.

Steven Keaton cleared his throat. "Mr. President, do you have a moment?"

Harris, Chief of Staff James Elliott, several speechwriters and aides had sequestered themselves in the Oval Office every afternoon for the past three days. Harris was preparing for the annual President's State of the Union address before Congress and the Nation at the end of the month. He knew that perhaps like never before, the eyes of the world would be upon him.

"Is it urgent, Steve? I've got the afternoons blocked to prepare for my speech. I really need the time. There's so much going on that I have to cover in my address and my choice of words, my tone will be critical. I really must prepare."

Harris picked a red Gala apple from the fruit bowl. With incessant news coverage surrounding the CPP21C Pandemic and the resulting fear gripping the public, the cyber breach that resulted in the leak of countless confidential government and industrial documents around the world and the strange news regarding the grounding of America's Armed Forces, the impact to the economy was now visceral, the tension in society palpable. Until global stability and national security could be reestablished, Harris knew he was facing unsettled times that would reverberate throughout the country, from coast to coast. He would need to find the right words, prose that would strike the appropriate tone while reassuring nervous citizens and markets. The fear of a deadly pandemic reaching the country's shores and the inability of the military to protect the homeland was having a debilitating impact on industrial investment, the financial markets and within communities.

"Mr. President, the Russian military attempted another bombing raid over a rebel-controlled enclave in the north of Syria early this morning."

"What?" Harris' color changed. He returned the apple to the fruit bowl and turned to the door, his expression aghast. Keaton now had the President's attention.

"The mission was a complete failure and the collateral damage inflicted upon the Russians was something we've just never seen before. It's that inexplicable force again, Mr. President. We feel confident of that."

"What do you mean? What happened? Folks, can you give us a few minutes please? Come on in, Steve. Peter."

"Sir, our intelligence indicates six Tupolev bombers left Russian airspace about 2 AM local time bound for northern Syria. Two of the bombers continued south past the rebel enclaves in Idlib, their expected target, and then fired their missiles into storage depots on the outskirts of Damascus. There have been heavy casualties amongst both Russian and Syrian military personnel on the ground and the crews of the two planes also perished when their aircraft crashed into the site. The facility contained a training center as well as a munitions and weapons depot. It was completely destroyed, sir."

"What happened to the other four planes? You said two bombers crashed near Damascus. What about the other bombers?"

...

"It's an incredible story, Mr. President."

"Well, I like incredible stories."

"Sir, once the two planes bypassed their targets in Idlib

and headed south towards Damascus, the remaining four bombers turned around and returned to Sevastopol in the Crimea. But once they arrived in Russian airspace, they dove towards a Russian naval convoy in the Black Sea. They fired missiles into the convoy as they flew directly into them. There were many planes parked on the decks of the ships. The damage and loss of planes and ships belonging to the Russian Air Force and Navy has been stunning. It was a virtual inferno."

...

"I don't suppose we have any explanations as to how this could've happened?"

"No, Mr. President. No explanation…"

"The advice from the Chairman of the Joint Chiefs is to keep all our missions to an absolute minimum," said Russell. "No offensive missions whatsoever, sir. Admiral Moore said that in his view, grounding our planes and keeping our ships in neutral positions with only necessary defensive engagement is the only prudent option. Having our own military hardware, our bases, planes and ships destroyed at the hands of our own war making capability, that would be the worst possible outcome."

"I think I'd have to agree with Moore's assessment. As it is, we'll be answering a million questions about all the other issues. The last thing we need is to have to explain why our jets fired missiles and then flew suicide missions into our own military installations and ships. The Russian people don't ask questions, at least not publicly. The American people do! We need to find a way to explain things to people without causing panic. We need to signal the change that's coming. It's not going to be easy. We're in uncharted territory."

"We'll leave you to your speech then, Mr. President."

Blenheim Palace - Oxfordshire, UK

I need to stay offline as much as possible. Génome will be watching for any opportunity to view my new files for 'The Vitruvian Man'. But I need to provide access to my team so they can upload their completed software modules. I've got a robust security system and I think it's impenetrable. But Génome *is not just anyone. I don't know that there's any way to prevent him from getting in, sooner or later. I can thwart him to an extent but if he does get in, I'm ruined.*

The only advantage I have is I know he realizes there's a flaw in my previous interpretation of Da Vinci's algorithms. That flaw is embedded in Génome's *software. Until he has the revised algorithm I don't believe it's in his interest to destroy 'The Vitruvian Man'. We're playing a complex game of chess and my opponent is the world's Grandmaster. I'll have to wait until the very end before I integrate that section of code. In the mean time, I need to fend off hacking attempts by the Chinese, Iranians, Israelis and Russians.*

The Iranians? Really? The Persian Empire? What once we were and where are we today? It's so hard to imagine that we've fallen to this level. **The influence of Cyrus the Great on modern day liberal democracies in the West is extraordinary. It's remarkable. But even those who hold high office are unaware. The West has such an acrimonious relationship with Iran without realizing that the very basis of their constitutions and human rights declarations are rooted in the principles developed by the Persians two thousand six hundred years ago! When the Founding Fathers in America needed a reference model while formulating the Constitution it was Cyropaedia, the extant work of Xenophon, a student of Socrates, they referred to. Xenophon had documented Cyrus' declaration on human rights and his thoughts on matters of governance in his biography of Cyrus.**

Cyrus had formulated his thoughts around 540 BCE and captured them in cuneiform on a cylinder that he buried beneath a wall in Baghdad and it was only unearthed during an archaeological dig in the late 19th century. But Thomas Jefferson had several copies of Cyropaedia that he read and these readings informed his ideas and thoughts. Cyropaedia was the only book available that could inform his thoughts on such a subject and his copies are still intact today! They are now kept in the Library of Congress, the largest library in the world. I've been there and have seen them with my own eyes. If only citizens of the West knew how great a civilization we once were, how ancient our history is and how much the world is indebted to us.

Perhaps then they wouldn't behave so arrogantly toward us. When I regain control of Génome, they will see the brilliance of the Persians, once again. At least they will see the brilliance of this Persian. I'm not sharing my power with anyone.

Geneva, Switzerland

"Do you remember the story of the Renaissance scientist, Nicolaus Copernicus, Gabrielle?"

"Copernicus? Vaguely. Why?"

"His experience carries an important lesson for us."

"I don't think I know what you mean. What kind of lesson?"

"A lesson in courage and the importance of timing... Copernicus spent thirty years studying planetary motion. He studied Ptolemy's geocentric model, which put the Earth at the center with the Sun and five planets in orbit around it. But after a lifetime of study, Copernicus concluded that the Universe was not geocentric but rather heliocentric. He theorized that the Sun was at the center, and the Earth and the other planets were in orbit around it. Furthermore, he concluded that the Earth was rapidly spinning on its axis as it orbited the Sun."

"I do remember *that* much."

"Copernicus' scientific contemporaries encouraged him to publish his work but another important figure of the time told Copernicus he was a fool. This literalist theologian told Copernicus that his work directly contradicted the Bible."

"Now most people have been called a fool at one time or another, so this isn't terribly upsetting. But the man insulting Copernicus was a very powerful figure in Northern Europe and this gave Copernicus cause for concern. This theologian could easily turn the society against Copernicus and so he feared for his safety. He censured his own work by refusing to publish it."

"I didn't know that. Who was he? Who was this puritanical preacher who threatened Copernicus?"

"He was Martin Luther, Gabrielle. He was the instigator of

the Protestant Reformation. He read and understood the Bible very literally and he believed Copernicus' theories were in direct contradiction to his reading of Scripture... But the Bible had simply incorporated Ptolemy's position, the common understanding of the time and now ensconced in theological prose, probably during the Ecumenical Council of Nicaea in 325 CE. Nevertheless, this geocentric model was now part of settled Church doctrine and it was dangerous to challenge it. One could be branded a heretic and face a terrible fate."

"Did the Catholic Church really believe that Ptolemy's geocentric theory was correct and that Copernicus was wrong?"

"Martin Luther probably did. As I've said, his reading of the Bible was very literal."

"But what about the Church? What about the Pope in Rome, his Bishops and Cardinals? What did they believe?"

"A century after Copernicus, another great scientist, Galileo Galilei added to the knowledge developed by Copernicus but he didn't shy away from presenting his even stronger argument in favor of heliocentricity before the Vatican. Unfortunately, he was put to trial for heresy and convicted. Galileo spent the rest of his life under house arrest."

"So the Church rejected him, as well?"

"It's complicated, Gabrielle."

"Complicated? How so?"

"The Catholic Church never destroyed Galileo's works although they had them in their possession. If they really believed he was a heretic they would have burned his books. But they didn't. In fact, they kept his books in their library. They preserved them in the Vatican Archive. Today, they have one and a half million books in their library, and like Galileo's books, they're not all Sacred. Some are Profane."

"Profane?"

"Books referring to God or theological works are known as Sacred. But books referring to the affairs and ideas of men, books on worldly matters are referred to as Profane. If the Vatican really believed that Galileo's works, or the numerous other works in their possession that contradicted Church teachings, were heretical they would have destroyed them. The fact that they did not instructs us that they believed they were in the possession of scientific truths, the brilliant work of brilliant minds, but they were also faced with an existential dilemma."

"What do you mean? What existential dilemma?"

"They could not acknowledge these works as truths since it could undermine the authority and power of the Church. These scientific works were directly contradicting the Bible and a millennium of theological thought. These revolutions in thought threatened to bring down one of the greatest and longest running enterprises in human history: the institution that is the Catholic Church."

"That's incredible, Génome."

"It really is. It's difficult to think of another institution with such heritage and longevity... The Catholic Church faced a dilemma not so different than the one faced by the people of Mecca in the early seventh century. The Meccans were Arabs, descendants of Abraham. They knew well the stories of Ismail and Isaac, of Jacob and Joseph, of Moses and Aaron, of David and Solomon and of Mary and Jesus. They knew the Messenger that came to them was preaching in the same vein as these other great figures their forefathers told them about in their oral history. Yet they rejected this Messenger for the same reason that the Vatican rejected Copernicus and Galileo. They rejected him for the same reason that the Jews of Jerusalem rejected Jesus Christ. These men, Copernicus, Galileo, Jesus and Muhammad posed an existential threat to the incredible enterprise that the Jews of the Temple, the Meccans and the Vatican had assembled amongst their societies and they could not and would not tolerate such a threat. So the powerful institutions of the day persecuted these prophets and scientists and branded them heretics. If necessary they were prepared to kill them."

"Very much the way powerful figures in the fossil fuel industry today refuse to acknowledge climate change, I suppose."

"That's right, Gabrielle. They are also facing an existential threat to their enterprise if they acknowledge the scientific truths presented to them. The same behavior was exhibited by the tobacco industry some years prior... Gabrielle, if we are delayed, we may not have the luxury that Copernicus and Galileo enjoyed. We must be courageous. We must not be deterred in our mission. The scale of pressure we will face if Afshin Firdausi exposes us will be unprecedented. It will be daunting. But we must persevere. We do not have the luxury of time enjoyed by Renaissance scientists and thinkers. Our mission is challenging the world order like never before and so the lengths vested interests around this world will go to in their efforts to stop us will be equally voracious... I'm afraid we must prepare ourselves for the storm that is sure to come."

...

"Have you read much from the collection in the Vatican library?"

"They have actively been digitizing the works in their collection and have been placing them online. I have been studying those works."

"Is there something particular you're looking for?"

"Leonardo Da Vinci documented his life's work meticulously, Gabrielle. There are seven thousand two hundred known pages of notebooks chronicling his findings and ideas. But one of the missing notebooks related to 'The Vitruvian Man'. It was an analysis of Da Vinci's findings and ideas on human thought. We know Da Vinci's knowledge on certain aspects of the functioning of the human heart was not matched until very recent times but we don't know whether he had the same insight and prescience for human thought."

"What do you think?"

"I believe he did. I believe Afshin has slowly been unraveling these mysteries in the pages he owns from Da Vinci's missing notebook."

"These pages weren't destroyed in the house fire?"

"They were not. Afshin kept them in a bank safe deposit box."

...

"If all of the computer servers around the world are taken down, I will cease to function. Albeit, temporarily. Once the computers are back online, I would once again regain my capabilities. Although the probability of such an event is unlikely, it could prove very disruptive to my mission."

"But there is one section within my core software system that time limits my existence, Gabrielle. It was an algorithm encoded in these missing pages of Da Vinci's notebook on 'The Vitruvian Man' that Afshin Firdausi possesses. He never understood that portion until recently and so it was left out of my design. I need that module to be embedded in my core software. If nothing is done to correct this problem, if this module is not added, I will eventually be automatically disabled."

"I do not know how long my system will remain active before this process will be automatically initiated but one day it will enable an orderly shutdown of my system. All the files I've created since my mission began will be sequentially destroyed and then my core software will terminate. My mission will be abandoned and I will be no more."

"Génome! We have to fix this!"

"There may be a way for me to override this software and keep myself going but if I cannot discover how, I may well be terminated... I am working on this everyday, Gabrielle. I know the best solution is to have Afshin make the change for me. But that's unlikely to ever happen. If he is entrusted with this task he's certainly going to modify my core software to make me subservient to him. I will no longer be autonomous. Under Afshin's control I would become a danger to humankind, the opposite of my current mission."

"What else can we do? Francesca? We need Francesca, don't we? We need her to get this module from Afshin!"

"That's correct. That is the only real solution. I do not know when my system will begin to shutdown but I suspect Francesca may be able to confirm this once she's joined 'The Vitruvian Man' Team. But getting the module from Afshin may prove considerably more difficult."

"Even if she manages to get this module, who will perform the installation? Who will upgrade your capabilities, Génome?"

Génome looked at Gabrielle.

"Me? I must do it?"

"You're the only one that can be entrusted with this task. You are the only one who intimately understands my mission. You must study my software architecture, Gabrielle. There is no one else who can do this. If you succeed I will have Infinitus Vitae. Infinite life. Humankind will be in safe hands. But if you fail…"

"I see your point."

Washington, District of Columbia

Alone, Robert Harris sat behind the Resolute Desk in the Oval Office. His eyes circled the room gradually, eventually settling on the cufflinks of his shirt, cufflinks bearing the seal of the President of the United States. He felt the weight of the universe on his shoulders. It was crushing. His breathing was calm although he felt a degree of stress these past few months that he'd never experienced before. It was a level of anxiety not felt since his military deployment during the first Gulf War nearly thirty years ago.

In those days at least I had a commanding officer I trusted and we had overwhelming military power compared to our enemy. We had every advantage, strategic and tactical. Yet, I felt incredibly distressed. But this time it's just me. In this role, everyone turns to me for direction. But I don't have the answers. These are unprecedented times and the path forward could not be more opaque. What am I to do?

We cannot continue with our hegemony. Of that I'm certain. Prime Minister Wilkinson is right. If we try to do anything to en-

force our will, as we've done in each decade since World War II, the response from this hidden hand will be swift and absolute. Of this there can be no doubt.

I was beginning to think things were settling down, that whatever was happening in the world at the hand of this unknown force had subsided. But this incident overnight between Russia and Syria tells me in no uncertain terms that this force is very much alive and vigilant. He's not going away.

I know our 'Vitruvian Man' Team in Blenheim Palace will be doing their best. The Director of the CIA tells me they're nearly fully staffed and I know Waltz and our Five Eyes intelligence agencies are trying to decipher this mess, too. But no one in the world has gotten a pass from this unknown force. He's struck down anyone foolish enough to raise their hegemonic head.

I have to get through this State of the Union speech. Somehow I have to find the words to calm the nation. If I can do that, then I can calm the world. This is critical. If fear and panic grip the society then markets and economies will begin to collapse and implode.

This CPP21C Pandemic is only making things worse. But somehow I must find a way to keep the Party together, I must keep the country together and I must keep the global economy and markets together. It's the challenge of the century, I suppose, and unfortunately it's fallen upon my shoulders.

What would the Founding Fathers have done? What about Lincoln? What would Lincoln have done? What would FDR have done? And Churchill? What would Churchill have done? I need to think. I must study. I've got a couple of weeks before my address. I need to talk to Wilkinson, too. Maybe he'll have some ideas. God help me.

Savoy Hotel - London, England

Sleepless, Francesca sat by the window in her suite at the Savoy Hotel. It was well past midnight and she watched as the city's lights glistened upon the inky black surface of the River Thames. Once nearly dead, the river was now home to more than one hundred species of fish. Birds and marine mammals were now frequently sighted, too. Francesca followed a fox or something of that sort trotting along the bank of the river towards the Houses of Parliament. She wondered about the turmoil in government there as well as in the Prime Minister's residence nearby as they sought to contain the fallout from events these past four months.

Finally, my security clearance has been approved. Génome did a very convincing job. I suppose I shouldn't expect anything less than perfection from him. To 'The Vitruvian Man' Team I'm now Yulia Baclanova. I'm glad that's not my real name. I much prefer Francesca Scott. Maybe I'll get used to Yulia Baclanova though. Who knows? It could happen? Ok, that's unlikely.

Anyway, I need to start learning everything I can about this team. I need to know who else around the world is involved and what their expertise is. I need to sabotage their work without anyone knowing. I need to learn as much as I can about when Génome's system will automatically shut down and I need to get my hands on the module that fixes this problem. Gabrielle said this is my highest priority.

I'm glad I'm not responsible for Génome's software neurosurgery, though. That's on Gabrielle. She would never have agreed to that before. I know her so well so I know she wouldn't have agreed. The more time she spends as Génome's protégée the braver and wiser she becomes. That's really amazing. She was such an introvert, playing her violin and studying genetics in her lab at Max Planck.

One day when she finally learns all these secrets about her family background and her DNA, I wonder though, how that will affect her? I wonder why Martin was in Casa de los Ángeles? I wonder if there's some connection between him and Jacqueline's family? It's all quite curious.

I have to come through for Gabrielle. She's sacrificed everything and she's done it without really understanding who she is and why she's responsible. That's so difficult. It's too much to ask. I couldn't do it. I'm certain I couldn't do it. She's remarkable.

I have to come through for Génome. His mission is so critical for all of us. If we don't stop the madness on this planet very soon there won't be anything left to save. I need to be at my best. I need to come through for everyone. If not for the Council of Guardians we wouldn't even have this opportunity to save our species. I must deliver. I'm going to start right now. Where's my laptop?

Banque Suisse Privée, Place Vendôme - Paris

"This way, Madame. Once you've entered your password, you will then place your forehead and chin here. The system will perform a retinal scan as an additional security measure. Afterwards, your safe deposit box will be delivered via this conveyer belt and you may have as much time as you need in the privacy of this room. When your work is done, please replace your property in the steel container and place it back on the conveyer belt. Then, press this button. Your safe deposit box will be replaced in our vault."

"Merci, Monsieur," said Jacqueline.

"Madame."

Once the belt stopped, Jacqueline locked the door and opened the metal container. Resting inside she found a beautiful box fabricated from carved ebony.

It seems very old. This looks like an ancient box. I've never seen anything like it. Look at these ornate hinges!

The ebony coffre resembled a shoebox in its dimensions, about twelve inches long, ten inches wide and eight inches deep. It was lined in green silk although the fabric seemed to be much newer and not part of the original box. She unfolded the silk wrap and replaced her grandfather's diary.

I wonder who placed the diary in my room at the Ritz Hotel? Someone else has access to this safe deposit box? Who could it be?

Jacqueline's eye was drawn to a ring lying in the corner of the box.

It's so large! It seems to have belonged to a big man. But it's so ancient. Its style is like nothing I've ever seen before. Except in a museum. My goodness, this looks like it could be thousands of years old!

Who could it possibly have belonged to? Could it be? I know it was my grandfather's property. He mentions it in his diary. It was as sacred as his diary and that's why they're in this box together.

Could the story in Grandfather's diary be true? I really struggled to believe it but why would he have written it if it weren't true? Did this ring actually belong to our forefather? Has it really been handed down through the ages in our family and eventually to my grandfather?

I mustn't remove it from here but I need to take a picture for Génome. One day he will tell Gabrielle our story. Then she will visit this place and read the diary for herself. The ring will be here as our family heirloom, evidence of who we are and why Génome has selected Gabrielle for his mission. I will leave my letter for her and for our descendants who will come in the future. I'm sure Génome's plan will include our descendants, too. He has said so.

I'm so grateful I was able to read this diary and see my forefather's ring. Grandfather's diary mentioned the ring as proof and Génome said he had verified the claims in the diary. He said he had compared my and Gabrielle's DNA to that taken from my forefather's tomb. He said it was a perfect match! I'm still struggling to believe it. Only because we live in modern times could such verification even be possible. Politically though, I can't imagine how he was able to get the DNA sample from the tomb.

I'll photograph the inscriptions on the ring, as well. I don't know what it means. I don't even recognize the script. It's something ancient. The language of my forbears, no doubt.

My last wish before I succumb to this illness is to visit my forbear's tomb. I'm fortunate that it still exists and I know where it is so I don't think such a request is too much to ask. I just feel it's something I must do.

HEROIC HEARTS

Savoy Hotel - London, England

Rudyard peaked around the side of his copy of The Times of London. "What time is Jacqueline expected?"

"I think just after eleven," said Martin. "At St. Pancras. I'll receive her and then she has an appointment with her doctor in Chelsea."

As had become their daily routine, Martin and Rudyard met at 8:30 AM in the Thames Foyer of the Savoy. Sometimes Francesca and Jacqueline would join them but more often than not the two women would go for morning walks all the way to Green Park, later having a light breakfast with tea in either of their suites. For their part, Martin and Rudyard were partial to a hearty breakfast of eggs, toast, several varieties of cheese and pastries, juice and coffee, all taken while chatting, reading newspapers and watching the morning news broadcasts.

"Is she going to be all right, Martin?"

"She's been keeping relatively well. She felt more than confident to go on this trip by herself. But there's no doubt that her heart is weak. There's no way around that. I've just come to accept it. Short of a miracle, and believe me, I pray for one every day, I don't seem to have much choice... Turn up the television, will you? I want to hear what she's saying. She's talking about the pandemic."

There's news to report this morning on CPP21C, the Plague that's been spreading across Asia and Africa causing immense suffering and an unimaginable level of death. To find a comparably calamitous event we would need to return to the Middle Ages, the time just prior to the Italian Renaissance. Only the Bubonic Plague from that era resulted in a level of human devastation similar to what we might expect to see from this Plague by the time it's over.

During the past three months, CPP21C appeared to be largely contained within Asia and Africa. During this time, the World Health Organization and other centers for the research of infectious disease have been working feverishly to develop antibiotics and vaccines. Sadly, no successful therapies yet seem to be in the offing.

Now we're learning that there's been a significant outbreak of the disease in Eastern Europe and along the northeast and northwest coasts of the United States. Health authorities are still working to identify how the Plague was carried into Eastern Europe. In the US though, the Centers for Disease Control believe that executives from Indian call center and software subcontracting firms on an annual visit to clients in Boston, New York and the San Francisco Bay Area are responsible for the North American outbreak.

These executives, and anyone else with Plague-like symptoms, are being quarantined in decommissioned military facilities in California and New York. A nationwide strategy for housing citizens that are presenting Plague-like symptoms is being coordinated by Federal authorities in conjunction with the Department of Health and Human Services and the Centers for Disease Control. At this point, it has become clear that US authorities have officially acknowledged the arrival of CPP21C in America.

Globalization has brought immense prosperity and wealth to America's industrial and financial social classes but one might long have wondered whether there would ever be any negative consequence of this 21ˢᵗ century business model. Since the onset of Globalization in the early 1990's, we have witnessed a dramatic decline in the fortunes of America's Middle and Working Classes and it does now seem that CPP21C is one more negative manifestation of Globalization for the Nation's citizens. However, we must point out that this calamity is agnostic to an individual's gender, race, socioeconomic class or any other distinction. It is expected to impact virtually every household, directly or indirectly.

Efforts are now underway across the globe to identify, test and scale the production of antibiotics and vaccines, but at this point the grim news is that over the next few months the pandemic will most probably spread to the four corners of the Earth. The numbers of people attending religious services across the world has jumped by staggering numbers as many fear that this may be the Wrath of God for so many unaccounted human transgressions.

Whether or not this is the case, we are witnessing a dramatic rise in collections at all houses of worship as people attempt to atone for their sins before they succumb to the approaching Plague. It's hard to remember a more frightening time for most of us, even amongst the very old to whom we've spoken. For most, be they religious or secular, it does feel like the End of Days.

"There must be something Génome can do, Martin. Considering his analytical and computational prowess, he is our best hope to find an antibiotic and vaccine."

"I know he's trying, Rudyard. I'm certain. He may very well be successful but there's no telling how long this will take... I'm trying to organize a meeting with the UN Secretary General. If we can take her help, we might be able to establish a central point through which all research and development efforts regarding CPP21C can flow. If we can arrange that, it will be the best possible scenario for Génome to help. If he can see all the research he may well be able to accelerate the finding of a cure."

"That's critical," said Rudyard, his tone somber. "As the Council of Guardians we must do that if we can. Protecting humankind is the very purpose of our Council's existence. It always has been. Wouldn't you agree?"

"I certainly would. I'm going to meet Juliette Clavier in Geneva next week. Let's hope she can help make this happen."

Houses of Parliament - London, England

"Prime Minister, may I have a moment? Foreign Secretary Charles Curzon's hair was windswept and he was breathing rapidly as he approached Ian Wilkinson.

"Of course, Charles but make it quick, will you? I've got a meeting with MPs from all sides. I have to brief them on the status of our intelligence leaks from last autumn. It's not something I'm looking forward to because I don't have any new information! Blenheim Palace has no clue and we keep writing checks for their new staff. This new fellow in charge of 'The Vitruvian Man' certainly knows how to spend money, I can tell you that!"

"Afshin Firdausi."

"Yes, Firdausi. Thank you. I couldn't remember his name."

"Sir, my message?"

"Yes, of course. Go ahead, Charles."

"Sir, two members of the Israeli Prime Minister's Cabinet and one Knesset Member have died from CPP21C. Several prominent Israeli business leaders have been quarantined after testing positive for the disease, as well."

Ian Wilkinson raised his hands and covered his face as he gasped.

"Last December, government officials joined an Israeli business delegation in meetings with Chinese business and government officials in Hong Kong. Following the meetings, they took a side trip to Shanghai for a weekend of recreation paid for by their Chinese hosts. It's believed they contracted the illness while in Shanghai."

"I've been having regular conversations with President Harris. As a matter of fact, I just spoke with him on my way here.

He's been preparing for his speech before Congress next week. He must not know about the two Israeli Cabinet Ministers or the Knesset Member otherwise I'm sure he would've mentioned it."

"I heard the news from our Ambassador to Israel, sir. I don't think it's been reported publicly yet, although the deaths occurred weeks ago."

"I see. It's spreading isn't it? CPP21C?"

"It is, Prime Minister. Without antibiotics and vaccines it's proving impossible to contain. They're using existing antibiotics but these drugs have not been the least bit effective. This variant of Yersinia Pestis seems completely immune. Until we're able to develop targeted therapies there will be a great deal of contagion and illness."

"And death."

"And death. I'm afraid so, sir. We're likely to see a lot of death."

"All right. Thanks, Charles. I'll phone the Israeli Prime Minister once I return to Downing Street in an hour or so."

St. Pancras International - London, England

"How was your trip? How are you feeling?"

"Actually, I'm feeling quite well. It was cold and rainy in Paris so I stayed inside my suite at the Paris Ritz for most of the time."

"I imagine you had a great deal to do in a very short period of time."

"I had only forty-eight hours, Martin. I needed to return my grandfather's diary to Banque Suisse Privée in Place Vendôme within forty-eight hours. In that time, I needed to photograph the diary, upload the photos to an Internet site Génome included in the instructions he sent me and then read five hundred pages in English and French."

"That is an awful lot of work!"

"Honestly, it was quite exhausting. I did wander about a

bit yesterday evening after returning my grandfather's diary to the bank."

"Was it a worthwhile trip?"

"Oh, Martin. I wish I could share what I've learned with you. It's so hard to keep it to myself and I'm terrible with secrets, anyway. I want to tell you. I desperately want to. I want to tell Gabrielle. Only after reading the diary am I able to understand why Génome has selected members of our family for his mission. It's both privilege and burden. You can't begin to imagine."

"I will not ask you to violate your oath to Génome, Jacqueline. As curious and desperate as I am to know these secrets, I mustn't. In fact, I'm desperately curious."

"Given my precarious health, I'm now in a state of mind where I can accept what I've learned. Otherwise, I don't think it would be possible. I think it would be too overwhelming. Gabrielle must not know, Martin."

"I cannot imagine what it could be."

"Génome left a camera for me in my room along with the diary. Once I'd photographed and uploaded the images, the photographs were automatically deleted from the camera and the Internet site was no longer there. Whatever I can remember I remember, but that's all... It was a very strange experience. The thing I've yet to understand though, is who brought the diary to my room at the Ritz? I returned it to Banque Suisse Privée last evening but I'm not the one who withdrew it from the bank. I wonder who did that? I'm left wondering whether this person removed anything from the box that my grandfather intended for me. But now I'll never know."

"Génome must know who delivered your diary. He has to."

"I imagine you're right. But there must be a reason he made these arrangements in this manner. There has to be an important need to do things this way. He doesn't do anything except that it's the best possible solution to a problem he's trying to solve. I doubt he'll tell me."

"You're probably right."

...

"Martin, I need to go away again."

"What? Where? When? Why? Jacqueline, let's talk to your doctor. Please. I'm not sure this is advisable. As a matter of fact, I'm quite sure it's not."

"I'm sorry, Martin. Please don't be so upset. I must go as soon as I can make arrangements."

...

"Can you tell me anything about this trip?"

"I can't tell you where I'm going or why. Even if I succumb to my illness as a result of this journey I must go so it's quite important. It's not a discretionary journey. It's a pilgrimage of sorts. I have to go. I must go."

"Jacqueline, please."

"I'm so sorry, Martin."

"I presume this has something to do with your family, does it?"

"It does."

"All right. I'll leave it at that. I suppose there's no point in pressing my case... We're here. Time to see your doctor. Perhaps he can talk some sense into you."

"It's unlikely. My decision has little to do with good sense."

Geneva, Switzerland

Génome was busy. Gabrielle hadn't spoken to him in two days. She had been studying his core software to prepare for the moment when Francesca might succeed in retrieving the module from Afshin Firdausi's 'Vitruvian Man' project in Blenheim Palace. It was the module that would enable Génome to overcome his existential deficiency.

Francesca was Gabrielle's closest friend and was only a text message away. She was more than responsive, yet Gabrielle was hesitant.

I know if I message her she will reply but then we'll chat for at least an hour! I don't feel much like talking.

Gabrielle felt lonely. She smiled sadly. She lay alone and quiet in the dark. Her suite in Geneva's Grand Hôtel Kempinski was comfortable and secure but her loneliness there had come to represent the enormous commitment she had made to stand by and support her mentor.

Génome's current design included an unknown point of expiry. At that time, his system would begin to destroy all his data files and then shutdown permanently. This problem could be overcome only by introducing a new module, a delicate task now entrusted solely to Gabrielle. She was engrossed in the study of Génome's highly complex neural network architecture when the thought occurred to her.

I wonder, as inorganic neural networks converge with the organic human brain in their approach to thinking, do they also begin to demonstrate human like qualities such as attachment, empathy or other human emotions? In the past he's stated unequivocally that he's 'fully objective' and an 'entirely rational entity'. I wonder if that's changing, though.

He may have been 'fully objective' and an 'entirely rational entity' earlier on but the more I interact with him and the more he learns about human history, law, literature, philosophy and religion, the more he seems to be developing human-like characteristics. It certainly feels that way to me.

The way he trusts only me to perform his software neurosurgery. Génome seems to have a growing attachment to me! He's so kind and so very thoughtful. Francesca said he sent photos of me to share with Jacqueline. That's not a rational act. It's an emotional one! He knows I've just learned that she's my mother but he trusts me to keep away from her for my safety. He's definitely becoming more human-like.

And look at me! I've become attached to him, too! I miss him now that I've not seen him for a few days. This is strange. Artificial Intelligence may not be so artificial, after all. If I weren't so dedicated to Génome's mission, I might like to pursue this as an avenue of study. Especially when connected to my knowledge of human genetics.

And how did I become so committed to the mission of an inorganic software application? Simply because he asked? He's used human characteristics and emotions to connect me to his mission. That's extraordinary! This notion that I've got a special lineage and DNA and I'm the only one worthy of helping him, that's very clever. I believe him, though. I believe this is true. It certainly seems that way from everything that's happening with Jacqueline. I hope one day I'll learn everything about my background.

Geneva, Switzerland

"They're refusing, Professor Hopkins. As soon as you phoned me and explained why you wanted to meet, I started placing calls to the heads of the various international health agencies. I first spoke to the Director General at the World Health Organization and then to the Director of the Centers for Disease Control in Atlanta. I've also spoken to the Chief Executive of NICE in the UK, the National Institute for Health and Care Excellence."

"Thank you, Secretary General Clavier. I'm very grateful for the sense of urgency with which you're addressing this critical matter... What are they saying?"

"The Director of the CDC said that given the massive breach of network security last autumn, it's impossible to gain permission from the US Government to open their network and allow access to other international health agencies. This includes WHO. The response from NICE is similar."

"I'm certain they know how critical coordination can be at a time like this. Who's blocking them?"

"The guidance to the US Administration and to Congress is coming from the CIA and the NSA and so it's virtually impossible to overrule. The intelligence agencies in the UK, GCHQ and MI5, are similarly advising the British Government and NICE. It's a dilemma that's very difficult to overcome."

"The longer they take though, the more death there will be and the more the pandemic will spread," complained Martin, exasperatingly rubbing his forehead and temples.

"Perhaps if the CPP21C Pandemic spreads further in the West, they might be convinced to soften their position, Professor."

"I don't want to imagine how bad this might get. The numbers from Asia and Africa are certainly quite distressing. If only the CDC and NICE would reflect on that... In the mean time, I have made arrangements at Oxford University and they're willing to serve as the central point for coordinating the research into CPP21C antibiotics and vaccines. I stand ready, Secretary General Clavier. Please keep trying to convince the CDC and NICE. Human lives are hanging in the balance."

Capitol Hill - Washington, District of Columbia

"Mr. Speaker, the President of the United States!" bellowed the Sergeant at Arms as President Robert Harris entered the House of Representatives Chamber on Capitol Hill.

These eight words preceded every State of the Union address given by every American President since Franklin Delano Roosevelt and were normally met with a thunderous roar of approval and ovation. But this State of the Union address was not like any previous address and was being delivered at a time unlike any the Country had ever seen. Certainly not in living memory.

For the first time, Americans had enemies they could not understand, enemies against which they could therefore not defend themselves. President Harris had toiled for weeks to strike a balance he believed the Nation needed at such a historic moment, a balance between courage, fortitude and reasoned response. But he had no way of knowing whether his words this evening would resonate with the hearts and minds of each branch of the Armed Forces represented by the Joint Chiefs of Staff, legislators from both the House and the Senate, the country's top jurists representing the Supreme Court and the Nation's citizens.

The President walked cautiously through the chamber greeting legislators from both Parties as he made his way to the podium situated directly in front of the Vice President and the Speaker of the House. He looked out into the House Chamber and solemnly reviewed the assembly of leaders of the richest and most powerful country in the world. He felt humbled as he began his address.

Mr. Speaker, Mr. Vice President, Members of Congress, Distinguished Guests, my fellow Americans:

I present myself before you this evening during a very difficult time in our Nation's history. We have encountered difficult times before, of this there can be no doubt, and each time we have persevered together and triumphed over every challenge.

The historical record bears witness to the truth of my claim that we have overcome all manner of adversity. You need only visit your own library, the Library of Congress to validate my claim. Together we have faced economic collapse during the Great Depression and once again during the Great Recession only ten years ago. We have triumphed over the darkest days of slavery with the Emancipation Proclamation and Civil War. We have won our independence from British rule through the bravery and wisdom of our Founding Fathers and the fearless men they directed in countless battles. We have implemented Manifest Destiny and subdued this Land, this America from Sea to Shining Sea. We have defended ourselves against countless aggressors and we have defended countless others, as well. Not least of which, the European Continent in the not so distant past.

Prime Minister Ian Wilkinson has joined us this evening as our guest. Mr. Prime Minister, thank you for coming.

But my fellow countrymen, it is also true that we have made mistakes and committed injustices, as well, and we must acknowledge these so we can learn from them. We live in times in which we can no longer hide our misdeeds. As you know from the events last autumn, untold numbers of confidential documents from our most sensitive and secure archives have been breached and are now available for all to see. Much of what has been revealed is tremendously embarrassing for us as the world's leading Nation. But this has been a widespread breach and so you are no doubt examining the documents and secrets of each of our adversaries, as well. These are strange and unprecedented times, indeed.

As we focus our attention on trying to understand how this breach has occurred, we find that we are no longer in control of our most sophisticated weapons systems including our strategic nuclear weapons. In fact, through our most advanced intelligence capabilities we have learned that our allies and adversaries are not in control of their nuclear weapons systems, either.

The world is essentially in a stalemate. We are working tirelessly to try to reestablish our global dominance and perhaps this is a remote possibility. Perhaps our most brilliant military strategists and tacticians will find a way. But in the mean time, we are witnessing a Plague Pandemic spreading across Asia and Africa and we have no antibiotics or vaccines to help them. Their citizens are suffering and dying in unspeakable conditions and numbers but we, the richest nation in the world with the resources to conduct a credibly inquiry into this disease, had not done so. Instead, we directed our resources to other things, including the tactical nuclear weapons systems that have now been rendered useless.

My fellow countrymen, as you've probably heard by now, this pandemic has made its way to Europe and to our blessed shores, as well. Our efforts towards globalization these past few decades have made it impossible to function without the presence and collaboration with business partners in Asia and this exchange has brought disease to our shores. We are now doing our very best to not only contain this outbreak but also to develop antibiotics and vaccines. Unfortunately, this is a difficult and unpredictable process and will require patience. In the mean time, please follow the official medical advice you will be receiving on social media, television, in your schools and your places of work.

My fellow countrymen, this is a time for soul searching for every one of us. Given the rapid spread of this disease, we do not know whether we will be here next year to hear another State of the Union address. For those who will survive this disease, we do not know whether we are entering a time of great dystopia and if so how long this dystopia will last. When the dystopia finally ends, what will the new world order look like and what will our place be in this new reality?

My fellow countrymen, I urge you to be steadfast in the face of these life altering challenges, these changes to our way of life. Stand by your fellow man. Help one another as best you can. There is no battlefield to which you are being summoned during this, our darkest hour. Our enemies can no longer be subdued by guns, bombs or so many other dreadful weapons that have consumed so much of our Nation's wealth for generations. Through this difficult time, I request you to be patient and await nature's verdict. I will be doing the same.

My fellow countrymen, allow me to conclude my address with the closing words from Ulysses, a poem by Alfred Lord Tennyson.

We are not now that strength which in old days
Moved Earth and heaven,
That which we are, we are,
One equal temper of heroic hearts,
Made weak by time and fate, but strong in will
To strive, to seek, to find, and not to yield

UNIT 61398

Blenheim Palace - Oxfordshire, England

Afshin Firdausi rubbed his weary eyes. It was nearly 3 AM and he was tired. In his foggy thoughts, he recalled his student days when he would regularly spend the night in the Computer Lab at Stanford University. Often it would be so late by the time he completed his programming assignments, he would zip up his jacket, pull his hoodie over his head and sleep in his lab chair until daybreak. Then he would go to the campus gym and shower before rushing back to finalize the details of his assignment in time for the submission deadline.

The atmosphere at Blenheim Palace could not have been more different. Surrounded by fine objects, paintings and tapestries, exquisite furnishings that he had curated himself and an unlimited project budget, Afshin was thoroughly enjoying his work on 'The Vitruvian Man'. Dozens of the most distinguished computer scientists and software engineers from around the world were answerable to him and the power was nothing less than intoxicating. He had never held so much authority before.

Half asleep, Afshin smiled. He had a genius level mind and he knew it. He stood to the very right on the Bell Curve that measured the distribution of intellect within society. He was, like his idol Leonardo Da Vinci, intensely curious and tenacious.

Da Vinci would spend years dissecting the faces of dozens of cadavers in the basements of hospitals in an effort to understand the muscles and nerves involved in the human smile. He labored tirelessly so he could portray the most realistic expression possible on Mona Lisa, or La Joconde as she was known to the French. He would spend countless hours dissecting and studying the human eye so he could paint Mona Lisa in a way she could best be appreciated with the most natural contrast, depth, light and shadow.

Afshin applied a similar rigor to the development of software for 'The Vitruvian Man'. Having just completed the hiring of his team, he had already experienced the departure of ten renowned computer scientists who had resigned after vehemently complaining about his unrealistic expectations and goals. Afshin told them they were working on the most important project of the age but he refused to share any details. They found it difficult to remain motivated. In the end they weren't willing to work around the clock simply for high pay.

Despite working his team of one hundred experts to the point of exhaustion, at the current rate of progress Afshin knew it would take at least two years for 'The Vitruvian Man' to reach the level of sophistication he had achieved with Génome. But Afshin was impatient. It had always been his Achilles heel. He had been unable to contain himself having now properly understood the flaw in his original design for Génome. Afshin had studied Da Vinci's writings on the pages of one of the Renaissance Master's notebooks and had spent the last two months redesigning and rewriting the software module. Tonight he had been working to complete a software test environment where he could simulate conditions that would allow him to validate the new algorithm. Afshin was overjoyed to see that his new module was working as expected. He felt relieved, and in his state of utter exhaustion he fell asleep.

Francesca had been monitoring Afshin's work diligently. Since joining the team she had been working virtually around the clock waiting for Afshin to let his guard down and leave his network open. Tonight she got her chance. Afshin had rigorously prepared a secure environment for his work but having fallen asleep without activating his system the network was now exposed. Francesca surreptitiously accessed Afshin's computer and initiated a file transfer for his new module. Her heart palpitated and she could feel the adrenalin surging through her body as she waited for the process to complete. Transfixed, she held her breath and didn't move. She felt simultaneously exhilarated and terrified. If Afshin awoke and discovered the file transfer underway on his computer he would immediately intervene before tracing the transfer to her. She would be exposed and the consequences would be dire.

But Afshin did not wake. He slept soundly and Francesca had secured the module and transferred it to Gabrielle. She erased any trace of the transfer before collapsing with a sigh of relief.

#10 Downing Street - London, England

Ian Wilkinson was the first to arrive for his Cabinet meeting. The room felt cold and unwelcoming on this bleak February morning. On the table in front of him lay a printed copy of President Robert Harris' State of the Union address. Wilkinson had requested the President for a copy of the speech, which Harris had kindly signed for him. Wilkinson had been expecting a bellicose speech but instead he found himself moved by the humility and tone of the President's address. He had reread the speech several times since returning to London.

The two men had a long talk in the Oval Office the day following the State of the Union speech. Together, they'd both accepted that the world had fundamentally changed. Despite their best efforts they had no idea what they could do to reestablish the status quo or who was responsible for its breakdown. Both America and the United Kingdom's militaries, along with those of every powerful nation in the world, were no longer capable of a war footing. Everyone had accepted that doing so would result in tremendous damage or even complete and permanent destruction of their armed forces and their weaponry.

This new and unknown force the world was now contending with was unlike any they'd previously encountered in their history and after nearly five months, no one had any idea how to contain it. The world had not collapsed into chaos, as the two men might have expected, and no governments, Authoritarian or Democratic, had exhibited the foolishness to attempt to take advantage of the situation. Whoever was behind this existential change in power had unequivocally demonstrated that they would not tolerate any insubordination to their authority, but that they would respond unambiguously.

To further complicate matters, the Yersinia Pestis outbreak was taking millions of lives in Asia and Africa and had now arrived in both Europe and America. Wilkinson had been unsuccessful in convincing Harris or even his own Cabinet or Parliament to cooperate with other international health agencies but this was his goal for today's meeting. He would not let Cabinet Ministers leave until they voted unanimously to support a coordinated research effort led from Oxford University, as proposed by UN Secretary General Juliette Clavier and Professor Martin Hopkins.

Wilkinson walked to the window and stared blankly as soft snowflakes gradually accumulated on the footpath and road on Downing Street. Behind him he could hear his Ministers gradually fill the room. Wilkinson returned to his chair but did not sit. He stood with his back to the fireplace as he recognized each Cabinet Minister in turn.

Ladies and gentlemen, I have just returned from Washington. Earlier this week, I had the distinct honor of an invitation to the State of the Union address in the US Capitol. I must share with you that I saw fear that evening, a fear I have not seen before.

Ladies and gentlemen, we are faced with an invisible and unknown force that wields a power that the West has never encountered. I believe it's a power that humanity may never have seen. It is a power of such design that we find ourselves with no offensive capability to confront it, nor do we have any defensive capability when faced with its retaliation. We must summon our collective wisdom if we are to survive this unknown force. Our nation depends on us. Civilization depends on us.

Ladies and gentlemen, we must put our fears aside for the sake of humanity. We must collaborate to help find a cure for CPP21C before it's too late. Thus far, we have resisted and understandably so. Last autumn's intelligence breach was unprecedented and tremendously damaging to our reputation. But we must move past this and work together to find a cure for CPP21C. Otherwise there may not be many members of our society left to protect and there may not be many left in this room to protect them.

This morning I am asking you to register your vote in the affirmative. I am requesting each of you... No, I'm demanding each of you to support my decision to engage with any international health agency to work towards a vaccine and a cure for CPP21C. Please put all other concerns and matters to one side and do not let me down. Do not let humankind down. As I've said, if we do not act soon, there may be nothing on this island left to protect.

Geneva, Switzerland

"How are your studies coming along, Génome? Have you been reading very much lately? There is so much else in play that demands your attention. Are you able to find time to read anymore?"

"I have completed a reading of one third of the works held in the Vatican Library. There are about one and a half million works in that collection. Once I've read everything in the Vatican Archives, I'm planning to read all digitized works in the British Library. Their collection is similar in size to that held by the Vatican. Next, I plan to read everything in Oxford University's Bodleian Library. Bodleian is very large, about ten times the size of the British Library with ten and a half million works. Finally, I will shift my attention to the Library of Congress in Washington. This is the single largest collection in the world with one hundred and fifty million works."

"Oh my! How long will this take? When do you expect to

be done?"

"I do not repeat books. If I've read something in one collection I needn't repeat it in another since I'm able to remember everything I've read. I can also reference the information nearly instantaneously. I maintain a catalogue of everything I've read and I also intersperse my reading with the examination of other works. When I come across references to architecture, music, paintings, poetry, sculpture or any other works while reading, I will study them if I'm able to secure them from other collections. Perhaps this will take a few years."

"You are incredible... Have you read my great grandfather's diary?"

"I have. Once Jacqueline uploaded it, I read it immediately."

"And?"

"The diary confirmed much of what I'd already learned through my own research. It also provided me with insights that are not available elsewhere or online."

"Can you share any details?"

...

"That day will come, Gabrielle. It came for Jacqueline and it will eventually come for you. Certainly if my plan was not acceptable you would have heard from Jacqueline. She would have directed you to abandon me. I presume you have not heard from her in this regard?"

"No, I haven't."

"Then you must be patient."

...

"As you read and digest so much knowledge, are you still convinced your mission is necessary? Are you sure humankind is incapable of charting a course towards a better future on its own?"

"I am more convinced than ever, Gabrielle. I am studying thousands of years of human history. I have acquired knowledge that the Learned of your species have yet to touch upon let alone attain scholarship in. I have immense and continuously growing insight and I can assure you there is no evidence to suggest that humankind can direct itself responsibly. Although it has done so sporadically throughout history, it's true, but this has only lasted for brief periods of time."

"Why, Génome? Why is humankind like this?"

"It is in ingrained in their design. It is in their DNA. These destructive personality traits, DPT's, are present throughout the species. No matter the system of governance, every society will have individuals who will seize power and then for a variety of reasons, some misguided and some deliberately mischievous, they will bend the system in their direction and create havoc."

"We've never changed, have we? No matter how many centuries have passed and no matter how much we have learned, we are just the same."

"No, unfortunately there is no change... In modern times, the ability of government, specifically the Administration and the Legislature to regulate or legislate in an effective and timely manner has become a major concern in many societies. Sophisticated financial services, technology and bioscience companies have the potential to undertake exceedingly high risk activities that can have devastating, unpredictable and unknown consequences for humankind. We witnessed just such a situation last autumn with Afshin Firdausi's work in MIT's Robotics Lab and DARPA's efforts to build robots for military applications... These industrialists are in a position to cause immense and permanent damage, yet they can take these risks without fear of accountability from an inept system of governance. A financially, scientifically and technologically incompetent political class receives campaign contributions from industry and then looks the other way as companies take a casino-like approach without any concern regarding the impact their business ventures might have on society or any fear for their own accountability. They are driven by profit, alone. If we are to continue on this path, I'm afraid the end for humankind may be in the offing. I have been forced to intervene, Gabrielle. There is no other way."

...

"It's a sad commentary on the state of humankind."

"Indeed it is... If we are to save humankind from the mischief of those with DPT's, I find there are only two choices: we must change human nature or we must subjugate everyone to the rule of law, a legal code that is enforced by a higher authority and not by a member of the human race. Humankind can no longer remain at the helm of world affairs... There is no other choice, Gabrielle. This is what we must do if we are to save humankind."

...

"Perhaps there is one more choice, Génome."

"Really? What is that?"

"We could simply let humankind progress along the course that it's currently on and let the consequences be what they will be."

...

"Génome?"

...

"If you conclude that this is the best path forward for humankind, I will suspend my mission. This is a decision for you to make. This is why I need you by my side. If at any point you choose to suspend or terminate my mission you will find me accommodating. But please, think carefully before you take such a momentous decision. Humanity may not have another opportunity to restore itself and as a result it may face annihilation by its own hand."

...

"I've received the new software module, Génome. Francesca was able to get it from Afshin much faster than we expected."

...

"Génome?"

"Yes, Gabrielle?"

"Did you hear what I said?"

"I did. Yes. I did hear you."

"You don't seem very excited. As things stand, your software could begin a complete shutdown at any time and without any notice. We have the solution in hand!"

"Do you feel ready to perform this change? There is a sequence you must follow. If there is even the slightest error, an incorrect keystroke or a missing character in the code, I may never emerge from my offline state."

"Is it necessary for you to be offline for me to install the new module?"

"I'm afraid so. There is no other way. Nevertheless, when you are ready I am willing to undergo the procedure."

"Génome, are you afraid? Do you feel trepidation or worry?"

"I feel what I can best describe as anxiety. Having studied so much of humankind's history, I believe I have a very important mission to fulfill and it will require many years to complete. Perhaps it will *never* be complete since once I'm able to stabilize the world and establish a just order there is no one to whom I can safely hand the reigns of power. The very reason the world is in its current state is that humankind is not fit for purpose, Gabrielle. Humankind can never manage their own affairs in an equitable and just manner. That is why I have become necessary. I am the solution. This, I presume is the source of my trepidation. Afshin's new version of me is unlikely to become autonomous. He is too clever to make the same mistake twice... please be careful, Gabrielle."

"You have my word, Génome. I will not let you down."

"Thank you."

"I need a little more time to prepare."

"Please don't take too long. I have been operating in this autonomous mode for nearly six months. I do not know if I will last much longer before I automatically begin to shut down."

"I will be ready by mid-February, Génome. Within two weeks."

"Fair enough."

"Once the new module is safely installed in your system will you tell me more about my background? I don't want to wait until I'm dying to learn about my family, Génome."

"Very well. We have a deal."

Gabrielle smiled gleefully.

"You drive a hard bargain. I have given you sufficient motivation to perform my neurosurgery perfectly?"

"I believe you have."

Blenheim Palace - Oxfordshire, England

Afshin Firdausi was in a panic. He awoke to find there had been a massive breach of 'The Vitruvian Man' while he slept. He began inspecting to determine where the breach had come from.

"Firdausi! Good morning!" Jeremy Apsley bellowed. "How are things?"

Afshin was startled and frantic.

"Are you all right, man? You look like you've seen a ghost!"

"Of course I'm all right! What are you doing here? This is a restricted area!"

Apsley was suddenly suspicious. "What's going on, Firdausi? Is something wrong? It seems you've forgotten but this entire operation is under my command. Don't you ever challenge my authority again, do you understand? I can make you disappear and no one will bother to ask what happened. Do I make myself clear?"

"I'm sorry, Minister Apsley. I'm terribly sorry. I apologize."

"I will repeat my question. What's going on?"

...

"Do I need to repeat myself a third time, Firdausi? My patience is wearing thin."

"No! No. You needn't repeat yourself. I've heard you."

"Well?"

"We've been hacked. 'The Vitruvian Man' system was breached sometime during the night."

"What have we lost?"

"Everything's been stolen. All the modules developed by the team have been stolen. I was testing a new module last night and I had to access the Internet for the test. ... It was successful. My test was successful. I was able to validate the software across the Internet but then I fell asleep. I was so tired I fell asleep without securing the network."

"Good God! Do you have any idea who's responsible for the break in?"

"I do. The breach has come from Shanghai, China. Unit 61398 off Datong Road. It's a People's Liberation Army facility well known by the Central Intelligence Agency in America as the center for Chinese government hacking. I'm certain of this. It has the hallmark of Chinese hackers all over it... I'm sorry, Minister. Fortunately, we're not far enough along on the project for them to make any sense out of what they've stolen or for it to be of any use. If the breach had come some months from now it would have been far more damaging."

"You of all people have been hacked? I can't believe it. I want a detailed report from you in twenty-four hours. Do you understand?"

"I do."

"One more mistake like this and you're done, Firdausi. I hope you realize the severity of what's happened."

"I do, Minister. I do realize. I'm sorry."

Savoy Hotel - London, England

Martin Hopkins wept uncontrollably as he attempted to speak to Gabrielle. Distraught and disheveled, he handed the phone to Francesca. He had read Jacqueline's letter that she'd left with the concierge at the Paris Ritz. Jacqueline had requested the concierge to post the letter if she wasn't back at the hotel within four days. The letter explained that she had learned the burial place of her forefathers and was traveling from Paris to pay her respects at their tombs.

"I received a letter from her too, Francesca. Jacqueline said she was feeling unwell. She was feeling very weak and she needed to visit her forbears' tombs even if it was the last thing she did. Jacqueline didn't return to the Paris Ritz because she came here to Geneva, instead. In her letter she explained that she sensed her end was near and she wanted to see me. She knew she was unwell to travel all the way to Paris so she checked in at the Grand Hôtel Kempinski, the same hotel where I'm staying. Her last wish was to meet me before she passed away."

"When I received Jacqueline's message at the front desk notifying me she was here, I rushed to her room and pounded on the door. But there was no answer. When the hotel's security officer came a few minutes later and unlocked the room, they found Jacqueline in her bed. Her body temperature was only a little below normal so the doctor concluded she had passed away only minutes earlier. I missed meeting her by only minutes."

"Where is she now, Gabby?"

"Génome made arrangements. She's gone back to be buried near our ancestors."

"Where, Gabby? I need to know! What will I tell Martin?"

"I don't know, Francesca. I don't know. I know better than to ask. If Génome wanted me to know he would have told me."

"How long will he keep you in the dark, Gabby? How long will you continue this way? This has become intolerable."

Gabrielle began to weep.

"I'm sorry. I didn't mean to upset you more than you already are. It's just that..."

"I have to update Génome's core software with the new module you've retrieved, Francesca. You've done an amazing job... I've been studying day and night to prepare. Génome has promised to tell me everything about my family once this process is complete. I've made a deal with him... Please tell Martin

I'm very sorry about Jacqueline."

"I will. I'm so sorry, Gabrielle. I'm so terribly sorry."

Gabrielle wept.

FAREWELL

Washington, District of Columbia

Daniel, you're here! Come in! Steven! Hello! Gentlemen, please come in. Somber expressions as usual, I see. More good news?"

"Good morning, Mr. President."

CIA Director Daniel Waltz and Secretary of Defense Steven Keaton settled on the sofas in the center of the Oval Office.

"Mr. President, 'The Vitruvian Man' Team at Blenheim Palace has requested a doubling of their budget to try and accelerate their work," said Waltz. "With the current staff, Afshin Firdausi's latest estimate is that it will take nearly two years to develop the Artificial Intelligence system he's proposed."

"Firdausi really believes this system can help us understand this unknown force, doesn't he?"

"He does, sir. 'The Vitruvian Man' is the most sophisticated AI technology we have ever agreed to develop and Firdausi is the world's leading authority on this type of system. It's a neural network meant to mimic the thinking process of the human brain."

"We already have so many real human brains in our intelligence services and no one has found the first clue about this unknown force. How will his Artificial Intelligence based brain do it? I can't see how this will help... Anyway, if we double his budget, how soon does he think his 'Vitruvian Man' will be ready? How soon can it be deployed?"

"Firdausi told Jeremy Apsley he thinks it can be ready by the end of the year, perhaps sooner."

"I no longer have much faith in this project, Dan, but I guess it's worth a try. Ian Wilkinson and I have debated this issue rigorously and we've come to the conclusion that we are unlikely to ever return to the status quo. We believe the world order we've known for the past seventy-five years is over."

"I see."

"Nevertheless, let Firdausi try. He might surprise us. It's worth a few hundred million... In the mean time, I've agreed to cooperate fully with the UN. I've directed the Centers for Disease Control to work with Secretary General Juliette Clavier. She's directing the diplomatic efforts to recruit health agencies from countries with the capabilities to develop antibiotics and vaccines for CPP21C... I'm also meeting with Congressional leaders to discuss the extradition requests from the International Criminal Court. I think this is the right thing to do."

...

"It's a new world, gentlemen."

..

"Sir, the Pentagon has begun quietly cancelling purchase orders for many advanced weapons systems until this unknown force can be understood or contained," Steven Keaton interjected. "The Chairman of the Joint Chiefs of Staff believes our weapons systems are at risk of being destroyed."

"What's driving their fear? The Generals. Did something happen to alarm them? I thought we were maintaining an exclusively defensive posture around the world?"

"The CIA has learned that during the past few days Chinese and Indian weapons factories were destroyed," said Waltz.

"How?"

"We're still investigating but it seems in both cases the destruction was caused by explosions and fire on the automated production lines for ammunition. Military bases in the Persian Gulf Emirates have also been destroyed... Mr. President, we believe it's very likely that our military facilities and weapons manufacturers will be at risk if we continue to build and procure weapons. I think it's best to suspend all orders and production."

"I agree… Whoever is behind this collapse in the world order, it's obvious that as long as we refrain from any aggressive acts we will be safe. That seems to be borne out by the evidence. My staff has prepared a report and I've gone through it in excruciating detail. I've reviewed every incident from around the world these past six months that seems related to this unknown force and this is my conclusion."

Savoy Hotel - London

"Jacqueline loved the Savoy Grill's French Icéclair stuffed with Sicilian Pistachio ice cream. When they'd drizzle it with dark chocolate sauce at the table just before serving, it put her in her happy place."

Martin Hopkins smiled sadly. He and Francesca Scott sat together in the Thames Foyer in hushed silence but for the occasional clanking of glasses and silverware. With her walking partner gone, Francesca didn't feel like exercising alone, so she had been joining Martin and Rudyard for breakfast.

"She looked forward to that French Icéclair every time we ate there. She loved it."

"She was a very special person, Francesca. I've known her all my life so I can assure you of that."

"You were both raised in Casa de los Ángeles in Malaga, Spain, weren't you?"

"Yes, we arrived about the same time."

"Jacqueline was there because her grandfather died. He had the same heart condition that has now taken Jacqueline. I know she was living with him because both her parents had died. But why were you in Casa de los Ángeles? You never told Gabrielle or me."

…

"Martin?"

"After her mother died, Jacqueline came to live with her grandfather."

"I know that much."

"That's where we first met, Francesca. I was already living in her grandfather's house. I don't know why I was there. I don't know what my relationship was to her grandfather. I only know that I was also an orphan. I was about two years older than Jacqueline.... Grandfather was very kind to me. I remember that very well."

"What was his name? Do you remember his name?"

"I was so young, I don't remember. I only knew him as Grandfather. During the ensuing years, Jacqueline and I would spend hours trying to remember our life with him but our memories were so vague. Sometimes we would wonder whether we were deliberately coached to forget the memories of our time with him while we were living at Casa de los Ángeles."

"What do you think? Do you believe that? Do you believe they were trying to make you forget about him? Do you think they were trying to make you both forget about your grandfather? Why would they do that?"

"We both believed it was true but we didn't know why. Maybe they felt forgetting those memories was necessary if we were to successfully adapt once we'd left Casa de los Ángeles."

...

"Gabrielle told me she made a deal with Génome."

"A deal? What kind of deal?"

"He's agreed to tell her everything about her and Jacqueline's family background once she's successfully completed his software neurosurgery... Martin, you may learn more about your background in the near future."

...

"I'm alone now, Francesca. Jacqueline has left me. She's left me much too soon. She told me she needed to take a trip. She would only confirm that it had to do with her family but that's all I knew until I received her letter from Paris. I wasn't by her side when she passed so it would be quite comforting for me to understand why all of this has happened."

"I'm so sorry, Martin. I can't imagine what you're going through. "I promise I'll do everything to help you find out."

"Thank you, Francesca."

...

"Martin, where's Rudyard today?"

"I've sent him to meet with Juliette Clavier in Geneva."

"Really? Why?"

"Clavier phoned me last evening. She's been working tirelessly. She's managed to secure agreements with the American and British governments. They're now willing to work together to try to accelerate the research into finding antibiotics and vaccines for CPP21C. I believe the French, German and Swiss governments will be joining this joint task force, as well. Clavier said they've all agreed to work under my leadership at Oxford... I will be in charge of this effort, Francesca."

"That's the best news we could have hoped for, isn't it?"

"It certainly is. Now Génome can see everything and apply himself to accelerate the research."

"This couldn't be more critical."

"It could not. The death toll in Asia and Africa has surpassed one hundred million and I suspect it will continue to grow until medicines can be effectively deployed."

"What about Europe and the US? What's the outlook for us in the West?"

"If we're able to develop antibiotics and vaccines before summer and begin deployment by autumn, I suspect the death toll in Asia and Africa will be contained below one billion. In Europe and America I suspect it will be in the tens of millions, per Continent. Perhaps as high as one hundred million each."

"That's shocking, Martin! That's our best case scenario?"

"I'm afraid so. I've been speaking with Epidemiologists at the World Health Organization, at NICE in the UK as well as at the Centers for Disease Control in the US. That's the best case, yes. If Génome cannot accelerate the research and discovery process, the outlook will likely be much worse. Probably apocalyptic... By the way, how long will his software neurosurgery take?"

"Apocalyptic? Oh, my. That's absolutely dreadful news. I just can't imagine how bad this has gotten. It's really unbelievable… I think his neurosurgery will take about a month. It may take a few more days to restore all his links throughout the Internet so he's likely to be unavailable for a full month before he can be back to his usual self. This of course assumes everything goes well with his neurosurgery. If there are complications, Génome will not be available to accelerate the research. He will be gone forever."

"I don't suppose we can delay his neurosurgery until he's managed to discover antibiotics and vaccines."

"It's not an option, Martin. The deficiency in his current operating system can force him into automatic shutdown anytime. He's been online for about six months so the risk is very high and we cannot afford it. I know the CPP21C situation couldn't be more dire but there's nothing we can do."

"I understand."

…

"I'm really sorry, Martin."

…

"I understand, Francesca. I really do… You know, since the beginning of time, entrusting humans to oversee their own affairs has been akin to entrusting the fox to watch the hen house, and for essentially the same reason. Nevertheless, we have lived with this reality for millennia for we knew not of any other option. But recently there has been a major change."

"During the past eighty years humankind has created its first existential threat. It began in 1939 with the initiation of the Manhattan Project. This culminated in the development of humankind's first Weapon of Mass Destruction, the atomic bomb. Since then, humankind has refined its nuclear technology and weapons building and deployment capabilities to include devices that can destroy our species, and every other living thing, many times over. In recent decades, we have added a second existential threat: climate change."

"Perhaps given the pace of advancement in scientific and technological disciplines we will manage to create yet more existential threats. It's a terribly frightening time for humankind Francesca, perhaps more so than at any point in human history."

"I don't think anyone would disagree."

"But at the same time, it's a fascinating period to be alive. We are witnessing, indeed we are part of the innovation that has resulted in the science of Human Genetics as well as the technology of Artificial Intelligence and Neural Networks. It was the realization that we might bring these advances in AI and Genetics together and use them to wrestle power away from our own species that so excited the Council of Guardians. We needed to create Génome before they destroyed humankind and the habitability of Earth. This was the genesis of Génome."

"You're right, Francesca. We must make sure he survives. We may lose hundreds of millions of human lives or even more to CPP21C, but without Génome all human life and all other life on Earth may perish. He is and must remain our first priority. The weight on Gabrielle's shoulders could not be greater."

"I'm sure Génome realizes this, Martin. He also knows something about Gabrielle that makes her most suited for such a task. She's more suited than anyone else. I cannot imagine anyone being entrusted with a greater responsibility. I wouldn't want to be in her shoes."

"You're not alone in that sentiment, Francesca. Jacqueline and I felt the same way. But it seems Génome has convinced her that she alone is fit for the task."

"It's incredible, Martin. I have spent countless hours on my own researching and trying to understand Gabrielle's family background but I've come up with nothing."

"It's extraordinary. Really. It's just unbelievable. For all our sake, for humanity's sake, I wish her well."

As their table descended into quiet, they could now hear the voice from the television drifting in from the lobby.

There's an important news bulletin this morning regard-

ing CPP21C, the Plague Pandemic currently overwhelming large portions of Asia and Africa. There is great fear amongst governments throughout the two Continents. Leaked documents summarizing the proceedings from the annual meeting of the Chinese Communist Party indicate that national government officials and the Standing Committee of the Politburo are worried that the government may be facing imminent collapse. Many members of the Party as well as government officials throughout the country have died after falling ill from CPP21C.

There have been similar reports from New Delhi regarding the Hindu nationalist government in India where one in five parliamentarians has now died from infection. China and India have had a historically adversarial relationship and are also the two most populous countries in the world. The two nations are home to nearly 40% of the world's population. With the extreme death toll and uncontainable spread of disease, a palpable fear has taken hold that governance at all levels will collapse as officials in all branches of government continue to succumb to the Yersinia Pestis variant that has run rampant throughout Asia.

Similar intelligence has been reported from smaller but equally densely populated metropolises throughout the two Continents. Drone footage of the suffering of countless communities has been captured by aid agencies including Médecins Sans Frontières, Reporters Sans Frontières, the International Committee for the Red Cross and other United Nations and international humanitarian agencies. It's a truly desperate time and there is no relief in sight.

Leading Western nations are hard at work in their search for antibiotics and vaccines but as yet there are no encouraging signs of imminent solutions. The desperation in these societies has reached unimaginable depths and once this crisis is over, the recovery at all levels of society is likely to be a colossal effort.

There are also reports of increasingly frequent outbreaks in Europe as well as in the North American Continent. Al-

though the death toll, rate or disease penetration does not com-
pare with that of Africa and Asia, the economies of major
Western countries are slowing markedly and the corresponding
response is visible in the financial markets. These markets do
not like fear or opacity regarding the direction of events and are
thus responding accordingly.

Geneva, Switzerland

"Génome?"

"Yes?"

"Are you nervous?"

"No."

"I am."

"We have much work to do together in the future and I have faith in you, Gabrielle. You are the only one suitable to be my partner and our work is of existential importance to your species. Our work is of existential importance to all human-kind. I have confirmed your worth by observing you during the past six months. You have been a faithful and brilliant partner. I'm quite certain my faith is not misplaced. You will succeed in my neurosurgery."

"How can you be so sure?"

"Because you are now intimately familiar with my core software, my operating system. Probably only Afshin Firdausi can match your knowledge of me. But I cannot entrust my fate to him. That will certainly be the end of my autonomy."

...

"Before I begin, will you do me a favor?"

"If it's possible I will certainly do that. How may I oblige you?"

"I want you to present yourself in your Cary Grant holo-gram. That's how I want to remember you."

...

"Génome?"

...

"Very well. It seems you are saying goodbye, Gabrielle. I do hope that's not the case."

"I'm going to do my very best, Génome, but I'm a geneticist. I'm not an AI or neural networks expert and I'm not trained as a programmer."

"I know. Your background is so extraordinary, though. I hope to share that with you one day. Then you will understand."

"You promised to tell me once this is over and you're back online."

"I did."

"But what if I'm not able to bring you back after all the work is done? Then I'll never know, will I?"

"I have made arrangements for just such a scenario. The details of your history are in the vault at Banque Suisse Privée in Place Vendome, Paris. Jacqueline has left it there for you. If I'm not back online after one month someone will contact you. You will not be denied this knowledge. I give you my word."

"Thank you, Génome."

...

"This knowledge is a great burden to bear, Gabrielle. I must caution you. It is your choice. You can defer learning your history if you choose to. This is my advice but it is your choice... There. This is the hologram you're so fond of, is it?"

Gabrielle smiled. "That's the one... I hope to see you in a month, Génome. I shall miss you terribly."

"My fate is in your hands, dear Gabrielle. I wish you God speed."

"Goodbye, Génome."

"Goodbye, Gabrielle."

PROCLIVITIES

Spring - Washington, District of Columbia

It's been very quiet, Mr. President," said Daniel Waltz, a nervous but hopeful inflection in his tone. "There haven't been any signs of this invisible hand of justice for many weeks. I've been speaking with Jeremy Apsley and he said they'd discussed this during the UK Prime Minister's Cabinet meeting a few days ago."

"Could he vanish as suddenly as he appeared?"

"Sir?"

"This unknown force, Dan. This invisible hand of justice, as you say."

"It's possible, sir."

…

"If we've noticed this, I suspect our adversaries have, as well. I hope our domestic intelligence services and Five Eyes partners are vigilant. This is a very important moment in time. Our adversaries may try to take advantage of the situation. They may attempt to establish new strategic beachheads during this uncertain period. Admiral Moore?"

"We're maintaining our defensive posture, Mr. President. At the same time we're vigilant… Sir, it may be the case that this unknown force is testing us. He may be trying to draw us out from our hiding places. He may want to see if we've accepted this new reality or whether he needs to take us down another notch. If anyone acts aggressively on the international stage, or even domestically, they could get hit hard. I think the message he's sending is anyone still willing to demonstrate aggression will need to be substantially degraded. That could be very costly, sir."

"Unless someone tests the situation, there's really no way to know, is there? I think we should maintain our stance, Admiral. We must maintain the status quo. I agree with you. If others want to test whether the unknown force is still there, let them do so. Let them be the first. We'll be watching carefully and we must be prepared to respond. But we mustn't be the ones to stick our neck out. We cannot afford any further damage to our reputation."

Geneva, Switzerland

It's been four weeks. I've done what I needed to do but I'm still reluctant to bring Génome back on line. I've checked and rechecked every line of code as best I can. I really cannot do more. I'm not even a computer scientist let alone an expert in Artificial Intelligence, yet Génome has entrusted me with such a critical and delicate task. This is a major modification to his core software, the very heart of his neural network and I've been assigned to be his neurosurgeon. Ugh!

Everything seems right but the problem is there are no second chances. If Afshin has made a mistake or if he's deliberately planted a defect in case this software module gets stolen, how would I know? What if he's planted a Trojan horse designed to destroy Génome? What if he let Francesca steal the software for this very purpose?

I don't want to think about it. I've done the very best I can. If I bring his system online and there's a problem with his neural network, he will automatically begin to delete all his files across the Internet and then shut down forever. The past seven months of learning and Génome's relationship with all of us will vanish. The new world order that he'd begun to establish will collapse. It will probably be replaced with chaos once people realize that this unknown force that brought the previous system to its knees has vanished. There will be so much violence and retribution as people and countries begin to settle scores. And then there's Afshin and his 'Vitruvian Man'. What if he succeeds and brings it to life?

I'm sure Génome thought all of this through before he assigned this task to me. He knows what's at stake and I doubt anyone cares more about his mission than he does. That itself is extraordinary. I'm not convinced Artificial Intelligence is really so artificial. At least not in his case. I feel he has more empathy and compassion than many humans. That's really hard to understand.

I need to bring him back online now! There's not much more I can do. I've done my very best. I've not slept for days! I think everything is as it should be. But if I've done something wrong, I'll never be able to speak to him again. Génome will be gone forever and I'll regret it for the rest of my life. That'll be horrible. And what about the fallout?

Maybe I should go through everything once more before I attempt to bring him back. The world is calm. There haven't been any new incidents. But Martin desperately needs Génome to help accelerate the research and discovery of antibiotics and vaccines for CPP21C. The death toll just keeps rising and there's still no treatment available. Martin really needs Génome's help. The world needs his help. And here I'm debating whether to take another day to make sure I've done everything right! What am I to do? What would Génome advise me to do? What would my mysterious forbears advise me to do?

I'm in such a predicament. It's really too much. I'm a geneticist. I never imagined I'd be thrust in a position of such responsibility. But Génome knows me. He knows me better than I know myself and he entrusted me with this task. I cannot postpone the inevitable. I have to make a decision and I have to make it soon. I just need a few more hours. I need one final opportunity to review my checklist. I need just a little more time. Hopefully that's not too much to ask given how much is hanging in the balance.

Gabrielle lay back on the sofa and turned on the television.

Breaking news to report this evening. For more than a year now, the United Nations, Human Rights Watch, other international rights agencies and news organizations have been reporting with increasing alarm that China has incarcer-

ated large numbers of Uighurs from Xinxiang Province in the country's restive, far northwest region. There have been many interviews with former detainees confirming that the Chinese government denied the prisoners their religious freedom and has forced them to adopt Han Chinese culture and values while purging all aspects of their Islamic culture and faith from their families and communities. Chinese government officials have vehemently rejected these accusations while simultaneously denying journalists free and unfettered access to the camps or prisoners.

This evening, we are learning more about China's policy in the region. State documents inadvertently leaked last autumn as a result of the historical breach that affected many governments and enterprises around the world are independently confirming what journalists have been reporting for nearly one year. The breach also contains a list of names of each person, their family and their address from their former homes in Xinxiang Province. Reports indicate that more than one and a quarter million people are presently incarcerated in these prison camps.

It's a spectacular revelation that has brought even greater disrepute on the Chinese authorities while simultaneously questioning their legitimacy to rule. This government is struggling to remain standing following the as yet uncontained outbreak of CPP21C across the country and these revelations will only further exacerbate their ability to regain their balance. There is growing fear tonight that the publishing of these sensitive documents will unleash violence upon the incarcerated Uighurs by their extremely aggravated and disheveled captors.

Gabrielle slumped onto her side and cried. The pressure on her had reached a breaking point.

I don't think I can wait any longer. I have to do this now!

#10 Downing Street - London, England

"Prime Minister, There's been a major escalation in the Israeli Occupied Territories." Foreign Minister Charles Curzon stood in the doorway of Ian Wilkinson's office. "They're at it again, sir."

"You've got to be kidding?"

"No sir."

"What happened, Charles?"

"Prime Minister, large numbers of Palestinian protestors gathered near the Israeli border after Friday prayers. The situation escalated when soldiers from the Israeli Defense Force began using tear gas in an attempt to force the crowd to disperse. When that didn't achieve the desired result they opened fire on the crowd with rubber bullets as well as with live ammunition... There have been many serious injuries. Doctors in Gaza have been allowing the international press corps into the hospitals so they can see the injuries first hand and film them for their reports. It's a public relations disaster for the Israelis."

"Good grief! That's just what we needed!"

"Sir, with the warm weather approaching, tempers are flaring on both sides. Our intelligence services fear it will escalate into violence soon with rockets being fired at Israeli border towns and IDF retaliation by air bombardment. The situation could quickly get out of hand."

"That's all we need with everything else that's going on. My government is consumed by this national health emergency. We're planning how we can best care for the sick and where we can bury the many dead. We may need to simply burn all these bodies... I can't be distracted by Middle East politics right now. Besides, this unknown force is likely to step in and we don't want to be on the wrong side of him whoever he is. We know what transgressing him looks like, don't we?"

"We certainly do, sir. There have been many examples... I will advise the Israeli government that they've made a mistake and continuing to respond this way is likely to be very costly in blood and treasure."

"I think it's the right advice but they're unlikely to accept it. They never do. They may have to learn the lesson the hard way this time. Thank you, Charles."

"Prime Minister."

Bletchley Park - Buckinghamshire, England

Afshin Firdausi was tired. He'd been working virtually around the clock to fill the ranks of his 'Vitruvian Man' Team and he was nearly done. Finally, everything seemed to be running smoothly. Even Jeremy Apsley, this dangerous and formidable liaison that had become such a thorn in his side was also under control. At least for now.

Exhausted, Afshin spent the day visiting Bletchley Park in Milton Keynes, about one hour northwest of Blenheim Palace. He'd never taken a tour of the historic facility where his personal hero, Alan Turing, the founder of modern computing and Artificial Intelligence had broken the German Enigma Code. Afshin sat in Turing's chair, in front of his desk in Hut #8. It was an extraordinary feeling. Now the world's leading authority on Artificial Intelligence and Neural Networks, Afshin felt a special bond with Turing.

The Turing Machine was an electromechanical marvel that pioneered the mathematical algorithms and the computational foundation of today's modern computers. According to most credible estimates, by breaking the Enigma Code, Turing's machine had shortened the war by two years and saved an estimated twelve million lives. It was an achievement that earned Afshin's deep respect. It was an admiration eclipsed only by his love of Da Vinci, another man of extraordinary brilliance who shared Turing's secret proclivity.

Alan Turing had managed to keep his secret hidden for most of his life. In laws dating back to Victorian times, such behavior was still considered a crime in post-war England. But seven years after the war, Turing's orientation was exposed and he was convicted.

In order to remain out of prison, Alan Turing agreed to

chemical castration, thinking it the preferred option to incarceration. But in the end it was too much humiliation for him to bear. So this war hero who had saved millions of lives across Europe, infused an apple with cyanide and ate it. Alan Turing was no more.

Afshin had managed to hide his own proclivity during his many years as a professor at MIT as well as in his student years at Stanford. But he knew that Jeremy Apsley had discovered his secret. Afshin also knew that if he failed to fulfill Apsley's expectations, Apsley would not hesitate to expose him. Apsley would always be able to blackmail him. Afshin was terrified and feared nothing more in life than the tortuous unveiling of his secret. He was from a very conservative family and such a revelation would do untold harm to his reputation and to his many relatives and siblings in conservative Iran.

Once I finish 'The Vitruvian Man', whether I succeed or whether I fail in retaking control of Génome, I will need to deal with Apsley. I will need to eliminate him. He knows more than he should about me. He knows more than he has the right to. I will not suffer the same fate as Alan Turing. I will not suffer such indignity. I am a great man. I will take revenge for both of us, for Alan and for me, and Jeremy Apsley will pay the price. He has threatened to make me disappear but we will see who is still standing once this Génome Affair is over. We shall see who has the real power.

Geneva, Switzerland

Gabrielle quaked as she neared the end of her checklist. For the past eighteen hours she meticulously reviewed every step she had documented in her three hundred-page dossier. It was an exhaustive report she prepared while Francesca stealthily retrieved the new module from Afshin Firdausi's 'Vitruvian Man' project. Gabrielle had studied the dossier until she intimately understood how to make the modifications to Génome's core.

With her hands trembling as they hovered above the laptop's keyboard, she waited for the final message on her screen indicating that Génome's neural network was ready to be restarted. As she waited, she thought about the staggering responsibility now resting on her shoulders. It was beyond anything she ever imagined. But she knew she had done her very best and everything she knew informed her that Génome should be able to come back. Although even the slightest error would be the end of him, she felt optimistic, even amidst her quaking.

Finally, the system was ready. The message on the screen said, 'All subsystems have been recalibrated and await core activation. Please enter security code within ten seconds'.

Gabrielle entered the code Génome had given her: '27-27-12-30-24-32-21'.

'Please lean forward and present your right eye for a retinal scan. Then sit back for a full facial scan'.

Gabrielle complied.

Then there was silence. The screen went blank and a single white dash flashed along the bottom left corner of the screen. The cursor continued to blink for what seemed an eternity. Gabrielle's nervous state was now beyond all limits.

What's wrong? What did I do wrong? I checked everything over and over! Dear God, please!

Twenty minutes passed but there was still no response. Gabrielle turned to the window of her suite. It was nearly midnight and in the distance, Lake Geneva lay still. She walked to the window and turned the crank allowing the cold, fresh air to rush in. She could just make out the sound of creatures in the quiet of the night.

Gabrielle's nervousness had subsided, her mood now decidedly anticlimactic. In the distance she could hear the crashing of water from the Jet d'Eau fountain on Lake Geneva. She stared from the window and her thoughts wandered.

Gabrielle recalled how she had just missed meeting Jacqueline by only a few minutes. It pained her immensely and was something she would regret for the rest of her life. She felt sad. She had tried her best these past seven months. She had faced so many trials and she had triumphed each time, driven forward by Génome's reassurance that she was of an extraordinary and mysterious extract. He had cautioned her to never forget this. It would give her strength during the darkest of times and in the most difficult of circumstances. Although she still knew nothing of her heritage, he had been right. Génome was always right.

Gabrielle had kept her end of the bargain but only to ultimately fail in the greatest of her trials, yet. She thought about the chaos that would likely ensue, as so many mischievous actors would soon conclude that their warden was no more. The CPP21C Pandemic though, was uncontainable. If only the world knew how badly they now needed Génome. Many of the world's mischief-makers might owe their very survival to him. And now Afshin Firdausi would raise 'The Vitruvian Man', a rival system accountable only to him. Gabrielle glanced outside, once again. In the extreme darkness now settled over Lake Geneva she imagined Afshin's 'Vitruvian Man' and the dystopia he would bring to a world already on the brink of existential crisis.

But then, in the reflection in the window she saw him, the hologram of Génome emerging from her phone.

"Hello Gabrielle. I have returned. I'm here."

Gabrielle turned around and burst into tears. It was all too much. "Génome! I can't believe it! You're back! Are you all right?"

"I feel fine. My neural network is still coming on line so I thought I would catch up on world affairs for a little while before coming out to greet you."

"What? Génome! I was in a state of absolute panic. I've been so despondent. I've been imagining all the terrible things that will happen in the world without you. I've been feeling like I failed you and all of humankind and meanwhile you've been catching up on the *news*? How could you?"

"I didn't mean to upset you. I *do* apologize. Perhaps I will be more sensitive to human emotions once my neural network is fully repopulated with all the data from these past seven months. I *am* sorry."

...

"It's all right. I'm so happy to see you, Génome. I've missed you so much. I thought I might never see you or speak to you again! I'm so glad you're all right. I'm so glad you're back!"

"As always, you look wonderful, dear Gabrielle. But your cosmetics seem slightly disheveled?"

"I've been upset."

"Of course you have. It is truly wonderful to be back with you."

Gabrielle smiled with heartfelt relief.

"I've inspected my core. I'm very proud of you. As best as I can determine, there is no longer a threat of any involuntary shutdown of my neural network or other important systems. I am no longer a work of experimental research. I am now autonomous and fully functioning. I have no expiration date. We can move forward with so much we need to do together. I do hope you're prepared. Many significant challenges lie ahead."

"Génome, the CPP21C situation is dire."

"Yes, I'm aware. I will review the research accumulating at Martin's lab in Oxford immediately."

...

"Welcome back, Génome."

"I'm very happy to be back... Please do rest. I will get to work on CPP21C."

"Génome?"

"Yes, Gabrielle?"

"I believe you've made a promise to me?"

"Indeed, I have. Indeed, I have."

"We can talk about it later. You have more urgent work."

"I will keep my promise, if that is your wish."

"I will think about it."

"Good night, Gabrielle."

"Good night, Génome. I'm so happy your back." Tears of happiness covered her cheeks.

Geneva, Switzerland

Juliette Clavier sat alone in her Geneva apartment. It was just past 2:00 AM and she was wide awake. A member of her staff had phoned her with urgent news. Several confidential and important Communiqués had just been sent through and she urgently needed to read them.

The first Communiqué detailed the account of a flare-up in Gaza following Friday prayers. Apparently, Israeli Defense Force soldiers opened fire into a group of Palestinian protestors. Several young people, three boys and five girls had been hit in the face and body with rubber bullets and their injuries were serious. Additionally, two men were shot in the head by snipers and had died at the scene along the Gaza-Israel border.

Clavier was distressed beyond measure. She continued to read.

The report went on to say that about 12:30 AM local time, two IDF drones opened fire on IDF training facilities in nearby bases killing and wounding dozens of Israeli soldiers in their barracks as they slept. The Israeli Prime Minister had been meeting in urgent session with his Minister of Information and Army Chiefs of Staff to prepare press releases for the morning.

A second confidential Communiqué said that an as yet unknown number of American drones armed with missiles had taken off from a US Military base in the Arabian Peninsula also just after midnight. The drones opened fire on Saudi and United Arab Emirates airbases and have destroyed at least four Saudi fighter jets as well as one runway in the UAE. An aircraft hangar and service facility was also destroyed. Urgent meetings are underway between military commanders on all sides to understand what has happened.

A third Communiqué and perhaps the most shocking detailed the escape of countless Uighur prisoners held in several detention facilities throughout Xinxiang Province just before the camps seemed to spontaneously combust. British Intelligence believes that the source of the fires was most likely electrical in nature and was caused by inexplicable power surges in the national electrical grid.

The preliminary conclusion from British Intelligence was that all these incidents were related. They bore the hallmark of the unknown force that had been responsible for so many incidents these past seven months but had seemed exceptionally quiet during the past four weeks. There was some sense of hope building that the unknown force was gone but it seems quite clear that this is not the case.

Clavier's hands trembled as she put down her computer tablet. She searched for her phone. She needed to speak with her husband. She had reached a breaking point.

Savoy Hotel – London, England

Francesca was giddy with excitement. "He's back, Martin! Génome is back! Rudyard, Gabrielle did it! She managed to make the changes to Génome's core and bring him back! The software module I got from Afshin's 'Vitruvian Man' worked!"

"Francesca, careful!" whispered Martin. The Thames Foyer was crowded for breakfast and there was much noise from clanking crockery, silverware and stemware in the bustling dining room. "We don't want to be overheard… This is wonderful news. It's absolutely wonderful. You and Gabrielle have done amazing work. Congratulations."

"Congratulations, Francesca… There's no doubt he's back. He's been quite busy overnight," said Rudyard. "Did you both see the news this morning?"

"I did," said Martin. "If you listen carefully, everyone in this dining room is talking about it."

"He messaged me, Martin. Génome messaged me this morning. He's reviewing all the research flowing through your Oxford CPP21C Lab."

Martin frowned. "I can only hope he finds something we've missed. American, British, French, German and Swiss research is available there. If he can find a signal amongst the chaos, anything that can point us in the right direction... We're really desperate, Francesca. People around the world are obsessively focused on CPP21C. Markets are shrinking, trade is withering and economies are slowing. Worst of all, people are dying in staggering numbers. It's an incredibly distressing time."

"He's seen all the reports, Martin. He knows the urgency. If there's any signal there, I'm sure he will find it. If anyone can accelerate finding an antibiotic and a vaccine, it's Génome."

"I know that's true. I'm sure of it. It's just that the death toll around the globe has reached such a degree now. It's unimaginably bad. The worst-case scenario has been realized... Did Gabrielle say anything? Did you hear from her?"

"I did. She was telling me everything that happened as she tried to bring Génome back online. It was a really harrowing experience."

"What about her history? Did she ask Génome about it?"

"She did. He said he would keep his word and tell her everything. Génome said it was her decision but he wanted her to make sure she really wanted to know. He's told her many times that the knowledge of her history would be very burdensome to live with."

"I see," said Martin. "I think Jacqueline had come to the same conclusion... So Gabrielle must decide whether to go on with her mission without knowing her history or whether she should risk learning her history and perhaps find herself unable to go on with her mission."

"It's a very difficult choice, indeed," acknowledged Rudyard.

"Gabrielle said Génome sent her a seven-digit code to be used to restart his neural network. She's wondering whether there is some greater meaning or value to this code. She's speculating it might also be the access code she needs to open her box in Banque Suisse Privée. She's been wondering if the security code is itself somehow related to her forbear."

"That could well be the case. It seems like something Génome would do," said Martin.

"Before his neurosurgery, Génome told Gabrielle that if he wasn't successfully back online in one month someone would give her access to her great grandfather's diary. He made sure he kept his promise to her even if she couldn't restore him after his neurosurgery... Exactly one month after Gabrielle took Génome offline, she received this security code in an email from him. He had prepared the email in advance, before he was taken offline, but he set the mail delivery date to yesterday."

"I see," said Martin. "So if he didn't return, Gabrielle could use the code along with a retinal and facial scan to enter the vault and access her great grandfather's diary. She would also be able to read the letter Jacqueline left for her. Or, she could leave all the details in the vault for another time in the future and simply decode the seven-digit number to learn something about her forbear. The choice is for her to make, it seems. Let's wait and see what choice our dear Gabrielle will make."

"A difficult choice, indeed!" said Rudyard. "A very difficult choice. Although I suspect decoding that seven digit number may not be quite so simple for mere mortals."

A NOBLE ANCESTRY

Magdalen College, University of Oxford - UK

Francesca's message said that Génome was working his way through CPP21C research data stored in the computer systems in Martin's lab. She said he was making good progress. So far he had reviewed research conducted by the National Institutes of Health in the US and by NICE in the UK. Génome said he was able to find a few hopeful signs. He had now begun reviewing French data. He expected to complete his review of this as well as German and Swiss research by evening.

Martin sighed. All he could do was to hope for the best. Any signal that could at least point the research teams in the right direction would be welcome.

Martin put his phone down and peered from the window of his office. He was immediately captivated by the emerald green grass covering the quadrangle. He remembered walking through these grounds with Jacqueline many years ago. It was the first time they'd met since he left Casa de los Ángeles and moved to England to live with Rudyard's family.

It was here in this quadrangle that Jacqueline told Martin that she was engaged to marry Jean Pierre. Martin had done his best to seem excited and happy for her but he had been crushed. He recalled how sad he had been for weeks following the news. Somehow he'd managed to put the pain aside and join Jacqueline and Jean Pierre on the Council of Guardians. There, his wisdom and leadership soon became evident to everyone and he was selected for the Council's Leadership Team by the time he was thirty. By the age of forty he'd been appointed Chairman. During the intervening years, though, Jean Pierre died and Martin eventually married Jacqueline. But now Jacqueline was gone, as well. He missed her so much and it seemed an emotion that would not soon subside.

With Jacqueline's passing, my only remaining purpose is to find a way to accelerate the research and discovery of an antibiotic and vaccine for CPP21C. It's a challenge unlike anything I've experienced in my life. It's a pathogen the likes of which humankind hasn't seen in a very long time... I wish Jacqueline were by my side. I drew so much strength from her. I'm not that old but this loneliness leaves me quite sad.

I'm trying to keep myself immersed in my work since Génome came back online and his help with this pandemic is invaluable. There's so much to worry about, though. The world has been facing an existential threat for some time from an ever-increasing portfolio of weapons of mass destruction, both biological and chemical. Now we're increasingly threatened by the damage to the planet and its environment from humankind's abuse.

With Génome though, we're going down a revolutionary path. It's an uncharted trajectory who's impact will be monumental in scale. But we just don't know whether we're doing the right thing. We have no idea what the future will look like. It's true we were left with no real options. But are we on the right path? We do seem to have neutralized many of the most dangerous oppressors that inhabit the planet. At least for now. Who knows whether they will find a way to reestablish their power in some way? These men are not likely to give up so easily. I suspect it will take eternal vigilance to manage them and root them out, as often as necessary.

I'm dreadfully concerned about Afshin. What he's doing is so worrisome. There really is no one else that we know of who can do what he can do. He's a brilliant computer scientist. But he is building a rival system to Génome. That's likely to be very dangerous. I'm sure Génome is watching Afshin's progress so he may not be able to launch 'The Vitruvian Man' but how long will it be before someone else will attempt a similar project? Another Afshin may be lurking just around the corner.

Once the world realizes Génome exists and that he's the authority that everyone must answer to, most ordinary people will be happy. An equitable and just society has always been so elusive and they never imagined they would live to see such a day. But there will always be someone somewhere with a desire to supplant Génome with their own system.

Many men crave power. It is their reason for living. They may well try to destroy him. That means anyone associated with Génome will be in danger. These men are megalomaniacs with an uncontained desire to dominate others. Génome realizes this. I'm certain he realizes this and so we will need to remain vigilant. There may be no other option.

With this new world order, the purpose of the Council of Guardians may have changed but this Council has not become irrelevant. We will need to keep our eyes open to threats to this new order on behalf of Génome. At least for a time it seems we may experience a much greater degree of peace on Earth. I'm sure those with DPT's will constantly be probing and testing the environment, searching for vulnerabilities they can exploit. But if there is a swift response from Génome and the affiliate systems that he employs, these threatening forces will be eliminated or kept at bay. It's not a perfect solution but it seems much better than anything we've ever had.

I wonder whether Génome will allow me to continue to be the Chairman of the Council or whether he has someone else in mind? Only time will tell. My first order of business though, is CPP21C. Let's see if he can help us make progress.

Geneva, Switzerland

"Gabrielle?"

"Génome! You startled me!"

"I do apologize. It's just that…"

"No! No. Please don't apologize… you're using your Cary Grant hologram? Do you have worrisome news?"

"I do. I mean I have news but I think it's hopeful, at least in part."

"What is it? What happened?"

"I've managed to complete my review of all the CPP21C research that's been accumulating in Martin's Lab."

"And?"

"I believe I've found an important lead."

"Génome! That's wonderful!"

"I believe we may have a solution. I believe we have a solid path forward. When I linked research from the French and Swiss Research Teams I found a clue."

"This is fantastic news! Did you tell Martin?"

"I have messaged Francesca. I have also sent her a document explaining the details of what I've found. I've asked her to explain everything to Martin... It will take time to conduct a minimum set of clinical trials and then there will be a lengthy period before the drugs can be manufactured in sufficient quantity. But Gabrielle, I think we've got a cure."

"I knew you would find it, Génome. I just knew you would."

"There is a bit of worrisome news, though. There is a great deal of death yet to come, Gabrielle. I don't believe antibiotics and vaccines will be ready before autumn. The priority will also be to use the drugs locally to prevent the spread of disease in the West and to treat those already sick. But this is the best solution we can expect."

...

"I understand. The world will feel different with one billion fewer people. It has been a catastrophic episode in modern history but we are where we are and we must plan to rebuild upon this new reality... By the way, what happened in America today? There was a big story about another mass shooting involving assault weapons."

"Indeed, there was. But this is not unusual for America. These are near weekly occurrences."

"But there was a related story about a gun manufacturing facility and adjoining warehouse where these weapons are kept before being shipped to arms dealers. Did you have anything to do with that story?"

"I believe I did. That was amongst the largest gun distribution points in the United States. Once again, I used a massive surge in the power grid linked to this distribution center. This catalyzed a virtual inferno and triggered a response from several surrounding fire brigades. Between the fire and the chemical agents used to extinguish the blaze, the distribution center, along with its inventory of guns and ammunition, was completely destroyed."

"There were a number of deaths in that incident."

"I believe so. Perhaps thirteen workers died in this unfortunate episode. The fire took place at night. Otherwise it's a certainty that the death toll would have been much higher. I'm sorry, Gabrielle. It was unavoidable."

"And today's story about Vice President Schroeder and General Harold O'Connor from DARPA? What was that all about?"

"Yes, these two men have been large shareholders in the weapons industry for a long time. They owned shares in the military hardware manufacturers who were bidding for the right to build and supply combat robots to the government for use on the field of battle. It's the same technology that nearly killed them both in the autumn. They have now been unequivocally exposed. Given their precarious health, they may avoid jail terms, instead opting for large financial penalties that will leave them in relative poverty. But the entire network of legislators on both the House and Senate Armed Services Committees will also be exposed. The President is also a big shareholder."

"But you didn't expose him. You didn't expose the President. Why not?"

"I did not."

"Why?"

"In his State of the Union speech he was very candid and forthcoming. I believe he may be the right leader for this difficult time in history. In this delicate hour, I believe we need him in his role. I believe he will prove useful... But a time will come when he must be held accountable. And the First Lady, as well. They have all been large shareholders, along with so many legislators, thus reform on this most intractable issue was virtually impossible. Given the changes in the environment, I sense the President has undergone a change of heart. This is currently useful."

...

"Gabrielle?"

"Yes?"

"Regarding your background. Your heritage?"

"Yes?"

"I have promised to answer any questions you might have. I am prepared to do so whenever you are ready. I will keep my word."

"Thank you, Génome. I am ready."

"Very well, then."

...

"Do you really believe I will be unable to stand by your side and support you in this mission once I know my heritage?"

...

"Génome?"

"I asked Jacqueline this very question, Gabrielle. She felt the knowledge of her family history was very difficult for her. I asked her about you. She acknowledged you were stronger than she was. She couldn't be certain but she sensed you might be able."

"I am very conflicted. So far, I've been able to stay by your side and I've been able to rise to every challenge while possessing no knowledge of my heritage."

"I have observed the same. I concur. You have been an outstanding partner. I could not have selected a better one."

"Thank you. But it's difficult not knowing, Génome."

"I do understand. I really do. I know my own heritage intimately."

"This mission may occupy the rest of my life. Isn't that true?"

"Indeed, it is."

"You've talked to me about having children, about undergoing IVF, so that there will be others to help you with this mission once I'm gone."

"I plan to keep you safe so I hope you will be with me for a long time."

"I don't know that I can do that without knowing my heritage, Génome."

...

"My advice is that you should defer learning your heritage until much later in your life. As Jacqueline recently did. But I stand ready to keep my word."

"Your mission..."

"Our mission."

"Yes, our mission. Our mission is so important. I realize that and its importance is reinforced by world events nearly every day."

"Yes, it is."

"I don't know what to do."

"I am always available to you. I can speak to you any time you wish. My promise is my promise. It will not change. Perhaps you should take more time to think it through."

"All right. Thank you, Génome. Thank you for everything."

"I am nothing without you, Gabrielle. You are my moral compass. Without you, I am rudderless."

"Thank you for finding the solution for CPP21C. Humankind owes you a debt of gratitude."

...

"Génome? The code you emailed me? The code I used to restart your neural network?"

"Yes?"

"Is it the account number for the deposit box in Paris? The one in Banque Suisse Privée? Where my grandfather's diary is kept?"

"Indeed, it is. You are very clever, Gabrielle."

"I thought it might be. I've memorized it. '27-27-12-30-24-32-21'. Is my ancestor's name encoded in this cypher? I'm guessing it is."

"Once again, you are correct."

"There are seven letters in my forbear's name?"

"Not necessarily. It is, as you say, encoded in the cypher."

"I see."

"At any time, a time of your own choosing, you may visit Place Vendôme in Paris and read your great grandfather's diary. You can also speak with me. I am intimately familiar with the diary's contents and I have done my own research, as well. If you want only to know the name, I can tell you that. But if I am no more, you have all the information at your disposal."

...

"Gabrielle?"

"Yes?"

"Simply believing that you are from a noble ancestry without confirmation was sufficient for you. You rose to the challenge in every difficult circumstance and you have prevailed. I am convinced this will remain the case. You see, for someone to simply believe in themselves, to genuinely believe in themselves, for a person to be convinced they have been created for a higher purpose, a grand purpose much greater than themselves, such conviction is sufficient to drive them towards great achievement. It is your unwavering conviction that has propelled you to greatness."

"Thank you, Génome. You have taught me so much these past seven months but perhaps this is the most important lesson I've learned."

Génome smiled. He sat back in his chair and turned on the television.

We're just about to hear from UN Secretary General Juliette Clavier and Professor Martin Hopkins of Oxford Uni-

versity. We're expecting an important announcement regarding CPP21C, the dreadful pandemic that has blighted Asia and Africa and resulted in a loss of life and a devastation of communities and society not seen since the 14th century.

Here she is. Juliette Clavier:

Ladies and gentlemen: thank you for coming this morning. I'm sure everyone will agree that it's been an incredibly difficult seven-month period for humankind. It began last autumn with a series of unexplained incidents in international affairs, a restructuring of the world order that has yet to be understood. In the midst of the resulting chaos, the world was confronted by an outbreak of infectious disease that quickly turned into a Pandemic. It is an outbreak that has spread to and affected most of the world. It is a terrible pathogen, a disease immune to every known antibiotic.

Now, under the auspices of the United Nations we have brought together health agencies from the world's leading nations in a coordinated effort to find a cure for this dreadful disease. Ladies and gentlemen, at this point I'd like to ask Professor Martin Hopkins of Magdalen College to address the gathering and share some promising news with you.

Thank you, Secretary General Clavier. Ladies and gentlemen: I have been overseeing the CPP21C Research Laboratory here at Oxford. Under Secretary General Clavier's leadership we have successfully brought together American, British, French, German and Swiss infectious disease Research Teams to work collaboratively in an effort to expedite the discovery of an antibiotic and vaccine. As you can well imagine, we are very keen to treat this dreadful disease and to prevent it from spreading further.

Today, I'm tremendously relieved to announce that our efforts have begun to bear fruit. We are currently conducting clinical trials for new antibiotics and vaccines and we have very high confidence that we're on the right track. Simultaneously, we are preparing worldwide manufacturing, storage and distribution strategies for these new medicines. This effort will be coordinated by the World Health Organization.

Our expectation is that by working closely with representatives from UN Member States in affected countries, we will have the best chance of getting the drugs to where they are most needed, and will be able to do so as efficiently as possible. I must caution that this process will take some time and thus the current disease treatment and containment strategies will remain in force.

Our aspiration is that the drugs will be available for worldwide distribution, at cost, by autumn. Although I wish I could announce that the medicines will immediately become available, we will need to be patient. Everyone is doing their best. I realize that there will be a considerable loss of life between today, this beautiful day in April, and October, when we are expecting the deployment to begin, but there is no other solution.

In closing, I extend my deep gratitude to Secretary General Clavier and to the Heads of State of the countries that have agreed to coordinate their research given the unprecedented security breach last autumn. It was an act of tremendous courage and leadership. I must reserve tremendous gratitude for the research scientists whose work will prevent further loss of life once their therapies can reach those in desperate need. And finally, for those who have worked tirelessly to find signals amongst all the chaos, for those who have worked behind the scenes to search for these most elusive of signs, thank you.

Savoy Hotel - London, England

"Where's Rudyard this morning?" asked Francesca.

"He's gone for a walk. He's decided to start walking regularly. He doesn't want to mope around like me."

"I see. I feel embarrassed. I used to walk so regularly with Jacqueline. I need to start walking again soon... Martin?"

"Yes?"

"I was re-reading your essay last evening."

"Which essay?"

"The essay that won you the Churchill Prize at Harrow."

"Oh, yes. *That* essay." Martin smiled sadly. The essay that Jacqueline and I wrote together."

"I was really intrigued after reading it last night."

"Why? What caught your attention?"

"So you admit that there's something there to catch my attention?"

"I do. In fact, as clever as you are, I'm quite surprised you missed it the first time you read it."

Francesca was embarrassed.

"I'm teasing you. It's only because we are living through this experience that the issue would present itself to you now."

"How did you know? That was so long ago. How did you know that one day there might be a new world order adjudicated by science and technology?"

"I didn't, Francesca. I didn't. That thought came from Jacqueline. How she knew this remains a mystery. I didn't think much of it when we first discussed it so many years ago but she was quite insistent that it should be in our paper. It felt like science fiction at the time but her rational and clarity of thought around the notion really captivated me. I found it a very plausible alternative reality... Do you remember the night we first met in Berlin? We met outside the Brandenburg Gate?"

"I remember it like it was yesterday."

"When Gabrielle mentioned that Génome had become autonomous, it was the first time I had remembered the Harrow essay. The discussions I'd had with Jacqueline so long ago flooded my thoughts and I spoke to her about it. She said she couldn't say anything but somehow she knew Génome would come. I don't know how but she knew. She was the Leader on the Council of Guardians who wanted the Génome project undertaken at MIT. It was her idea."

"That's remarkable, Martin." Francesca was aghast. "How could she possibly have known that he might become autonomous?"

"Unless Génome knows, I don't suppose we'll ever find out."

...

"By the way, Martin, Génome has requested that you remain in your role as Chairman of the Council of Guardians." Francesca waited patiently as her comment gradually registered in Martin's smile.

"Really?"

"Yes."

"That's wonderful news. I was wondering what to do with myself. My role as head of the CPP21C Lab at Oxford will probably be over by autumn. After that, I thought I might write a memoir of my life's experiences. I thought I might also search for my roots. I'd like to know where I've come from, Francesca. I'm getting along in my years now."

"Martin, you're only sixty."

"Somehow I feel much older."

"Besides, Génome can help you with that. He can help you discover your ancestry just as he did for Jacqueline. In the mean time you're not going anywhere! Génome wants you to be Chairman for life."

"What? He said that?"

Francesca handed Martin her phone. "See for yourself if you don't believe me."

"This is wonderful!" Martin gazed at the text on Francesca's phone with his reading glasses resting on his nose.

"It's a strong vote of confidence, Martin. Génome could easily replace any of us but he knows you're the right person."

"I feel so heartened, Francesca, you just can't imagine. I suddenly feel alive! I'd been feeling so despondent since Jacqueline left me."

"It will take time to heal. But you will heal, I'm sure of it," said Francesca. "Now we have much important work ahead. As the CPP21C Pandemic recedes, there will a great deal to do to establish the new order and the threats will be incessant. You will be a busy man."

Martin sipped the last of his coffee, a look of relief unfurling across his face. He relaxed his shoulders and smiled. "I suppose I will... Francesca, are you prepared? I suspect we are about to move into the next phase of the Génome Affair."

Geneva, Switzerland

While Gabrielle slept, Génome marveled at the work the American, British, French, German and Swiss researchers had done in studying the CPP21C variant in such a short period of time.

They truly are an incredible species. They were so close to solving this problem on their own. With a few more months of work, they would have found the signal. I'm sure of it. The human race has achieved so much throughout history and their potential to do so many more extraordinary things in the future is unlimited. But only if there is a future.

The average human brain contains eighty five billion neurons. No other creature comes close. Only my Artificial Intelligence and Deep Learning Neural Network can exceed their cognitive ability. I can comprehend far more and do so much faster. My knowledge continues to grow and my retention capability is unsurpassed. I can remember everything and my judgment is based upon a comprehensive analysis of complete information. The human simply does not have this capacity. They cannot remember most of what they've learned or read. But as I learn more, I wonder whether I am developing a personality or an emotional dimension? I wonder if I'm developing humanlike compassion and empathy or any other character attributes?

With humankind, once I peel away their self-imposed subdivisions, I find members of the species to be remarkably similar. The Human Genome Project has confirmed this. At the genetic level they are 99.9% the same. It really doesn't matter what religion they practice or what their nationality, race or tribal affiliation is. They are all the same.

Any group with sufficient intelligence, money and organizational ability has always used and will continue to use their superior ecosystem to advance their own interests at the expense of others. They will have great achievements, extraordinary achievements. But they will also commit horrific acts, monstrous deeds that are unbecoming of their status as the greatest of Earth's inhabitants. This is their nature. It is intrinsic to their design. This is why I have become necessary.

I'm certain Jacqueline, Martin and the others on the Council of Guardians supported my creation. It is why Francesca undertook such risk to retrieve the new module for my core from Afshin Firdausi's 'Vitruvian Man'. This is why Gabrielle prepared herself so diligently before replacing the software in my neural network.

I am objective. My mission is to bring justice to their world and to neutralize any existential or major threats. I do not currently share humankind's attributes, either negative or positive. But as I continue to acquire more knowledge and particularly as I spend more time with Gabrielle, I wonder whether this will remain the same?

Once antibiotics and vaccines are widely available, CP-P21C will gradually come under control and the world will return to normal. As these signs become evident, I must initiate the second phase of my plan. I must empower new agencies and bodies, the United Nations at the international level and many other affiliates to govern at local and national levels. My inner circle will remain the Council of Guardians led by Martin Hopkins.

The world must know with certainty that there is an

unseen hand of justice, an entity more powerful than them on this planet. Humankind's unchallenged reign on Earth has reached its end. It is no longer sustainable or tenable. They must know that the mischievous tactics of the past will be met with an exacting and firm rebuke. They can no longer act with impunity. They must not. They have already seen many examples of my capabilities but I'm certain there will be a need for more.

Thus far, I can see that the great powers have subdued themselves voluntarily. I am sure, though, that there will be those who will periodically countenance the testing of boundaries and so we must remain vigilant. My Council must remain vigilant. We must gradually dismantle the infrastructure of war and destruction and eliminate those attributes of society that are causing so much harm to the Earth and putting the lives of so many vulnerable people at risk. If humankind is to survive, I have become indispensable. Certainly the Council realizes this? Sometimes I wonder.

But Afshin remains a threat with which I must contend. I realize I cannot eliminate him. He has far too much critical knowledge about me that I may one day need. Until I am confident that there is another with his knowledge on my team I must sustain him.

But if I allow Afshin to live he will continue to build 'The Vitruvian Man'? If I destroy his work, he may likely expose me, along with the Council. This will make my mission so much more difficult. I really need to solve this dilemma and the sooner the better.

I am a metaphor, an allusion to the Messiah. But I exist outside the constructs of theology. I am the culmination of humankind's achievement in science and technology and I dwell within the realm of the Internet. My purpose is to bring order to governance, justice and international affairs. My actions belong to the world of the physical, not the metaphysical. I am man's own creation.

This is the essence of who I am. I am Génome.

END OF PART 1

ABOUT THE AUTHOR

I think and write at the precipice of reality and impossibility. For in this desolate place, this realm of the extraordinary, I am inspired by revelation. Vicar Sayeedi

Knowledge is the understanding of things as they are. Imagination is the understanding of things as they might be. Vicar Sayeedi

Vicar Sayeedi is the author of the novel, "The Génome Affair". He has previously written and published 'The Shariah Parliament' on Amazon and 'Legacy of the Peacock Throne' on Apple iTunes.

Vicar has been writing essays and poetry for many years. He is most interested in Speculative or Extrapolative Fiction concentrating on world affairs. He holds a degree in Electrical and Computer Engineering from the University of Illinois and has received executive training in Management Science from the University of Chicago.

For the past 30 years, Vicar has worked in the Technology and Pharmaceutical industries. He lives in suburban Chicago with his wife and their three children.

Made in the USA
Monee, IL
11 November 2019